Worth the Trade

Books by Kristina Mathews

Worth the Trade

Better Than Perfect

Published by Kensington Publishing Corporation

Worth the Trade

Kristina Mathews

LYRICAL PRESS
Kensington Publishing Corp.
www.kensingtonbooks.com

LYRICAL PRESS BOOKS are published by

Kensington Publishing Corp.
119 West 40th Street
New York, NY 10018

Trade Paperback Edition: May 2015
ISBN-13: 978-1-61650-945-3
ISBN-10: 1-61650-945-7

10 9 8 7 6 5 4 3 2 1

Printed in the United States of America

Also available in an electronic edition:

eISBN-13: 978-1-61650-541-7
eISBN-10: 1-61650-541-9

To my two sons.
From the time you were each just "a player to be named later" to your first baseball games to watching you both find your own interests as you've grown, it's been a pleasure to be your mom.

Chapter 1

"That's him. Over there." Hunter Collins recognized her new left fielder by the body language, posture, and raw physical power of a professional athlete.

"The guy in the plaid shirt?" The limo driver shook his head in doubt. "Are you sure? He doesn't look like no baseball player. He's too tall."

Marco Santiago was indeed tall. And dark. And—she hated to admit, even to herself—incredibly handsome. The expert tailoring of his shirt emphasized his broad shoulders, long, strong arms, and slender waist. Dark denim hugged slim hips, clung to muscular thighs, and she'd put good money on what they did to his taut backside.

His tattered duffel bag was slung carelessly over his left shoulder. A small leather case lay at his feet. The casual observer might interpret his relaxed pose as lazy, bored, or perhaps a little worse for the wear. But she'd watched him on the field enough to know he could spring into action with panther-like reflexes at the crack of the bat.

"He's the one." Her heart rate quickened. A little more than three months ago she'd inherited forty percent ownership of the San Francisco Goliaths. At twenty-seven, Hunter was the youngest president of one of Major League Baseball's oldest franchises. She brushed off the pain of losing her father, focusing instead on her first official player acquisition. Together they would make their mark on the new era of Goliaths' baseball.

As the driver pulled up to the curb, she noticed the slight change in Santiago's stance. His shoulders straightened and he rocked back on his heels like he was ready to chase down a fly ball. There it was, the instinct that had her drooling over him for some time. As a ballplayer, nothing more.

Her driver got out, opened the passenger door, and Santiago ducked inside.

"Whoa, you scared me. I didn't expect company." He smiled at her, flashing a set of dimples and startlingly blue eyes. He let his gaze travel the length of her body, inspecting her, before nodding his approval. "But this might turn out to be a good trade after all."

Excuse me?

"Are you saying you're not happy about the trade?" He had no idea how hard she'd worked to make this deal happen. For the past few weeks she'd practically slept with her cell phone attached to her ear, when she'd slept at all. She'd tuned out the sports talk show hosts and beat reporters and bloggers who claimed she was too inexperienced to make a deal. As if *inexperienced* was a euphemism for *female*.

Not to mention the embarrassing and insulting offers initially given by the other team. They'd wanted her to give up half her farm system, thinking she didn't know the wealth of talent she had in the minor leagues. But once they realized she actually did know what she was doing, they were able to strike a fair deal.

"It came as a surprise." He settled into the leather seat. "Sure, I heard rumors. But there are always trade rumors this time of year. I really didn't expect to walk into the clubhouse this morning only to be told I was no longer wanted in St. Louis."

"You'll be welcomed with open arms here in San Francisco." Hunter gave him what she hoped was an encouraging smile.

"Is that so?" He looked her over as if she wore something low-cut and see-through. Or nothing at all. "So are you the welcoming committee? If they'd done their homework they'd have known I usually prefer blondes. But I can make an exception, just for tonight."

He cocked one eyebrow up and drew his mouth into a grin that stopped just short of a leer.

"I don't see why my hair color should matter to you." She tried not to roll her eyes. He wasn't the first athlete to assume the only place for a woman in pro sports was underneath him and naked. "Your last owner was fully gray. And the one before him was completely bald."

At his stunned silence, she smiled and held out her hand.

"Hunter Collins. President and Managing Partner of the San Francisco Goliaths Baseball Club." She avoided referring to herself as the *acting* president. A role she'd served in during her father's long illness. Hell, she'd served in that role since she was old enough to read a box score. Unofficially, of course. Henry Collins had always been the face in the meetings, the name on the contracts. But she'd been right there with him, working behind the scenes. This was as much her team as anyone's.

"My new boss." He gave her a firm handshake before sinking back into the seat and letting out a frustrated sigh. "Can we start over?"

He turned toward her, a forced smile on his face. The kind of smile he'd give a reporter after a tough loss.

"Don't bother telling me how happy you are to be here." She had to admit, she was more than a little disappointed. Why wouldn't he want to be here? The Goliaths were a first class organization. Her father had saved the team from being moved to Florida. He'd taken on partners in order to build the state-of-the-art ballpark without using public funds. The fans came out to fill the seats night after night, and the ownership did its best to offer the fans their money's worth, even though they hadn't won it all. *Yet.*

"I am happy to be here. I just . . ." He ran his left hand through his hair. She didn't need to check for a wedding ring. He was single, no family to uproot for the cross-country move. "My flight was delayed. I lost half my luggage. And I haven't had a good night's sleep in weeks. So I apologize if I seem less than thrilled."

"I suppose you'll be happier when you can get out on the field." She'd been around athletes her whole life. Enough to know they were creatures of habit. Rain delays, schedule changes, and especially trade rumors could wreak havoc on their routine. Those distractions upset their rhythm and could only be remedied by getting back to work.

"I wish I could have been here in time to get out there tonight." He leaned forward, resting his forearms on his knees. His thighs trembled with nervous energy. "But maybe a day off will do me some good."

"You didn't have the best series against Philly." She'd followed his career closely. Probably knew his stats better than he did. "I imagine the trade rumors had something to do with it. I know you guys say you don't pay any attention to that kind of thing, but it's got to be a big distraction. Not to mention, a little hard on the ego."

"So I take it you're a hands-on kind of owner." His voice was smooth, rich, sensual. The thought of his hands on her body popped up into her imagination. Not what she needed right now. His hands were going to make good catches, good throws, and big hits. His hands were going to make them a lot of money if they made the playoffs. *When* they made the playoffs.

"I like to keep up with my players. It's good for business." She had to turn away from him, from those blistering blue eyes. Where'd they come from? He had the dark hair, dark skin, dark stubble of a Latino player. He should have dark eyes, too, not neon blue ones.

"Don't worry, I won't disappoint you. You'll get exactly what you paid for." He looked down at his hands. Long, straight fingers. Short, well-manicured nails. Thick, strong wrists.

Oh my.

"My father always thought highly of you. He wanted to trade for you last year, but St. Louis beat us out." She needed to remember why they were both here, in this limo that felt so much bigger before he slid into the seat next to her. Now it felt like they were thrown together into the back of a Smart Car. Not that a Smart Car even had a back seat. "So, I decided to carry out his wishes and make the deal happen. I'm sure you'll prove yourself. On the field."

"Your father?" He edged away from her. "Your father was Henry Collins."

She just nodded, unable to speak past the sudden lump in her throat.

"I'm sorry for your loss." His voice lost all traces of teasing. "He was a class act. The league will miss him."

She chose to take his words as a compliment for her father, not an indication that he thought she wasn't up to the job.

"Thank you." She needed to pull herself together. The last thing she wanted was for him to see her as soft or weak. "Let's get you to your hotel, get you settled in so you'll be fresh for the game tomorrow."

"Is the game over?" Santiago pulled out his phone, scrolled though the screen. "Nope. It's the bottom of the seventh. Goliaths on top three to one. Why don't we swing by the ballpark? I'd like to meet my new teammates tonight."

"Right now?" She hadn't expected him to want to get out there tonight. Especially after a long flight, lost luggage, and his disappointment at her not being a blonde.

"Unless you have something else planned for me." He raised an eyebrow and flashed one of his dimples. He knew all too well how irresistible that smile was. "Because you own me now. So . . ."

"The ballpark it is." Hunter leaned forward to alert the driver of their change of plans. She didn't want to think about what she could demand of him, other than a division title. That was the only thing she wanted from Marco Santiago.

The limo driver pulled up to the players' lot and checked in with the security guard who waved them inside.

"I'll see that your bag is sent to your hotel." Hunter's—Ms. *Collins'* tone was cool. Very impersonal and businesslike. "I'll send the driver back around when the game is over."

"Aren't you going to stay?" Why that disappointed him, he had no idea.

"No. I've had a long week." She heaved a sigh, sinking back against the seat. "I think I'll go home, take a nice long bath."

Marco closed his eyes, trying not to conjure up the image of her slipping naked into a tub full of warm water. Bubbles. Perhaps some scented oils. Damn. He shifted in the plush leather seat, his jeans becoming uncomfortably tight.

Please don't let her notice. She was his boss. The worst thing he could do would be to get all worked up trying to picture what kind of underwear she wore under her various shades of gray. Her loose-fitting charcoal pantsuit was a little on the drab side. Almost as if she'd borrowed it from her father's closet. Her blouse, the color of fog, was buttoned up to the hollow of her throat. But it was just soft enough to hint at the womanly curves she was trying to hide.

Still, something about her drew him in. Her eyes were a warm, golden brown. Her hair was pulled back in some uptight updo, but a single loose strand that curled behind her right ear looked soft, silky, and entirely too touchable. Like the delicate skin of her neck. He couldn't help but wonder how she'd respond to the lightest brush of his lips, right there. Would she shiver? Sigh? Moan?

He'd made the innuendo about her being his own personal welcoming committee. Talk about stupid. Just put her on the defensive. But it had also injected a charge into their interaction. A sexual energy that might have stayed under control if he hadn't opened his big mouth.

This wasn't the first time Marco had experienced lust at first sight. But usually it was for a woman who had all her feminine assets on display. Showcased in tight, revealing clothing. Flashing tons of makeup and broadcasting her availability for a night or two of fun.

Hunter was the opposite. The way she dressed was the least of it. She wore hardly any makeup. Her lips were bare. Pink, soft, and lush enough to make him wonder what she'd taste like. No artificial cherry-vanilla flavoring, or glossy chemical taste. Just pure, unenhanced woman.

Who was one hundred percent off limits.

"Well, thanks for picking me up." He winced. Every word out of his mouth tonight dripped with sexual undertones. "From the airport. And . . . uh . . . thank you for bringing me to San Francisco. I'll make it worth your while. You'll see."

"I'm counting on it." She glanced down at his lap and quickly turned away, color spreading across her cheeks. Damn. She'd noticed the effect she had on him. "Are you going to get out of the car? Or should I tell the driver you've changed your mind?"

"I'm going. I'm going." He slid away from her. Reached for the door to make his exit, but he couldn't quite pull the handle.

"Have dinner with me?" Maybe it was jet lag. Sleep deprivation. Or some seismic anomaly affecting his brain waves. Maybe going more than six months without sex had been a really bad idea.

"I'm sure you'll find plenty to eat at the post-game spread." Did her hesitation mean she was rattled? "We have an excellent caterer."

"No. I want *you* to have dinner with *me*." He leaned toward her, knowing she'd deny him, but he wanted to linger near her a little bit longer.

"I can't." She squirmed, avoiding his gaze. "It would be a conflict of interest."

"You're only conflicted because you're interested." He kept his smile to himself. He was getting to her. Almost as much as she was getting to him. Even though she wasn't at all his type. Or maybe she was, she just worked so damn hard trying to hide it.

"I'm only interested in winning the division and making a strong run in the postseason." She turned her head to look out the window as if to show she was unaffected by the chemistry between them.

"Aren't you a rotten liar?" He chuckled softly. Oh yeah, he was definitely getting to her. "Don't join in the poker game at the next owners' retreat. You'll be wiped out."

She whipped her head around so fast the car shook. "I happen to be a very good poker player. I can hold my own against anyone. Any time."

Interesting. Her strong reaction told him two things. She was insecure about her place among her fellow owners. And yes, she was interested in him on more than a professional level.

"That explains your wardrobe." He leaned back, not ready to leave her just yet. "You dress like you do to fit in with the old boys' club. But you can't hide the fact that you are all woman."

"And you can't hide the fact that you don't want to be here." She dared look him straight in the eye, but couldn't hold his gaze.

"I'm starting to come around." He gave her one last smile. "I think I'm going to like San Francisco. I think I'm really going to like it here."

Marco slid out of the seat and headed into the ballpark acting like he owned the place.

The game had ended by the time he got through security and onto the field. The Goliaths had held their lead and a good portion of the crowd lingered, singing along to Tony Bennett. One of the on-field reporters recognized him and rushed over to be the first to interview him.

Showtime.

"Rachel Parker here, with the newest member of the San Francisco Goliaths, Marco Santiago." The crowd cheered, as word of his arrival spread and they played the interview on the scoreboard. "Did you come straight from the airport?"

"I sure did." Marco flashed his million-dollar grin. He earned the rest of his salary with his bat and his glove. "I'm just so happy to be here. In this ballpark. With these fans. And this team . . . This team has a real good chance of going all the way. I can't wait to get out on the field and make a contribution. To thank the ownership for bringing me here."

"We're happy to have you here in San Francisco." The reporter was friendly, almost too perky. "What does your family think of the change?"

"I'm sure my mother will be happy for me." Guilt hit him at the realization he hadn't talked to her since the trade went down. She had to hear it on the news like everyone else. "But she's always been proud of me."

"You're not married?" Was she asking for herself or all the single ladies who might be watching the broadcast?

"Just to my job." He hoped she would drop the subject of his personal life. He didn't have one. Didn't want one. Not until he was settled more permanently. "My focus is on helping my team get to the postseason. The ownership and management took a chance on me. I won't let them down. I won't let the fans down."

He didn't want to let anyone down.

The rest of the night was a blur. He signed quite a few autographs, took tons of pictures, and introduced himself to his teammates. His manager, Juan Javier, made him feel welcome, as did the coaches, trainers, and support staff. It probably didn't hurt showing up after a victory, when the whole ballpark was buzzing from the win.

The atmosphere had a much better vibe than in his former clubhouse these last few weeks. They weren't officially out of it, but with such high expectations the season had been more than disappointing. When management started trading away all their star players it started to feel like they were giving up. *Rebuilding.* In other words, dumping big salaries and trying to salvage their financial asses.

He knew it was just business. Nothing personal. This trade had nothing to do with how anyone felt about him. The St. Louis owners thought they could make more money without him and the San Francisco group thought they could make more money with him. Hopefully they were both right.

But he felt bad for the fans. They'd embraced him in St. Louis. There were bound to be folks who felt let down. People who worked for a living and spent their hard earned money on seats in left field. It didn't matter whether they made it to one game a year, or all eighty-one. The fans made signs, shouted his name. They bought the T-shirts, jerseys, and bobble heads not to add to the team's profits, but because they loved their team. Because they wanted to be a part of something bigger than themselves.

Maybe he wasn't too crazy about being traded once again. But now that he was here, he'd give it everything he had. For his teammates. For the fans. For the lovely Miss Hunter Collins.

Since he couldn't sleep, Marco pulled out his iPad. Good thing he'd kept it in his carry-on bag. After sending a quick e-mail to his mother letting her know he'd arrived safely in his latest temporary home, he decided to do some Internet research on his new team. Who was he kidding? He wanted to know more about his new owner. He hoped to satisfy his curiosity and move on. Instead, he became more and more intrigued by the woman as he watched her life unfold through a series of pictures, videos, and articles about the little girl who was raised by her single dad and the entire Goliaths organization.

What was he doing? Hunter Collins was his boss. Hadn't his family suffered enough at the hands of an employer who'd taken advantage of his employee? He couldn't risk it. No matter how much he wanted her. He'd be a free agent at the end of the season, looking for a team he could finish his career with. He had to make a good impression. On the field. Only on the field. He didn't need any distractions. Especially not one with the power to end his career right when he was hitting his prime playing years.

Still, he went to a little extra trouble with his appearance the next day before heading to the ballpark. He put on his best semi-casual dress shirt. The one that made his eyes bluer than a summer sky. Or so he'd been told. And not only by the salesgirl who sold him the overpriced garment. He spent a good half hour debating whether to shave or go with the scruffy look. He shaved. Since he was starting with a new team, he decided his face needed a fresh start.

Besides, it's not like they were going to hop into bed right away. No. He liked to take his time. Get to know a woman. Draw out the seduction over a period of weeks. Some guys preferred the easy in, easy out approach to relationships. But a woman wasn't a drive up window. He didn't want to just toss her aside after a quick taste. He liked to savor a woman. Leave her with no regrets tainting the memories they'd made.

He wondered what kind of memories he could make with Hunter Collins. She was different than any of the women he usually dated. For one thing, she wouldn't be impressed by what he did for a living. She was around professional athletes all the time. She'd surely known too many ballplayers who thought they were God's gift. He'd need to show her how he was different from every other man in that dugout.

What an idiot. He probably wouldn't even see her. It's not like she'd be hanging out in the clubhouse. If she even came to the game, she'd be sitting pretty in a luxury box, looking out over her investment. He'd do well to remember she was an owner. She was only interested in him because he could make her money. He should only be interested in her signature on his paychecks.

He needed to focus on getting ready for his first game as a Goliath. He needed to prove he was worth the trade. This was his fourth team since making it to the majors. He hoped it would be his last. He'd spent far too much of his life moving around. As a kid. Again in the minors. When he was drafted in the second round, he thought he'd finally found a home. Texas would keep him around. People loved the local boy makes good story.

But he'd quickly learned that baseball was more than the national pastime. It was a business. Big, big business. Loyalty only went as far as the bottom line. And the investors were restless. Every team started the season hoping this would be their year. For the twenty-eight clubs who didn't make it to the big dance, someone was to blame. Players were shuffled. Free-agents signed. Salaries taken on and dumped. All in the hopes of a share of the postseason pool.

Marco had been called up, sent down, brought back up, and traded three times in the last six years. In the process, he'd become somewhat of a streaky player. One who could turbocharge the lineup for weeks at a time. Then he'd hit a plateau. His average would dip. Run production taper off. And the pressure would get to him. He tried not to listen to the talk shows or read the blogs. But he knew what they were saying about him. Knew it was only a matter of time before someone else started looking better.

He needed to make sure that for the last two months of this season, the grass was greenest in left field beneath his feet.

Marco went about his usual pregame routine. He'd eaten two bananas, a peanut butter and honey sandwich on whole-wheat, and washed it down with a quart of chocolate milk. He filled his back pocket with sunflower seeds and put on his new jersey—number 9. After donning his new cap, and picking up his trusty glove, he headed out to the field.

Standing on the sidelines, hat over his heart, he took in the sights and sounds of the ballpark as the national anthem rang out over the loudspeakers. He closed his eyes, letting the words and the music fill him. He knew how fortunate he was to be standing here instead of on the street outside the stadium. He could easily be the guy cleaning up after the game, instead of the guy hitting cleanup.

When the song ended, he happened to glance into the stands. Hunter Collins sat behind home plate. She caught his eye, held his gaze for a moment, and then tried to busy herself with the scorebook on her lap. But she dropped it. He was close enough to notice a blush creep across her cheeks.

He'd gotten under her skin. And she was now in his head. He just hoped he could get her out of it before he came up to the plate.

The top of the first inning went quickly, with the first three batters striking out. In a way, Marco was glad nothing came to him in left field. But the longer he went without making a play, the more nervous he got about making a good impression. On the team, the fans. And of course, on Hunter Collins.

The Goliaths leadoff man got a base hit. He stole second and avoided a double play when the next batter grounded out. Shortstop Bryce Baxter stroked a double down the left field line, scoring a run. Could be a rally. It was up to Marco to keep it going.

Too bad he struck out on three pitches.

He shook his head, feeling the shame of letting her down. No it wasn't just Hunter, he'd let the whole team down. Not to mention the forty thousand fans in the stands and the countless others catching the game on Bay Area Sports Net or listening to it on the radio.

Shake it off. It was only the top of the second and they had a one run lead. Marco grabbed his glove and took his place on the field. With a runner on second and one out, the next batter hit a deep fly ball, heading for the gap in left-center field. No way was he going to let it get away from him. He dove, snagging the ball inches from the grass. The crowd roared and he felt a little better about his blunder at the plate.

He finished the night hitless, with two strikeouts, a pop fly, and finally, grounding into an inning-ending double play. Way to make a good impression.

At least it hadn't come with a loss. Johnny Scottsdale had pitched a gem and Baxter hit two home runs and an RBI double to clinch the win and draw media attention away from him.

Marco had done part of his job. He made some good plays in the field. He hadn't committed any errors and he'd saved what could have been a run-scoring double. The night hadn't been a total loss. But it hadn't been anywhere near what he wanted to accomplish in his first game as a Goliath.

Chapter 2

He'd gone zero for thirteen. Hunter couldn't believe Marco Santiago was hitless after three games. Was he doing it on purpose? To let her know he really didn't want to be here?

No. Of course not. He was a professional. He might not have been enthusiastic about the trade, but surely he wouldn't sabotage his career because of it.

Still. She felt like there was something personal about his performance. Like she was somehow responsible for his lack of focus at the plate. Because he looked like a man who had something other than baseball on his mind every time he stepped into the batter's box.

He'd look over at her. His damn blue eyes boring into her, then he'd shake his head and dig in. He was distracted. Frustrated. And since he was her first official player acquisition, she took his struggles at the plate personally.

Hunter wasn't too surprised to find him in the batting cages before the game the next afternoon. He was doing the right thing. Trying to work his way out of his slump. She had to give him credit for that. She watched him take cut after cut. His swing looked good. No major flaws in his mechanics. It didn't appear to be a physical problem. So it had to be at least half mental.

Hunter settled in to watch his extra batting practice. He was starting to look a lot more comfortable as the session went on. She relaxed a bit, enjoying the simple pleasure of watching a talented athlete hone his craft. He really did have a beautiful swing.

Until he caught her watching him. He shook his head and completely missed the next pitch. He fouled off a few more balls, and it became clear that he was rattled. No more clean contact. No more smooth, easy swing. No more poetry in motion. She was in his head.

She should go. Her presence was only making things worse. For his game and for the sexual tension that surrounded them like fog whenever they were near each other. But she couldn't quite make her feet move. Couldn't quite tear her gaze away from the way the muscles in his arms and shoulders flexed as he swung the bat. The way the thrust of his hips added power to his swing. Not to mention the way his ass looked in those almost-tight white pants.

As if he knew her observation wasn't entirely professional, he set the bat down, grabbed a towel, and approached her with a scowl on his face. A frustrated yet incredibly sexy scowl.

"What are you doing down here?" His blue eyes blazed with annoyance. And desire. "I'm trying to work."

"I thought I'd take a look and see if we can figure out how to get you back on track." She tried to keep her voice as professional as possible. To not betray the fact that a few minutes ago, she was simply admiring the view. "There's a reason I traded for you and I think if we work together, we can get this team to the postseason."

"Oh yeah? And what can you do, besides distract me, to get me hitting again?" He gripped the towel around his neck.

"I distract you?" Her heart tripped, stumbling over his intense stare. "How do I distract you?"

"I think you know the answer to that." He stepped closer, making the space seem entirely too small. They were in a large, underground facility, with room for batting cages, pitching mounds, and weight rooms. Yet she felt like she was trapped in an elevator whenever she was near this man.

"Is it because I'm a woman?" Her hackles rose. When she was little, her gender hadn't mattered. She was Henry Collins' kid. Always at his side. She was as much a fixture at the ballpark as the left field bleachers. It wasn't until she got older that she realized she was the only girl in the clubhouse.

"Yes. You're a woman." He said that last word in such a way that every single one of her womanly parts tingled. "And you're my boss."

"You don't think I can do my job. Simply because I'm a woman. I may not have ever played professional baseball, but I know as much about this game as anyone. My father trusted me. He listened to me. Valued my insight and instincts."

He'd never made a trade or signed a free agent without asking her thoughts on a player. She used a combination of sabermetrics and instinct. Going with her gut when the two offered conflicting advice.

"I grew up in this clubhouse. I've played catch with more Hall of Famers and all-stars . . ." She fisted her hands on her hips. "I actually do know what I'm doing."

"I'm sure you do." He was mocking her. His eyes twinkled. His dimples teased. His lips curled in a half-smile. "I'll bet you're very good at your job. But that's not the problem."

"So what is the problem?" She folded her arms over her chest.

"You're my problem." His smile faded. "You're my boss. I shouldn't want you . . . but I do."

Their eyes met. The connection between them impossible to deny. Pure, physical attraction.

"And that's why you're distracted at the plate?" She wished he was joking. That he was only toying with her because he knew it wouldn't lead anywhere. Couldn't lead anywhere. It was all part of his game, and once he realized he was out of her league, he'd let it go.

Except it didn't feel like he was playing her.

"Yes. You sit there in the front row, taking notes." He dropped his gaze to her blouse, and the way his eyes blazed, she wondered if she'd forgotten to button it. "In your buttoned up suits. And your pulled back hair. It's like you don't want anyone to know what's underneath. But it's all I can think about."

"My suits?" She could feel the heat rising in her cheeks. "You think about my suits?"

"What are you hiding?" His voice was deep, rich, and way too sexy.

"I'm not hiding anything." Her pitch was too high, making it sound like she was indeed covering up something.

"So you're naked underneath all that black and gray?" A grin teased his lips.

"No. Of course not." Her cheeks weren't the only part of her to flush. "But that's none of your business, anyway."

"I know. It is none of my business." He closed his eyes and exhaled in frustration. "Yet I can't help but wonder."

What did he want her to do? Show him? Do a little strip tease right here in the batting cage?

"It's driving me crazy." He opened his eyes and stared straight at her. Through her. "You're driving me crazy. I can't . . . I can't get my head in the game because you're there, taking up space."

"Why?" She hadn't meant to ask the question aloud, but since she had, she continued. "I mean, I'm not the kind of woman men fall for. Never have been."

"What? Because you don't dress in skimpy clothes and wear a lot of makeup, you don't think men notice you?"

"Not usually." And she was fine with that. For the most part. She'd been just a girl, in a man's world. But none of the players were ever bothered by her. They looked out for her, sometimes even teased her, like a kid sister. But they never took her seriously. Even when she came back from college, she was still Henry Collins' little girl. Not even a consideration.

"Idiots." He clenched his jaw muscles. His fists, too. "Or maybe I'm the idiot. I know all the reasons I shouldn't want you. But I do."

She felt a strange flutter in her chest. He wanted her. Even though they both knew it was a bad idea.

"So if I wasn't sitting behind home plate, you'd start hitting?"

"Maybe." He stepped closer. Close enough that she could smell the faint scent of soap and sweat. And pine tar.

"If I move to the luxury box with the other owners, you won't be distracted?"

"It depends. Are any of the other owners men?" His eyes burned with suspicion.

"They all are." She was all too aware of that fact. "But Marvin Dempsey is old enough to be my father. And Clayton Barry? He doesn't like me very much. I think he's intimidated by a woman with equal power."

"He's attracted to you." He stepped even closer. Just short of touching her.

"No. He's married. With kids." She laughed at the absurd idea. "His wife is a supermodel. He's definitely not interested in me."

"Wanna bet?" He smiled, taking a step back.

"Not really. Besides, we work together. And we never agree on anything. Even you."

"What about me?" His gaze narrowed.

"He didn't want to trade for you. Thought we should get someone flashier. With a bigger name. And a bigger price tag."

"Like who?" His ego had been pricked. Good. Maybe it would spark a hot streak.

"It doesn't matter." She smiled sweetly. "I wanted you."

"Oh?" He raised an eyebrow. Flashed a dangerous grin. "And you always get what you want?"

"Yes. When it comes to helping this team win." At some point she was going to have to admit she wanted Marco Santiago, the man. But she wanted the ballplayer even more. She needed him to be the player she knew he could be. "I want this division. I want the pennant. And I really, *really* want the World Series. I believe you can help us get there."

He nodded, serious once again. "I want all of that, too."

He lifted his cap. Raked his hand through his hair. Replaced his hat.

"Typical female." He shook his head, mumbling to himself.

"Excuse me?" She couldn't pretend she hadn't heard him.

"You only want a ring. One with a ridiculous amount of diamonds." He grinned. A crooked, cocky smile that reached his eyes. "I'll get you that ring. Don't you worry about that."

"You'd better. I gave up my youth to get it." She was referring to the pitching prospect and the rookie outfielder she'd traded, along with a veteran relief pitcher, to bring him to San Francisco. Those guys would probably make an impact in the next few years. She wanted to win now. She needed to justify her father's faith in her. And this team.

"I'll do my best," he promised.

"I'll be watching. From the owner's box." She would sit up there at the Club Level. Watch the game on the big screen. Make nice with Clayton Barry, even though he coveted her position.

She would keep her distance from Marco. Treat him like every other player. He was just another part of the team. They were already a good team. Good enough to win the division. Marco could help get them there.

She hoped.

Damn. Was he really so hot for his boss that he couldn't hit a freaking baseball in her presence? Even worse, he'd admitted it. At least he had the restraint not to take her right there in the batting cage. Barely.

Today's torture device—or conservative pant suit—was black. With another gray blouse buttoned to the neck. How he itched to undo those buttons, one at a time. Slowly revealing what he was certain to be hidden treasure. He couldn't help but wonder if her undergarments were more of the same muted colors or if she was hiding a jolt of color. Bright red satin, for instance. Like those art films in all black and white except for the one colorful detail. A red umbrella, perhaps, or a woman's sapphire-blue eyes.

He now had a mission to find out. But she wouldn't let him anywhere near her bed until he started hitting. She was the one who'd brought him here. He couldn't disappoint her. He'd have to come through on the field. She wasn't the kind of woman he could wine and dine or shower with expensive trinkets.

Hunter Collins was the kind of woman he would have to seduce with action. A plan. And yes, diamonds. Both the dirt-covered kind and the ones set in platinum. She wanted a ring and he was going to be the man to give it to her.

First, he had to help the team make it to the World Series. And in order to get them there, he had to start hitting. He had to be the man she thought he was when she traded for him. If she could fight for him before she'd even met him, surely he could fight through this slump for her.

Marco's teammates arrived shortly after Hunter left. He needed to work a little harder at getting to know the rest of the players. But it was hard to be too friendly when he was letting his teammates down. Already.

A few of the guys had tried to reach out to him. Offering advice and encouragement. Suggesting everything from prayers to getting laid. He'd been advised on where to get slump-busting takeout for any kind of food. Chinese, Mexican, Italian, or even vegan restaurants that had done the trick for one or more of his teammates. Or, if he was looking to blow off some steam, he'd learned the best bars to meet the kind of women who were more than willing to give a certain kind of fan support.

He didn't need enchiladas or groupies or a chicken bone cross. He needed to get his head on straight. To find his focus. His control. There was only one man who could cure what ailed him.

"Hey, Johnny." Marco approached veteran pitcher Johnny "The Monk" Scottsdale. The man was known for his composure. He was a Zen master when it came to keeping his focus on the game. He'd also been known for keeping monk-like control off the field, but that was before he married his college sweetheart after a fourteen year separation.

Marco waited until they were alone to ask for advice. "Can I ask you something?"

"Sure. What do you need?"

"Wisdom." He also didn't seem like the kind of guy you danced around. You got straight to the point.

"Wisdom?" Johnny repeated. "I'll do my best."

"I need to regain my focus." Marco hated to admit weakness. Especially to another man. Even a future Hall of Famer and leader of this team. But Marco was desperate. There was too much riding on this.

"It's never easy coming to a new team. Particularly one with such high expectations." Marco was glad he didn't have to explain.

"Every team starts the year hoping to win it all." Still putting up walls. He'd never become a true teammate until he put himself out there. Acknowledged that sometimes he didn't know what the hell he was doing. "I think this team has a real shot at the pennant. But you already knew that. You gave up a long term deal with Chicago to come here."

"We're still in the race. That's for sure." They were three games back. With fifty left to play. Still very much in the race.

"Yeah. But every single one of us has to make a contribution." And Marco knew he hadn't done that since coming to San Francisco.

"True. But we don't all have to do it at the same time." Johnny made it sound so simple. It was for him. After so many years in the big leagues, he was having his best season yet. "We have twenty-five guys on this team. We pick each other up, encourage each other, and keep working for each other even when it feels like it's not going to work out. We show up. Every. Single. Day."

"I want to be that guy," Marco admitted. He wanted to be the guy who stuck around. Who made a contribution on the field and beyond. "I want to keep showing up. Every day. Every year. I want to be someone people can count on."

"So be that guy. Step up to the plate like you own it." Johnny exuded confidence. Composure. Wisdom. "No one can beat you unless you let them."

If it was only that simple.

"Look. I know what it's like to be the new guy on the team. To heap that much more pressure on yourself. But you don't carry this team. This team will carry you. If you'll let us."

Johnny wasn't pitching today. He laced up his cleats anyway. Gave Marco an encouraging nod and headed to the field to support his teammates.

Marco tried to let Johnny's advice soak in. The entire season did not rest on his shoulders alone. He had twenty-four other guys who wanted a shot at the postseason just as much as he did. He'd have eight men on the field with him at any given time. Every single one of them was capable of driving in the winning run. Even the pitchers. All of their starters had at least one RBI this season. He did not have to do this on his own.

Marco stood for the national anthem. He glanced behind home plate. Only the old guy, in the bow tie and sweater vest, sat in the prime seats. Dempsey was his name. Hunter wasn't there. She'd made good on her promise not to distract him.

He needed to make good on his promise.

Hunter sat in the luxury box above the field. They had all the amenities one could wish for, food, drinks, Wi-Fi, and big screen TVs. But she couldn't smell the grass from up here. Couldn't hear the crack of the bat as it made contact with the ball. She couldn't feel the buzz of the crowd around her. She was isolated up here. Separated from the fans, the players, and her father. He'd never sat in a luxury suite. Always in the seats behind home plate. Always right where the action was.

The suite included a balcony, with outdoor seating. She sat down, trying to at least catch a whiff of garlic fries. After standing for the national anthem, she settled into her seat with her scorebook and a notepad to jot down anything that stood out about her team or their opponent.

Clayton Barry was busy entertaining his wife and five-year-old twin daughters. They seemed to be more interested in the catered meal and playing video games on the big TV than the actual game.

The Goliaths got the first two outs easily. But then the pitcher walked the third batter, bringing their cleanup hitter to the plate. Sure enough, he got a hold of a ball that was up in the strike zone, launching it deep into left field. A collective gasp was followed by cheers as Marco leaped into the air, snagging the ball just inches above the outfield wall.

Her heart continued to thump as he trotted back to the dugout. Maybe a spectacular play like that was just what he needed to build his confidence. Hunter hoped it would carry over into his next at bat.

She wasn't going to panic just yet. He'd only been in town three nights. Still living out of a suitcase. He hadn't had a chance to acclimate to the city, the clubhouse, or the contours of the outfield. A week ago, he'd been looking forward to Marco Santiago bobblehead night at his old stadium. Now he was sporting a new uniform, a new number, and a new set of expectations.

Besides, she'd acquired him for his defense as much as anything else. He was fearless in the outfield. Making impossible plays look routine. And routine plays spectacular. He'd just saved them two runs. That was worth plenty in her book. They would have needed to score three if he hadn't made that catch.

In his first at bat, Marco hit a soft line drive that squirted past the second baseman into the outfield. Baxter scored from third base and the Goliaths took a one to nothing lead. Hunter breathed a sigh of relief as Marco recorded his first official hit and his first RBI since the trade. She started to relax. He was settling in. Showing signs of the player she'd put her faith, and several million dollars, into.

She watched him standing on first base. He glanced over at her usual seat behind home plate, and shook his head. He then lifted his gaze up to the suite level where she now sat. Even though he couldn't possibly have picked her out of the crowd, she felt the connection. Those damn blue eyes that haunted her dreams. Made her feel naked when he looked at her. And made her want to be naked. With him.

The next batter struck out and she watched Marco trot back to the dugout. He grabbed his glove and hustled to the outfield, ready to play. She watched him cover the large expanse of left field. He would shift his body at the crack of the bat. Somehow he knew which direction the ball would go before it left the bat. Instinct.

She had that kind of instinct when it came to her players.

Usually.

She watched Marco make several routine and not-so-routine plays. Her gut feeling about his defense was spot on. She hoped her faith in his batting would play out eventually.

But when he got to the plate in his next at-bat, he hit the ball hard, right into the glove of the diving center-fielder. On his next trip to the plate, his frustration showed. He hit a weak grounder to third. He shook his head as he walked back to the dugout. This time, he didn't look up.

"Your boy toy is turning out to be a bust already." Clayton slunk into the seat next to her. He leaned back, stretching his legs as if he owned the place. Right. He had a thirty percent share of ownership. He was her business partner, but he saw her more as competition. He'd been threatened by the players' loyalty to her father and now her.

And he wanted her position as president and managing partner. Vice president wasn't enough for him. She wasn't sure if he wanted more power or if he wanted to be more powerful than her. Some men couldn't handle a woman who knew more than they did. He'd expected her to be a spoiled little rich girl, only interested in her daddy's money to keep herself in designer shoes and spa treatments. Instead, he'd been shown up by her business savvy and determination to improve the team.

"And we gave up a hot pitching prospect to get him." He didn't like the fact that she couldn't be pushed around. That she knew more about the game than he did, and a lot more about the players, both on her team and around the league. He only cared about numbers, statistics, and name recognition. She sometimes wondered if he chose players based more on jersey sales over actual production on the field.

"Marco Santiago will come through for us." She hoped. No, she truly believed in him. "I'm sure of it."

"Oh really?" Clayton leaned toward her, the Scotch on his breath making her a little nauseated. His wife, Annabelle, had left after the third inning to get the girls ready for bed. "You want to bet on it?"

"What would you like to wager?" She hated that he could bait her so easily, but she couldn't let him think she was intimidated by him. Or that she had any doubts about her choice. "A hundred bucks?"

"No. Not cash. I've got plenty of that." He gave her a patronizing laugh. "But I'd be more than willing to wager, say five percent."

"Five percent?" If she won, that would give her more of an advantage when it came to negotiations. Dempsey trusted her and usually went along with her decisions, but it would be nice to have the added leverage over Clayton. "And just how would we measure Santiago's contribution?"

Would he have to lead the league in RBIs? Batting average? He'd already been named an all-star. Just not for their team. But there was only one thing she wanted from Marco. From her team.

"MVP?" Clayton suggested.

She laughed. No one had ever won the most valuable player award after being traded. She wasn't going to fall for a sucker bet.

"Nice try. It would be quite an accomplishment, but not likely enough to give up a percentage of my team." She narrowed her gaze. "I want something more. I want the division. I think Santiago will help us get there."

"L.A. has picked up several big names." He was still pouting about losing out on one of the megastar free agents last winter. Even though he hadn't quite justified his enormous salary. "It's going to be tough to win the division outright."

"But it can be done." She folded her arms across her chest. She couldn't back down. For one thing, her partner didn't know shit about what it took to put together a winning team. But more importantly, she had absolute faith in her new left fielder. He would contribute to the team's ultimate success. "Marco Santiago is the key. I would bet five percent, no make it ten, that the Goliaths will make it to the post-season."

"The division title. Not a wild card berth?" He gave her a shit-eating grin. "That sounds like a definitive measurement."

"Looks like we have a deal." She leaned across the armrest and shook on it. She got a shiver down her spine at the contact. But it wasn't the good kind of shiver. Not at all like the kind of tingling she felt when she touched Marco.

That kind of tingling must have short-circuited her brain. She'd just bet ten percent of her team—her legacy—on a player who didn't want to be there in the first place. A man who was more interested in hitting on her than hitting a baseball.

What could possibly go wrong?

Maybe she wasn't ready to run the team. No. She was ready. She'd been doing it long enough. Marco Santiago was a good acquisition. He was a good player and once he had a chance to settle in with the team, he could be a great player. One she could count on. What she hadn't counted on was the crazy attraction between them. It had thrown her off her game, but she'd shake it off. She had to.

Chapter 3

After his last at bat, Marco glanced over at the empty seat behind home plate. Even without her sitting there, he still felt the overpowering presence of Hunter Collins. He wanted her. Wanted her more than was good for him. Or the team.

The Goliaths had a six game road trip coming up. He was already packed, ready to head straight for the airport after the game. He hoped getting away for a few days would give him the space he needed to get his head on right. To work out the flaw in his swing. Yeah, sure, the flaw was in his swing. In the swing of his head toward Hunter's seat. Then up toward the booth, where he imagined the owner's box was located.

A road trip was just what he needed to clear his head. To get back in the game. And every other cliché guys like him used to excuse their poor performance.

Hunter believed in him. Or she had until he got one look at her, and he'd somehow forgotten everything he'd ever known about hitting a baseball. It couldn't come at a worse time, either. Not when his contract was up at the end of the year.

This was supposed to be his chance to sign the big deal. He hoped it would be here, in San Francisco. In the short time he'd been in the Goliaths clubhouse, he'd noticed the guys had something special. A camaraderie that he hadn't found anywhere else. Instead of a collection of players, all doing their own thing, they were a *TEAM*. They backed each other up. And not just when the spotlight was on them. It was like they were more than teammates. More than friends, even. It was like they were a family.

But he was still the outsider. The new guy who wasn't quite cutting it. Wasn't pulling his weight. And that was one more reason he needed to stay as far away as possible from Hunter. He didn't need to sleep his way onto the roster. That wouldn't do either of them any good.

He needed to forget about her. Starting now. He'd board the plane for Atlanta, and when he returned, he wouldn't be bothered by her presence behind home plate. Wouldn't even think about unbuttoning her stuffy shirts or unpinning her uptight hairdo. He wouldn't wonder if she was as soft underneath as she pretended to be hard on the outside.

And he damn sure wouldn't worry about her partner, married or not, sliding up next to her in the luxury suite, laughing at what a mistake she'd made in bringing Marco Santiago to San Francisco.

No. He couldn't let that happen. Couldn't let him put her down. Couldn't give him the satisfaction of saying *I told you so.*

Marco would just have to work harder. Smarter. And better than anyone else on the team.

Six days later, Marco was the last one to board the plane back to San Francisco. He'd improved his batting average, gotten his first extra-base hit, and two more RBIs. But he still wasn't in his groove. Most of those hits were just plain lucky. Weak ground balls that squirted through the infield. Bloopers that fell just short of the outfielders. He wasn't making real good contact, and he had far too many strikeouts.

His concentration was still shot.

It helped a little that Hunter wasn't sitting behind home plate. But she was sitting there in his head. Tormenting him. Tempting him. Torturing him.

He'd never let a woman come between him and his game. Not in high school, college, or the minor leagues. Especially not when he'd made it to the majors. He'd always kept his personal life separate. Any time a woman even got close to coming between him and base-

ball, it was always easier to let her go than try to juggle her needs
with the needs of his team.

Ever since he stepped into that limo with Hunter, he couldn't get
her out of his system. Must be pheromones or something. How else
could he explain an intense sexual attraction to a woman who was not
only his boss, but was sending seriously non-sexual signals?

The way she dressed, for example. He couldn't think of one thing
he liked about her wardrobe. She dressed like she was going for a job
interview at a funeral home in a black-and-white movie. He'd only
seen her in black and gray. Conservative. Boring. Like she was trying
to hide something. Her femininity. Her passion. But he saw right
through her. Or rather, he felt something, an underlying sensuality
that she couldn't quite keep hidden. Not from him.

And he wanted to uncover that sensuality in the worst way.

But despite their mutual attraction, she'd made it very clear she
wasn't interested in him.

Time to let it go. To take the advice of the master of control. The
man. The myth. The Monk.

"Hey Johnny, I'll bet you're looking forward to getting home."
Marco sat down with an empty seat between him and his teammate.

"Yeah. It wasn't a bad road trip." They'd won four out of six
games in Atlanta and Milwaukee. "But I'm definitely ready to sleep
in my own bed."

"For me, one hotel is the same as the next." He wasn't complaining, just stating a fact.

"You're still at the hotel?" Johnny shook his head. "Man, you
need a place of your own."

"I haven't had time to look." He was too busy trying to get Hunter
out of his head. Trying to get his swing back. "Besides, at this point I
don't even know how long I'm going to be here. Kind of hard to find
a decent place willing to rent for only two or three months."

"You could sublet my apartment," Johnny offered. "It's right
across the street from the ballpark. Now that Alice is over her morning sickness, we never stay over. It's just sitting there. Vacant. It
would be perfect for you, if you're interested."

"That might help me feel a little more settled." Anything was better than staring up at the ceiling in his hotel room that was so like any
other hotel room in any other city. A bed. A shower. A minibar. He

hadn't even bothered to unpack his suitcase. He'd given up a long time ago trying to ever make himself at home.

"Why don't you come by tomorrow morning and take a look. If you want it, it's yours. Through October. This team has come too far to go home at the end of September."

"Sounds like a good deal." Marco leaned back in the seat. Having a place to live was only part of his problem.

"Anything else I can do to help you settle in?" Johnny asked. The man must have noticed Marco's lack of concentration.

Marco leaned forward, resting his forearms on his knees. "So how do you keep your head clear? Your concentration is legendary."

"Well, to tell the truth, a lot of it was not having anything else to think about. I didn't have anything else to care about."

No woman getting under his skin.

"Well, you've got a lot now. A new wife, a teenager, and a baby on the way." Marco was surprised by the little stab of envy. "You still manage to keep your head in the game."

"Now I've got even more reason to keep my focus." Johnny's face lit up with the mention of his family.

Again, Marco felt like he was missing out on something. Not that he was looking to get married any time soon. But he thought he'd want a wife. A couple of kids. Someday. When he had a long term contract. When he could offer security. Stability.

He knew he wouldn't want to uproot a family every couple of years. He'd done enough of that growing up. He'd always hated being the new kid. Having the teacher assume he didn't speak English because he was one of those migrant worker's kids. Sometimes they wouldn't even bother to check his birth certificate to see that he was, in fact, here legally. He was born in Texas, just like two former presidents.

"I need to find my focus," Marco stretched his legs out in front of him. "Otherwise, I won't need to bother unpacking my bags. My contract is up at the end of the year. Then I'm a free agent."

"So you want to make sure you finish strong." Johnny knew the game. The whole game, both on and off the field.

"I want to help the team finish strong." What he really wanted was a long-term contract. "The postseason bonus would be nice, too."

"Not to mention make you more marketable."

"Hey, maybe if I get my act together, they might want to keep me around." Marco threw it out there as a joke, but yeah, he'd like that. He'd like that a lot. "It seems like a good organization. A team that's only going to move forward."

"Yeah. I've loved playing with these guys this year. More than being a collection of all-stars, it really feels like a team, you know?"

"I haven't quite felt like one of the guys yet." Marco had never had trouble fitting in with his teammates. But not this time. Mostly because he felt like he was letting everybody down. He didn't want to be the reason they didn't make it to the postseason.

"You will. You've been with the team, what, a week?"

"Ten days." Ten days and he hadn't done shit. Other than hit on his new owner, struggle at the plate and keep to himself. Yeah, that was a good way to fit into the clubhouse.

"You'll feel like one of us by the end of this home stand. They traded for you for a reason. I'm sure you'll be a key member of this team by the end of October."

"Easy for you to say. You're The Monk. You're sure of everything."

The other man just laughed.

"What looked like confidence on the outside"—Johnny turned and gave him a serious stare—"was just a way of covering up my fear. For most of my career, I was too scared to get rattled. Afraid if I let up for one game, one pitch, the whole world would find out I was a fraud."

"You're hardly a fraud." Marco had a hard time picturing future Hall of Famer Johnny Scottsdale as having any doubts. "You're practically perfect."

"I was perfect. Once. For nine innings. I got over it." Johnny also had two Cy Young Awards. "Besides, I still had to come out to the ballpark week after week. Play my game, even though I knew I wasn't going to be perfect. I knew I'd make mistakes. And it wasn't until I realized that I didn't have to be perfect that I was able to relax again. I just have to go out there and be the best I can be on that day."

"You know, that's probably the best advice anyone's ever given me."

"Anytime." Johnny stretched out his legs, leaned back in his seat, and tried to relax a little.

"How'd you do it all those years?" Marco needed to know about the non-baseball stuff. "How did you stay a monk off the field?"

Johnny chuckled. Shook his head and pulled his legs up so he could rest his elbows on his knees.

"It was actually a lot easier than you'd think." He gave Marco a sideways glance. "For me, anyway. I could resist temptation because there was really only one woman for me."

"Your wife." Envy shook Marco like a blast of turbulence. "How did you know she was the one?"

"I just did. It's hard to explain, especially since she married my best friend right after I left for the minor leagues." Johnny leaned back, stretching out again. "But it was already too late. She had me the first time we met."

"And you never even looked at another woman?" Marco was starting to understand what that felt like. There had been women on the road trip who normally would have caught his eye, but he wasn't interested. Not now. He could tell himself it was because of the slump, but he'd busted out of slumps before with the help of a little female companionship.

"You ever play any other sports?" Johnny asked. "As a kid?"

"Sure. I played soccer a couple of years." Marco wasn't sure what this had to do with his question. Maybe Johnny was just tired of the whole monk thing. "But after a while, I gave it up."

"Were you any good at it?"

"Sure. I was fast. Aggressive. Could kick the ball pretty hard."

"So why did you quit?" There was something in Johnny's voice that made Marco think he was leading him somewhere.

"I didn't love it." Marco shrugged, still not sure what soccer had to do with his problem with Hunter. "I knew baseball was it for me."

"But you could have kept playing soccer, right? You might have been really good."

"True. But why take a spot away from someone who really wanted it?"

"Why be with a woman if she's not the one you really want?" Johnny asked.

Okay, he got the picture now. Mostly.

"I don't know, man. If I got cut from the baseball team, I might have taken up another sport. How'd you do it knowing you couldn't have her? It would be like if you'd quit after throwing your perfect game, knowing you'd give up a hit again."

Johnny folded his hands behind his head. "I guess you could say I gave up on women, but I never really gave up on Alice. My secret, or whatever, was to channel it all into my game. The night I threw the perfect game? It would have been her tenth wedding anniversary."

"Really?" Marco was even more impressed now.

"Yeah. So I did the only thing I knew how to do, I pitched my heart out." Johnny chuckled. "Good thing I had some of it left when I found out she was no longer married."

"I think I will take a look at your apartment tomorrow." Marco felt a little like he'd walked in on a private moment. Johnny's very public perfect game had a personal meaning behind it. "But call me when you're ready. You need to spend time with your wife."

"Don't worry. We're pretty good at making up for lost time." He grinned, obviously looking forward to reuniting with Mrs. Scottsdale. "So tell me, is there someone back in St. Louis? Someone you're trying to figure out if she's more like baseball or soccer?"

"No. Not in St. Louis. Or Florida or Texas." Marco couldn't admit that he was hung up on a woman he couldn't have. He knew she wasn't like soccer, just a way to get his kicks. But he didn't know if Hunter could be it for him. Could she be more to him than the game itself?

The road trip hadn't been a total disaster. They hadn't lost any ground. But they hadn't gained any. Every time the Goliaths won, so did their rivals. Every time L.A. lost a game, San Francisco dropped one, too.

Hunter was getting anxious as the remaining games became fewer and fewer in number. It was still too early for either team to start thinking about the magic number—that mathematical combination of wins by the leading team, losses by the second place team, and games left to play—but the tension was mounting.

She'd feel a lot better when the team was back on home soil. More in control of things. The players each had their own pregame rituals, and she had hers. Intellectually, she knew it didn't change the outcome of the game if she didn't line up the bobbleheads in her office just so, or forget to pat the large foam finger proclaiming *We're #1!* as she left the office for the day. She knew turning her broom bristle side up after winning the first two games of a series wouldn't guarantee a sweep, but she did it anyway. It couldn't hurt.

And maybe, just maybe, a little pregame warm-up might be necessary to get Marco Santiago out of his slump.

She'd known the man ten days. And after tossing and turning in her bed for ten nights, she realized she couldn't deny the attraction that sizzled between them. He'd made it very clear that he was game for a little outside the park action. She'd shut him down. And he'd admitted that her denial was at least contributing to his lack of production at the plate.

She decided she couldn't deny him any longer. She couldn't deny herself any longer either. It had been more than two years since she'd last gone out on a date. Since her father's cancer had returned. She didn't want to think about how long it had been since she'd last had sex.

She wasn't a prude or anything, it was just that most of the men she'd gone out with didn't really do it for her. They were nice, decent men. On paper, just what she was looking for. But she hadn't felt that spark. That sizzle. That something extra that went beyond stats.

Until she looked into Marco Santiago's eyes. She felt it then, the hyper-awareness, that same nervous anticipation she felt when the Goliaths held the lead in the bottom of the ninth and they were down to the last strike.

She felt it so much that she'd filled a prescription for birth control pills, picked up an extra-large sized package of condoms, and put fresh sheets on her bed.

Now all she had to do was figure out how to seduce the sexiest man in baseball.

She drove to the ballpark to meet the team bus. Most of the players left their cars in the secure players' lot, rather than the airport's long-term parking. Many of the wives and families who lived in the area would meet the team bus. There were always a few fans who stood just outside, hoping to catch a glimpse of their heroes and let them know they'd been missed while on the road. There were usually large crowds after a long road trip or an important series.

Hunter stood off to the side. She didn't feel like she belonged with the players' wives and girlfriends. Even if they knew who she was, it didn't mean they would accept her into their circle. She was just their husband's or boyfriend's boss.

Besides, this was their time. Time to welcome home the men they loved. The men with whom they shared a life outside of baseball.

As she watched couple after couple reunite, Hunter felt a pang of loneliness that went deeper than just not having a man in her life. She missed her father. The thought of going back to her empty house was almost unbearable.

He'd died not long after opening day. She'd known it was coming, but it still hit her pretty hard. She was grateful he'd hung in there until after the season started. So she'd have something to focus on other than her grief. She could surround herself with her team. Her family. The only family she had left.

Alice Scottsdale approached her as they waited for the bus to unload.

"I don't know if you remember me, we met a few times through my work with the Harrison Foundation."

"Of course, I remember you. And congratulations." Hunter hoped her smile hid her feelings of envy. "On your marriage. The baby. Everything."

"Thank you." The other woman actually glowed with happiness. "I wanted to extend my condolences. Your father was a good man. I enjoyed working with him through the foundation."

Hunter couldn't speak past the familiar lump in her throat. Grief was something that would sometimes hit her all of a sudden. She tried to push the feelings aside. To save them for the offseason. She didn't have time to deal with it now, she had a team to run. Too many people were counting on her. Not just the players, but also coaches and support staff. Even the people who worked at the ballpark—the concessioners, ushers, and parking lot attendants—all needed the Goliaths to be successful.

She had nightmares of losing control of her team. Of someone like Clayton Barry running the franchise into the ground or deciding it would be more profitable to try and move the team. She couldn't let that happen.

"I've always been impressed with the way you've run things from the top down. The Goliaths have always been a first class organization." Alice was talking to her, but her focus was on the bus. "And I know that this team means more to you than just a business."

"This team is all I have left." Hunter didn't mean to say that out loud. Even if it was true. "What I mean is, this team is like my family. I grew up around these guys. Well, not these guys. But the men who came before them. It was like having twenty-five brothers who all looked out for me. Only now, I'm the one looking out for them."

"And you are doing a great job." Alice put her hand on Hunter's shoulder, but then her attention was drawn to the last two players to emerge from the team bus, Scottsdale and Santiago.

Chapter 4

As the last man off the bus, Marco was forced to watch his team-mate fling himself into the arms of his awaiting bride. The woman who had been the force behind The Monk's success this season.

Marco was almost able to brush away the envy. But standing next to Mrs. Scottsdale, was the one woman he was determined to forget. Hunter Collins.

What the hell was she doing here?

Other than the fact that it was her team, her bus, and her ballpark. Hell, for all he knew, she owned half the city. Including him.

Maybe he could slip past her. Get a cab back to the hotel and take the world's longest, coldest shower.

"Marco." Too late. She'd spotted him.

"Polo." He tried to joke. To pretend her rejection hadn't hurt. Hadn't messed with his mind.

"Can I give you a ride to your hotel?" She smiled. A real, open and warm smile. Warning bells sounded in his head. He should run the other way. Catch a ride on the Muni. Walk. Take a cable car or hitchhike.

"Sure. Why not?" Damn. He wished he had his Mustang. Then he could drive his own sad self to the hotel. But it was still in St. Louis. Apparently along with his pride and his ability to hit a fastball.

"Great." She smiled again. He wanted to go running to The Monk.

To have the other man teach him the ways of the celibate competitor. But The Monk had his arms wrapped around his wife.

Marco shouldered his bag, following Hunter like a lemming going off to certain demise but unable to help himself.

She walked across the parking lot with determined steps. He supposed if she'd wanted him to get back on a plane to St. Louis, she would have met him at the airport. When she stopped in front of a red Mini Cooper convertible and disabled the alarm, he threw his head back and laughed.

"What?" She spun around so fast that a few strands of hair shook loose from her uptight hairdo.

"I just never would have matched you with this car." It was red. And fast. And kind of sexy in an offbeat sort of way. "I would have pictured you as a BMW, Mercedes or . . . I don't know, a Bentley kind of girl."

"A Bentley?" She drew her brows together. She was cute. And far too sexy. "Seriously?"

"I don't know." He shrugged. Almost forgetting the vow he'd made to himself. The vow of forgetting her. "It seemed like a good guess. When you're not riding around in a limo."

"It's fun to drive." She didn't really need to defend her vehicle choice, but she did anyway. "Easy to park, and on those really fabulous Northern California days, there's nothing like driving a convertible up the coast."

"But it's red." He swept his gaze over her gray pantsuit and ivory blouse and black shoes. Her outfit made the red car seem that much brighter. And it made him wonder even more if she was hiding something. The image of a red lace bra and matching panties popped into his head. He had to shove that thought down deep into his subconscious. He was only asking for trouble by even imagining it.

"Yes. It's red." She placed her hands on her hips. "What's wrong with that?"

"I was starting to think you were color blind." He walked around to the back of the car. "Is this open?"

She opened the tailgate so he could toss his duffel bag inside. She slammed it closed and marched around the front of the car. Great. He'd pissed her off. Maybe it was for the best. Maybe she'd stop trying to help him.

"Thanks for the ride." He squeezed himself into the front passenger seat. At six-four, he wasn't exactly comfortable in the compact car. Another inch and he'd need to ask her to put the top down. "I really do appreciate it."

"Yeah. Sure." She didn't even look at him as she put the car into reverse. "Sorry it's not in a Bentley."

"Look, I like the car. It's cute." He shifted, trying to get comfortable. Trying to keep from putting his foot in his mouth, but that seemed to be the only place it fit.

"Cute? Huh? What do you drive?"

"A Mustang." At least she was still talking to him. "A '65 classic."

"Convertible?"

"Of course." Something they actually had in common. They both understood the amazing freedom of hitting the open road with the wind in their hair.

Hunter laughed as she maneuvered her little car around the city streets. She zipped around obstacles and whipped through traffic like Matt Damon in *The Bourne Identity*. She seemed to be enjoying herself. Of course, her knees weren't pressed against her chest and she wasn't fighting a most unwelcome erection.

Finally she pulled up in front of his hotel. Marco bit back an invitation for her to join him. He already knew he'd strike out. Again. He'd had enough of that at the plate. So with a heavy heart and too tight jeans, he unfolded himself from the passenger seat. He stretched before he headed around to retrieve his luggage.

"Aren't you going to ask me to come up to your room? Join you for a drink? Or something like that?" Hunter rolled down the window and smiled. Was she teasing him?

"So you can explain to me once again why it would be a bad idea?" He knew she was out of his league. No use continuing to make a fool of himself. "I'll save us both the trouble, and just say goodnight. And thanks for the ride."

"That's too bad." She set the parking brake and got out to unlock the back. "I might have said yes this time."

She opened the tailgate, pulled his bag out of the cargo area, and handed it to him. He hoisted the strap over his shoulder and stood there like an idiot, watching her get back in her car and drive away.

Was he supposed to take that as encouragement? Like getting a foul tip instead of a complete swing and miss? Or was she just teasing him? Now that she could see he was giving up.

It didn't matter. Either way, he was going up to his room. Alone.

Until she showed up in his dreams. Now he had even more fuel for his imagination. That sporty little red car revealed a side of her he'd suspected was there all along. A playful, fun, adventurous side. And at least in his dreams, it would be physically possible to get it on in the front seat of her car. In real life, he'd end up on the disabled list if he even tried. They both would.

Well, that didn't go as she'd planned. Hunter pulled into her garage, frustrated, embarrassed, and more than a little discouraged. He'd shot her down. No. That wasn't quite right. He never even gave her a chance. He just gave her a hard time about her car, and then thanked her for the ride.

She felt like a fool. Here she'd thought he was truly interested in her, only to find out that he was just, what? Flirting? Or was it just that he was so used to women falling at his feet he didn't know any other way to relate to her?

At least she hadn't made an obvious sexual overture. She'd offered him a ride. And if he had asked her to join him in his hotel room, she would have said yes. But would she have been able to laugh it off when he admitted he wasn't serious?

At least she didn't have to find out.

Everything could just go back to normal. She could concentrate on her team. On making sure she did everything in her power to keep them on track. She could return to her seat behind home plate. She wouldn't have to suffer through another game up in the luxury suite with Clayton Barry.

Ugh. The bet. She'd bet ten percent of her ownership share that they'd win the division outright. Ten percent that would make it that much easier for him to wrestle control of the team from her. Marvin Dempsey, the third partner, had always been loyal to her father. A friend even before he'd become a partner. He'd been there for her, too. Helping with funeral arrangements, writing the obituary, and setting up a scholarship fund in her father's name. But she knew it was business. And if Barry wanted to play hardball, Dempsey would do what was best for his bottom line. He had a family of his own to support. He owed his loyalty to his children and grandchildren.

She had a feeling he'd be disappointed in her for taking that bet. All because her pride, and her uncontrolled attraction to Marco Santiago, wouldn't let her admit that she might have given up too much to get Santiago. Maybe he wasn't the missing piece, after all.

She needed to find out. Needed to know what really had him so distracted his shoulders crept up around his ears every time he settled into the batter's box. Gone was the fluid easy swing that she'd coveted for years. Professionally speaking, of course. She had only started wanting him in other ways since meeting him in person. Since feeling his stare. The way he looked her over as if she was the league MVP, batting title, and Gold Glove Award all in one.

She needed to let it go. She walked into the home she'd grown up in. The mansion that was now hers. It was too big for one person. She could house half the team there, and still have room for company.

That's what she needed. To have the players over for a relaxed get-together. She'd invite the single players, and the married guys who didn't have their families here in California. She'd offer them a chance to relax with their teammates, away from the public eye.

Her father had always hosted an informal barbecue on off days in the middle of a long home stand. He'd wanted his players to get to know each other off the field and away from clubs and hotel bars. He wanted them to feel a part of something bigger than the game. Wanted them to know they were more than just a business to him.

She could carry on that tradition. She would carry on the tradition. They had an off day this coming Monday.

She picked up the phone.

"Hello, Hunter, what can I do for you?" Dempsey answered on the second ring.

"I wanted to have some of the guys over. Informally, like back in the old days." The days when she'd been just a girl. Like a kid sister, hanging around, trying not to get too excited when the baseball players paid attention to her. She'd learned a long time ago that charm was just part of their game.

"That sounds like a fine idea."

"There are quite a few new guys." She hoped it wasn't obvious that there was one man in particular she wanted to entertain. "And a lot of players who might be missing their families. Who are starting to feel the grind of a long season."

"Yes. It can wear a fellow down after a while."

"But I don't want to give anyone the wrong impression." Didn't want to make any of the men feel uncomfortable being invited to the home of a single woman. A single woman with undeniable attraction to one of them. "I thought it might be nice if you and Helen could be here, as well."

"Certainly. Would you like Helen to give our caterer a call?"

"No. I was thinking of keeping it casual. Burgers and dogs. Chips and dip."

"Okay, I'll pick up some dessert."

"You mean, Helen will pick up some dessert."

He laughed. "So what about Clayton and Annabelle? Are they included in this party?"

The last thing she wanted was to spend more time with the man, but she supposed he should be included. He was part of the team, as well.

"He probably won't want to come, but, yeah, I'll invite him."

"He'll drop by, but he won't stay."

"You're probably right."

They finished up the details. A team get-together was a good idea. In theory. But Hunter still had butterflies in her stomach. Even though she wouldn't be alone with Marco, she was still attracted to him. Very attracted to him. So he'd moved on. She was afraid she couldn't.

Marco walked around Johnny's apartment. Nice place. Just across the street from the ballpark. He could walk to work. No more rides from Hunter.

"So what do you think?" Johnny had a big grin on his face. He obviously hadn't spent the night tossing and turning because of some woman. No, he'd spent the night with his wife and his family.

"I'll take it." Marco looked out the big picture window at the ballpark. He could spend as much time there as he needed to get back on track. Extra batting practice, running the bleachers, whatever it took. "I need a place of my own. I'll have to make my own bed, but it's a small price to pay for privacy."

Stability.

"I'm glad. It's nice and quiet here. The parking garage is secure."

"I haven't had a chance to bring my car out yet. Another reason to live close to work. If I keep hitting—or rather, not hitting—like I have been, I wouldn't want to cause a riot on the bus."

"You'll get it back. We're all behind you. Just remember that."

"Thanks. Having a home base will help me settle in." He hoped.

"Anything for a teammate," Johnny offered.

"Just keep runs off the board, and maybe I won't feel like I have to hit a three run homer every night."

"You don't." Johnny sat on the leather sofa.

Marco took the recliner opposite. "Yeah, I keep forgetting that. Things had gotten pretty bad in my old clubhouse. Everyone blaming each other for the recent skid."

Now that he was out of that locker room, he realized just how high the tensions had mounted. They were a good team, full of all-stars, and plenty of big egos. It was great at the beginning of the year. A lot of people predicted they'd go all the way. Then a few key injuries, a collapse of the bullpen in late June, and the last month had been one bad hop after another.

"It's different here. Sure we've got a lot of talented players. But every single one of us plays for the name on the front of the jersey, not the name on the back." Johnny didn't seem like the kind of guy to spout the company line if there wasn't something to back it up. "I know it sounds a little cliché to say we're a team with a capital T, but it's true. I've never experienced anything like it."

"Just one big happy family, huh?" Marco wanted to believe in it. Wanted to be a part of it.

"We have something special here. And it starts at the top. Losing Henry Collins could have put this team in a tailspin. You'd expect some instability with a change in ownership, even if it's just one of the partners. But his daughter stepped right up. She's young, but she's been in the business her whole life."

"She seems to know what she's doing." Marco felt his heart rate spike at the mention of Hunter. "And she's passionate about this team."

That should be enough.

He'd never cared about any of his previous owners. He certainly hadn't cared about what kind of car they drove or how they dressed or where they sat in the ballpark.

"So, do you need help bringing your stuff over?" Johnny asked. "I can fit a few things in the back of my Jeep."

"I don't have much. Just a couple of duffle bags." Marco had long ago learned the art of traveling light, even before his baseball days. "But now that I have an actual address, I can ship some of my things from my apartment in St. Louis."

He could hire someone to pack up his stuff, but he didn't need much. This place had all the essentials: TV, stereo, exercise equipment.

He'd like to have his Mustang. But there just wasn't time to drive it cross country. And there was no way he was going to trust his most valued possession to some stranger. So it would remain in storage until the season ended.

He needed to keep his libido in storage until the end of the season as well.

Not a problem as long as he stayed away from Hunter.

Marco checked out of his hotel room and hung up his five shirts, two pairs of dress pants, and his one suit in his new apartment. He packed his jeans and T-shirts away in the dresser and took a walk over to the ballpark. There was plenty of time to suit up and hit the batting cage before the official warm ups.

After several good cuts in the cage, he felt pretty good by the time he took the field for warm-ups. Getting a place of his own was just what he needed.

Determined to get to know more of his teammates, he reached out to his shortstop. A free agent who'd signed in the offseason, Bryce had spent much of his career with Pittsburgh, and the two men had crossed paths while playing against each other.

"So, it's good to be home, huh?" Marco had long ago stopped associating the word with anything other than the need to wear white pants. They wore the gray uniforms on the road.

"Yeah. It is." Bryce looked like he'd be more at home on the beaches of southern California than the city streets of San Francisco. A golden boy with thick blond hair that fell almost to his shoulders, he had the laid-back attitude of a surfer on spring break. Until he stepped on the field. Then he was all business. With his Gold-Glove winning defense and power at the plate, he already had people talking about the MVP.

As an opponent in the same division, he was the kind of player you wanted to hate, yet you couldn't help but respect him. He was the guy who'd kick your ass on the field and then buy you a beer afterward.

As a teammate, Marco imagined he'd be the guy to help you celebrate the victories along the way, but he'd be the first guy to dig in and help you work through your slumps. He needed a workout partner in the worst way.

"How do you like living in San Francisco?" Marco asked. "I imagine it's very different than Pittsburgh."

"Yeah. It's different. But once you find your way around, it's a great city." Bryce stretched, rolling his head from side to side. "I like the hills. It's great for getting off the treadmill and changing up your workouts. Plus, the scenery is better out on the street, if you know what I mean?"

"Yeah. I haven't had a chance to look around." Nor did he want to. He was no longer interested in the kind of women who were into professional athletes. The kind of women who were fascinated by his job, his income, and his moments in the spotlight.

"Hey, I'd be more than happy to show you around," Bryce offered. "There aren't enough single guys on this team."

"I'm not really looking to party," Marco admitted. "Besides, the last thing I need is to strike out off the field, too."

"Sure. Let me know if you change your mind, though," Bryce added as he finished his stretches.

They seemed to run out of things to talk about. Maybe Marco should have taken Bryce up on his offer to show him around. No one said he'd have to go home with anyone if he didn't want to.

"Are you going to the team barbecue?" Bryce put his glove on, ready to take some ground balls.

"I guess so." Marco had glanced at the invitation only briefly before tossing it in his locker. The last thing he wanted was to stand around talking about how much he sucked.

"You want share a cab with me?" Bryce asked. "I hear they used to be quite the tradition. Before Henry Collins got sick."

The name "Collins" pricked his attention.

"So, where is this party?"

"At the Collins' estate." Bryce grinned. "It's supposed to be casual: barbecue, bocce ball, that kind of thing. It might be fun. Get a chance to see her let her hair down."

Marco knew the her he was talking about. No way he was letting Bad-boy Baxter get anywhere near Hunter. Not without him.

"Yeah. I'll go with you." Marco decided. "I'll definitely go with you."

Chapter 5

So far, the casual get-together was just what Hunter had envisioned. Several groups of players stood around chatting, sipping cold beers, and generally relaxing. A couple of guys were playing a heated game of bocce ball, and she'd managed to keep from spending all her time tracking Marco's movements.

It was time to start cooking the burgers. Hunter lit the grill and went inside to retrieve the tray of hamburger patties she'd prepared ahead of time. She came back to find Marco scraping the grates on her built-in gas grill.

"What do you think you're doing?" She would have been more open to him stepping in if he'd said more than two words to her this afternoon. Okay, so maybe "Thank you for having us over." was actually six words. Still, he'd pretty much avoided her all day. Now he was making himself at home?

"Manning the grill." He grinned, flashing his deep dimples. She couldn't see his eyes behind his sunglasses. That was a good thing.

"I've got it." She tried to step in, but he shook his head.

"Sorry. Red meat. Open flame. Man's job." He pounded his chest and grunted for good measure.

"Really? Does that work for you often?" She crossed her arms over her chest and wasn't too surprised when he dropped his gaze to her breasts. What a caveman.

"Look, I know you've busted your tail doing all the prep work. Getting everything ready. You should relax for a bit. Put your feet up. Have a beer." Now he was being charming. He lowered his voice, making the conversation that much more intimate. "Give me a chance to feel at least somewhat useful."

Fine. She could do that. If his ego was so fragile he needed to grunt, pound his chest, and char meat to feel manly, who was she to get in the way?

She went back into the kitchen to retrieve a platter for the cooked meat. As she reached for a brightly colored dish, she was startled by the sharp sting of memory. She fondly recalled dragging her father to the open market in the Dominican Republic during one of their many scouting trips to the Winter Leagues.

Taking a deep breath, she swallowed the grief before heading back outside.

"Here, you can put the manly meat on this." No, that didn't sound cheesy. Oh, damn it. She'd forgotten the cheese.

"Wow. Colorful." He was teasing her again. And checking her out as he flipped the burgers. "I think there's more to you than meets the eye."

Before she could come up with a clever retort, every head in the back yard turned. Clayton had arrived, with his wife, Annabelle. She'd been featured in the *Sports Illustrated* swimsuit issue three years in a row. Twice on the cover.

"Thank you so much for inviting us." Annabelle swept across the yard in her oh-so-stylish emerald green silk blouse that dipped elegantly in the front and tied in a big bow in the back. She wore crisp white linen cropped pants and wedge-heeled sandals. "What a great idea to give the players a family style picnic."

"I'm glad you could come." Hunter wiped her hands on her cargo pants. She'd wanted to take a break from the suits and go with a more casual style. So she wore a black three quarter sleeve T-shirt, graphite cropped hiking pants, and light-as-air trail shoes. She'd pulled her hair back in a simple braid instead of her usual twist. She was trying for the carefree going-for-a-hike-on-Mt. Tam look. Next to the supermodel, she felt more like she was wearing a digging-through-the-dumpster-for-aluminum-cans kind of style. "You're part of the Goliaths' family as well."

"Aw, that's so sweet of you to include me." Annabelle brushed an air kiss across Hunter's cheek. "I haven't really paid too much attention to the team since the girls were born."

The girls were five-year-old twins, Sophie and Olivia. Two perfect little princesses.

"Did you bring them?"

"Oh, no. They had a play date. Besides, the last thing a bunch of single ballplayers want is to have little girls underfoot."

Hunter used to be that little girl underfoot. When her father had first bought the team, he took her with him to every game, scouting opportunity and media event. She was kind of an unofficial mascot.

"Maybe when we have a get-together for players and their families, you could bring them."

"Sure. Or we could host the next party," Annabelle suggested. She turned to survey the rest of the crowd. She smiled graciously as some of the players recognized her. Then she broke into a huge grin as she caught sight of one player in particular.

"Marco Santiago!" The supermodel practically launched herself at the left fielder. She kissed him lightly on the cheek. "How long has it been?"

"Seven years." He smiled that charming grin of his. "You're beautiful as always."

"Please, I've gotten so out of shape since having the twins." She patted her perfectly flat abs. "But look at you. You've been working out."

She actually reached up and squeezed his biceps.

"Yes, well, that is my job." His cheeks colored slightly.

"Oh. My. God. I can't believe I didn't know you were a Goliath." She shook her head, making her perfect golden locks bounce. "I guess I should pay more attention."

"So what are you doing here? Are you a friend of Miss Collins?" He met Hunter's eyes, offering a slight smile.

"Oh, no. My husband is one of the owners. Can you believe that?"

"He's a lucky man." Marco stepped back, hooking his thumbs in his jeans' front pockets. "I hope he appreciates what he's got. Well, it was good seeing you again, Annabelle."

"What, no hug?" She pouted, and Marco leaned in for a quick embrace.

"Get your hands off my wife!" Clayton chose that moment to make his presence known. "Who the hell do you think you are?"

"Oh, Clayton . . ." Annabelle let go of Marco and went immediately to her husband's side. She placed a soothing hand on his arm. "Don't be dramatic. Marco's an old friend of mine."

"Old friend, huh?" Clayton glared at the other man. His jaw twitched, and Hunter was sure he was about to lunge for Marco's throat.

"Um Marco, I need you in the kitchen." At the moment she didn't care if he took that as an invitation. She just wanted to separate the two men, before she had to scrape blood off her patio.

"Sure. No problem." He stared down the shorter man and followed Hunter back into the house.

"So, what do you need?" Marco looked around her kitchen, waiting for direction.

"I need you to not get into a fight in my backyard." Her heart was still pounding, both from the fear that the two men would go to blows and the thought of Marco and Annabelle as once-upon-a-time lovers.

"I'll behave. I don't know if I can say the same about your partner." His mouth twitched into a little smile. Not enough to bring out his dimples, but enough to show her that he found this amusing.

"You don't understand . . ." She couldn't tell him about the bet, but . . . Oh, she had a bad feeling this was going to end in disaster.

"I think I understand well enough." His expression lost all hint of amusement. "The guy didn't want me here in the first place. And now that he knows I have a history with his wife . . ."

"A sexual history?" Damn, it was none of her business. Except for how it could affect her business. Her team.

"If I didn't know better, I'd think you were a little jealous. But that would mean you were interested. And clearly, you're not."

Hunter felt a warm flush creep up her cheeks. She knew if she tried to protest, he'd see right through her. He seemed to have x-ray vision where she was concerned.

"We dated, briefly, when I was first called up to the majors." He chuckled, clearly enjoying this.

"So you did sleep with her?" Her cheeks flamed.

"Does that bother you?" He moved closer, his damn blue eyes boring right through her.

"I think we should check the burgers on the grill." She tried to move past him, but he caught her arm.

"Hunter, the burgers are fine." His hand was warm, his voice even warmer. "You're jealous."

"She was on the cover of *Sports Illustrated*."

"Now, I'm jealous," he teased. "I've never made the cover."

"She does look better in a bikini." Hunter tried to laugh it off. Pretend her gut wasn't twisting at the thought of him and Annabelle together.

"You think so?" His features became more serious.

"She's beautiful." Hunter couldn't help but sigh. What woman wouldn't be envious of the two-time cover model who looked like she could make a third appearance—even after giving birth to twins?

"She's not the only one." He stared directly into Hunter's eyes. "But I haven't thought of her once since we broke up all those years ago."

"Oh." Hunter had to wonder how many other gorgeous women he'd replaced Annabelle with.

"Yet, I can't get *you* out of my mind." He reached out to touch her hair. "You, with your pulled back hair. Your drab wardrobe. Your barely there makeup. You haunt my dreams."

He muttered something in Spanish. A crude, suggestive remark. He obviously didn't realize that she'd been around enough Latino players to have picked up on slang.

But before she could tell him she also spoke Spanish, his tongue was in her mouth. Hungry. Insistent. Possessive.

He kissed like he played: full throttle. He explored her mouth as thoroughly as he covered the outfield. Diving deep. Lunging. Taking her breath away. He slid his knee between her legs. Instinctively, she pressed against his hard, muscular thigh. He ran his hands up her back. Rubbing. Pressing. Claiming. He shoved one hand through her hair, loosening the carefully braided strands while his other hand continued to pull her closer.

"Marco." She gasped, trying to catch her breath.

He kissed her again. Harder. Deeper. He rubbed his thigh against her most sensitive spot, sending small shudders throughout her body. She was *this* close to having an orgasm, fully clothed, with a yard full of people just outside.

"Marco. Please." She pulled away, even as her heart—no, her body—wanted to protest. "Someone could walk in here any second."

"Right. Sorry." Marco let her go with a heavy sigh. Then he muttered a curse in Spanish.

"*Yo hablo Español.*" She barely managed a smile, her lips were so swollen from his kisses.

"I should have known." He stared down at her. Stared right through her. It was almost enough to make her forget she had company, including her partners, several members of the team, and Marco's former lover.

"I need you to take out the trash." She indicated the cabinet door that hid the kitchen garbage can and showed him the back door.

"You're the boss." Marco gave her a quick nod.

Hunter made a dash for the bathroom. She ducked into the nearest powder room, hoping she could make herself presentable.

Damn.

Damn. Damn. Damn.

He shouldn't have done that. Shouldn't have kissed her. Not here. Not now. Probably not ever, but the damage had been done.

He grabbed the trash bag and headed outside. He needed the fresh air. If he didn't get himself under control, he'd be making a call to his doctor in four hours. And that was without the aid of modern medication. Even without the little blue pill, Marco knew he was in for a long, uncomfortable state of frustration.

When he could no longer avoid the crowd, he washed up and made his way back to the party. All eyes were on him as he returned. Shit. Had someone caught him and Hunter making out in the kitchen?

Bryce walked up to Marco, and handed him a beer. "So you and Annabelle? Damn."

Right. They'd all witnessed Annabelle fling herself into his arms. They'd all heard her husband's display of jealousy. And they'd all seen Hunter step in to keep the peace.

He'd repaid her by sticking his tongue down her throat.

"It was a long time ago. When we were both young and . . ." Marco wished he had something to talk about besides a seven-year-old affair.

"Still, she's pretty hot." Bryce had that locker-room talk down pat.

Sure. Annabelle had that classic all-American beauty. The kind that sold magazines. The kind that young men fantasized about. But Hunter was even hotter. And now that he'd kissed her, he was going to have even more trouble getting her out of his head.

"Annabelle's married. To our boss," Marco reminded him. "And he's not real happy about the connection."

"He'll get over it." Bryce clapped him on the shoulder.

"I hope you're right. Otherwise, this could be a very long season." Thirty-nine games left. Not much time to make an impression. But he realized it didn't matter. He could hit four hundred or a buck forty. He wouldn't be back in a Goliaths uniform next year. So he might as well make the most of it while he was here.

"I'm still new here, but I got a feeling about these guys . . ." Bryce lifted his bottle in salute to their teammates. "They've got something special. No, *we've* got something special here."

But Marco still felt like an outsider. He sat in a quiet corner, munching on a burger, slaw, and some fresh fruit. He sipped the beer Bryce had given him and watched Hunter interact with his teammates. Every smile, every laugh, every nod of her head was like a sharp line drive to his gut. Jealousy flared like a grease fire.

Intellectually, he knew she was just being friendly. Wasn't that the purpose of this little get-together? For her and the other owners to meet with the players, make them feel like part of the family. He'd been here less than two weeks, and he'd already picked up on the sense that making this team feel like family was important. At least it was to Hunter.

For her partner, Clayton Barry, not so much. The man had been latched on to his wife's side, warning off all the other men and sending glaring daggers toward Marco the whole afternoon.

Who would have thought that a couple of weeks spent cavorting with a model at the beginning of his career would end up biting him in the ass all these years later? Even if he got his swing back, there was no way in hell that man would offer Marco a long-term contract. He might as well accept the fact that this would be his only stint with the San Francisco Goliaths.

"Yeah, I think we could go all the way this year." Bryce seemed oblivious to the fact that Marco had lost interest in conversation. He'd lost interest in everything except Hunter. "It started a little rough, with Cooper's suspension. And then Henry Collins passing away. But his daughter has done a good job filling his shoes."

"And his suits." Marco hadn't meant to make that statement out loud, but damn. What he wouldn't give to see Hunter in the flashy outfit Annabelle wore. Or one of the swimsuits from her modeling days. Or nothing at all.

"Well, for a suit, she's pretty easy to talk to, don't you think?" Bryce drained his bottle. "I never shared burgers and beers with any of my other owners."

"Me, either." He'd certainly never shared a kiss with any of them.

"It's just one more thing that makes this team special." Bryce looked at his empty bottle. "You want another one?"

"Nah. I'm good." He didn't need more alcohol to make an ass of himself. He'd already nearly started a fight with one owner and then made out with another. Maybe he could knock Marvin Dempsey on his ass, possibly break his hip. Then he'd be three for three.

"I'll catch you later." With that, Bryce sauntered off to the cooler to grab another beer.

Marco noticed that most of the burgers had been devoured. He picked up the nearly empty platter and carried it into the kitchen. Man, he must be in a real state if he preferred washing dishes to hanging with his teammates. He rummaged around the spacious kitchen, searching for a container to put the leftovers in. He found some foil and carefully wrapped the two uneaten patties before sticking them in her Sub-Zero refrigerator.

"Thank you." Hunter came up behind him, making him nearly jump out of his skin. "I do appreciate your help with the grill."

"Anytime. Maybe when my contract's up, I can get a job at one of the concession stands at the ballpark." He said it as a joke. He just hoped he wouldn't have to resort to that. Ideally, he'd play four or five more seasons. Then hopefully get hired on as a hitting coach on his way to ultimately becoming a manager.

"That would be making good use of that college degree of yours." She had done her homework. Of course she had. She'd taken the time to discover that he was one of about three percent of major leaguers who actually finished college.

"Yes. I went back to school so I'd be qualified to flip burgers someday."

"Well, they were pretty tasty." She walked over to the sink and started filling the sink with hot water. "I'll see what I can do about the concessions job."

"Wouldn't you have to run it by your partners first?" Meaning, the man who had been giving him the stink eye all afternoon.

She made a noise that gave him the impression she wasn't on the best of terms with the younger of her two partners.

"I thought this was one big happy family." Marco needed to know just how tight the ownership group was. "At least, that's what they tell me."

"That's the way my dad ran things." She had a wistful tone in her voice. "I know it probably seems a little strange to consider a billion dollar enterprise as a family business."

He lowered his voice, even though no one was there to overhear. "Does that make me the black sheep?"

"No. Just one who's trying to find his way." She patted him on the shoulder. Not in any way meant to be sexual, yet it sent a jolt straight to his groin. Yeah, he wanted to find his way, all right. Straight to her bed.

"I'll finish these dishes." Marco needed to stand at the sink for a while. With his back to Hunter so she wouldn't notice the way she affected him. "If there's any more out there, just bring them in."

"You think you can just make yourself at home in my kitchen?" She sounded slightly pissed off.

"I must be the only man in America who gets scolded for wanting to help in the kitchen." He plunged his hands into the soapy water. What he really wanted to do was plunge himself deep into Hunter.

"Marco, you don't have to work so hard to impress me." She gathered up a few stray dishes, stacking them on the counter before leaving him alone with his thoughts and his dishpan hands. Not to mention a hard-on that just wouldn't quit.

Chapter 6

Annabelle swept into Hunter's office the next morning, gorgeous as always. Now that Hunter knew she was once Marco's lover, her envy cut a bit deeper.

"I hope I'm not interrupting too much." Annabelle removed her oversized sunglasses and made herself comfortable in the guest chair. "But I wanted to apologize for my husband's behavior yesterday."

"There's nothing to apologize for." At least not to Hunter. If anything, the man should have apologized to his wife for acting like an ass.

"Still, I wanted to make the effort." Annabelle leaned forward. "I guess I should have paid closer attention to the team. And its players. I was so surprised to see Marco again after all these years."

"Were you two serious?" Not that she really wanted to know the answer.

"Oh no, not serious. We were together maybe a couple of weeks." She sighed. It must have been a good couple of weeks. "We had fun, that's for sure. Marco's a great guy. A really great guy. But you know, he'd just been called up for the first time and neither of us were looking for anything serious. Even if we were, it wouldn't have worked out. Not with my career. His career and, well . . . his background."

Hunter tensed, wondering if there was a skeleton in his closet she needed to know about. As his employer, of course.

"As wonderful as he was . . . is . . ." Annabelle closed her eyes, leaning back into the chair. "My father wasn't like yours. He's . . . Well, he would have never allowed me to bring home a man like Marco Santiago."

She looked up at Hunter, then broke the eye contact. "At the time, it was more important to go along with my father than, well you know?"

"I'm sorry. I really don't know. Why would your father have anything to do with your relationship with Marco?" And then she realized the other woman's problem.

"My father would have flipped if I brought home a Mexican guy. The illegitimate son of a maid." She sounded horrified, but Hunter wasn't sure if it was at Marco's heritage or her father's prejudice. "As far as he was concerned, someone like Marco was only good for one thing. Cheap labor."

Cheap? She would have to come up with several million more than he was making this year if she wanted to keep him.

"He had his opinions about immigration. Let them come here to tend crops, mow lawns, make beds." Annabelle rolled her eyes, as if she knew his attitude was wrong, but she couldn't do anything about it. "You know, the jobs real Americans wouldn't want."

"Marco's a real American. Just like us." Anger burned at the assumption that certain jobs were only for certain kinds of people. That one's race, or gender, would preclude someone from being able to perform.

"I know that. You know that." Annabelle shrugged, as if ignorance was no big deal. "But I knew my modeling career would be short lived, so I couldn't afford to be cut off. You know, with nothing but my face, and my body to support me."

"Your father would have cut you off if you'd gotten serious with Marco?"

"He would have cut me off if he'd even found out I was dating Marco." She leaned closer, as if she was about to reveal a huge secret. "I wasn't twenty-one yet, so I had that as an excuse for not going to clubs and places where we'd be photographed."

"So what did you do together?" She shouldn't have asked.

"I'd watch his games. Then we'd hang out. Order room service." Annabelle sighed deeply.

Hunter really shouldn't have asked.

"But mostly we'd talk. He was the first guy who actually noticed I had a brain. And interests of my own." She fidgeted with her sunglasses, twirling them around by one earpiece. "You know, he's really smart, too. He'd been working on finishing his degree even while playing in the minors. Did you know that?"

"Yes. I did."

"He wanted to be sure he had something to fall back on. Wanted to make sure he could take care of his mother."

Was there something wrong with his mother? Maybe that was something else adding to his distraction.

"She always took care of him, sometimes working two jobs to make ends meet. The biggest reason he wanted to make the big leagues was so that she'd never have to worry about money again." She sighed. "Isn't that sweet?"

"Yes. That is sweet." Hunter's heart did a crazy little lurch, both at the thought of Marco as a mama's boy and the reminder of her own loss.

"I forget sometimes that not everyone grows up like we did." Annabelle placed her sunglasses on the top of her head, like a headband.

"I'm pretty sure most people didn't grow up like I did." Hunter had mixed feelings about her childhood. "When I was a kid, of course, I thought everyone spent all their spare time at the ballpark. Then as I got older, I realized I was missing out on things. A dinner table. Chores. A mom."

"That's right. You lost your mom when you were little. Like six or seven?"

"Seven." But her mother had been almost a ghost even before then. She was often shut up in her room with the blinds closed, not feeling well or too tired to play with Hunter most of the time.

"And twenty years later, you lost your father. I'm so sorry."

"Yes. Well, it is what it is." Hunter blinked back the tears and started shuffling some papers on her desk."

"At least you had a great relationship with your father." Now Annabelle was the one to blink back tears. "The kind every girl dreams of."

"I don't know about that. I always got the feeling he wished I'd been a boy." Hunter knew she was loved, but he'd loved the game more. "And I don't know how many girls wished they could spend their childhoods in a locker room full of sweaty men only to be banned once they got their breasts."

"He was just trying to protect you. At least your boobs aren't sitting in your father's friends' desk drawers. Or worse, framed in their office." She shuddered. "When I graduated high school, my father couldn't tear himself away from work to show up. But when I made the cover you'd think he was the one who spent hours out in the freezing cold wearing nothing but a skimpy piece of cloth and being spritzed with cold water to make it look like sweat."

"Aren't you proud of your work?"

Annabelle gave her a puzzled look. "You're the first person to realize modeling is actually a job. No. I guess you'd be the second."

One good guess at the first. Marco.

"So? Are you proud of your work?"

"Yes," Annabelle said softly. "Yes, I am proud of my work. And it was hard work. You have no idea how hard it is to try and look sexy when there are all these people watching you and giving you directions. Sometimes it was hard not to feel ridiculous."

"But you pulled it off. Beautifully." Hunter didn't even try to hide her admiration of the other woman's looks. "You still could."

"Thank you. That's sweet. But I'd have to train, like ninety hours a week, in order to get that body back. When would I spend time with my girls?"

"How are Sophie and Olivia?"

"Priceless." There was genuine awe in their mother's voice. "I can't believe they start school in only a few weeks. They're off with some friends we met at the twins' group. We're taking turns, so the mommies can get used to the idea of having a few hours to ourselves each day."

"That sounds like a good idea."

"It's killing me."

They chatted for a few minutes more. But it was clear that Annabelle was anxious to go pick up her twin princesses.

"Maybe sometime we could go shopping together." Annabelle stood and offered a hopeful smile.

"Shopping?" Right, like Hunter wanted to step into a dressing room with the former model. "I'm not really much of a shopper."

"Oh, I just thought maybe you were still in mourning or something." She cast a glance over Hunter's wardrobe.

Yes. It was dull. Hadn't Marco mentioned her colorless wardrobe a time or two or every time they were alone? But she hadn't realized it was that bad. That someone would think she was in mourning.

"I guess I could use a little update, but nothing too flashy." She still had to fit into a man's world.

Marco figured he had nothing to lose. He should be able to relax at the plate. No pressure. Right?

Wrong.

Hunter was back in her front row seat. She had her usual drab suit buttoned up tight. Her hair pulled back. The only color was a blush that appeared on her cheeks when he caught her eye.

Damn. Now he couldn't stop thinking about that kiss. About how she tasted. How she felt. How she responded.

What the hell had he been thinking? That he'd be satisfied with one kiss? No way. He wanted her more than ever. His suspicions had been confirmed. She was a fireball underneath all that gray.

He struck out looking in his first at bat. Didn't even get a swing off. He couldn't look at her as he walked back to the dugout. He knew he'd let her down. So yeah, he still had something to lose.

Her respect.

It only got worse. A misplay in the outfield cost them a run. He struck out swinging in the fourth, killing a rally that would have at least tied the game. Then in the bottom of the ninth, with two on and one out, he grounded into a game ending double play.

He couldn't remember a worse performance in twenty years of playing baseball. Not even the time he was in Little League and forgot he was the runner. When the next batter hit a slow roller to first base, Marco had picked up the ball and proudly stepped on the bag, making an out for the other team.

His Goliaths teammates tried to boost him up. They'd all been there. Every man in that clubhouse had been the goat at one time or another. The only way to not fail at this game was to not play it.

Marco took a long shower. As he watched the water swirl down the drain, he couldn't help but wonder if his career might be heading in the same direction.

He'd never had a slump last this long. Never been so distracted that he couldn't just work it out in the cage. But this time it seemed like the harder he tried, the worse he performed. The more he wanted to impress Hunter, the more he let her down.

Oh, yeah, he was screwed.

By the time he got out of the shower, the locker room was nearly empty. Only his manager was still around. He called Marco into his office.

"What's up?" Like Marco needed to ask.

"I've noticed you're always the first one to the ballpark. The last to leave." Javier had been an all-star catcher back in his day. He'd also been traded a time or two before finally calling it quits due to injury. "Your work ethic is admirable."

"I try." Marco shrugged.

"Maybe you're trying too hard," Javier echoed Hunter's words. "Do me a favor. Take tomorrow off."

"You're benching me?" He shouldn't be surprised, but still . . . It was a blow to the old ego. He hadn't been benched since junior high, when they still had mandatory playing time.

"No. I mean take tomorrow off from the extra batting practice." Javier put a hand on his shoulder. "Don't come to the ballpark until you have to. Take a cable car ride. Go see a movie. Do something not related to baseball."

"Yeah. I'll think of something." Marco wasn't sure if it would help, because it wasn't baseball that was screwing with his head.

"There's your problem right there." Javier tapped his forehead. "You're thinking too much. You need to relax. I know it's hard coming to a new city. A new clubhouse. A new routine. You need to find some way to ease the tension."

"Yeah. Well, I usually do that by hitting the batting cage."

"Try something else." Marco didn't need his manager telling him he needed to get laid. He'd been fine for months without sex. Had the best start of his career by forgetting about women. Focusing on his career. Working out a little more on the off-season. Coming into spring training leaner, stronger, and ready to make a run for it.

Sex was the furthest thing from his mind.

Until he set foot in that limo. Until he met Hunter Collins. Until he kissed her and only made things worse.

* * *

Hunter wasn't surprised to find Marco was the last one in the clubhouse. He'd been the first to arrive, the last to leave every day since he joined the team. He worked harder than any other player, but he wasn't getting the results they'd hoped for. He was officially in a major slump.

Looking at him hunched in front of his locker, it was easy to see why. The tension in his shoulders was obvious even from clear across the room. No wonder he couldn't get a good swing off. He was too tight. Too wound up.

She needed to help him loosen up.

The carpet softened the sound of her footsteps. But he was so far into his own head, she doubted he would have heard her approach wearing tap shoes on ceramic tile.

She placed her hands on his shoulders, and he tensed even more.

"What are you doing here?" His voice was just as tight as his shoulders.

"Trying to help you relax." She slowly started to knead his rock hard muscles. They didn't give. She tried again, but she didn't have enough strength in her fingers.

He held his body stiff, unable or unwilling to give in to her.

She moved her hands to rub the back of his neck. Then she ran her fingers through his thick dark hair and started massaging his scalp.

A nearly inaudible groan came from deep in his throat.

Progress.

She moved closer, her breasts pressed against his back. His muscles tightened. The opposite of what she was trying to do.

"Marco," she whispered into his ear. "Relax. I'm not going to hurt you."

She brushed her lips across his neck, just below his ear and he trembled.

He smelled so good. She couldn't help herself. She flicked her tongue out to taste him.

"Mmmmm." That's better. Some of his tension released as she moved her mouth down his neck.

"You're going to kill me, woman." He groaned.

"I think I'd rather seduce you."

He reached around, pulled her onto his lap, and captured her mouth with his.

She dug her fingers through his hair as he plunged his tongue in her mouth. She could taste his desperation, his need to prove himself to her.

He grabbed her hips and positioned her over the thick hard ridge of his erection. She was getting through to him. As he deepened the kiss, she moved against him, sending little quivers of pleasure straight through her body. Even through their clothes, she could feel him throbbing. Straining. Pressing her into him. Bringing her to the edge before lifting her to her feet.

"Let's get out of here." Marco's voice was rough, desperate, as he tugged on her arm, leading her to the door.

"I'll drive to the hotel," she suggested, wanting to finish what they'd started.

"I found an apartment." He threw open the door. "It's just down the street."

"Great. That's just great." She was excited for him. Excited for them, because she didn't want to sit through traffic.

Once he got her inside the building, Marco pressed the button for the elevator, but when it didn't provide immediate gratification, he yanked her toward the stairwell. Together they sprinted up the three flights of stairs and burst into the hallway leading to his apartment.

"I'm subletting the place from Johnny Scottsdale," Marco told her as he fumbled for his keys. He found the right one and slid it into the lock. He turned the key and shoved the door open.

He pushed Hunter against the door and pressed his mouth to hers. She opened, allowing him inside. He clutched the back of her head, pulling her closer. He felt around for a way to let her hair down, but he couldn't quite get a grasp on whatever held the knot of her hair so tightly.

She groaned, wrapping her leg around his and sliding up his thigh. She was as needy as he was. He lifted her and she encircled his waist with those long legs of hers. They moved together toward the bedroom where he dropped her to the king sized bed.

"Did I ever tell you how much I hate this suit?" Marco kissed her neck as he unbuttoned her jacket and slid it down her shoulders. He went to work on her blouse, but didn't get past the second button before becoming too impatient and popping the buttons off.

"Oh. White cotton." He shook his head, tsking under his breath before unhooking the front clasp of her bra. "I was kind of hoping for something more exotic."

"This is the real me." She sounded almost apologetic.

"Mmm, beautiful," he murmured as he drew her nipple into his mouth. He flicked his tongue over the tight pink bud and grazed his teeth over her flesh, just enough to make her squirm beneath him, but not enough to hurt her.

"You're so hot." He moaned, moving his mouth across her skin so he could give her other breast the same attention. "So, damned hot."

She made sexy little noises as he moved his hands and his mouth down her body. After undoing the top button of her slacks, he kissed a trail down her belly as he slid the zipper down and pulled her pants off.

"More white cotton. We'll have to do something about that." He grinned as he slipped his hand beneath her panties.

"Marco." She gasped when he slid one finger into her center. She was so wet. So ready. And so responsive. He'd barely gotten a feel for her when she started to buck against his hand. She whimpered and shuddered as an orgasm overtook her. "Oh my. I wasn't quite ready for that."

"Well, get ready." Marco reached for a condom from the bedside drawer. "Because I'm just getting started."

"You can start by getting naked." Her voice was so sexy and seductive.

"You're the boss." Marco tore his shirt over his head while she reached for his jeans. She undid the buttons and zipper and shoved his jeans down over his hips.

She licked her lips as she slid her hands beneath the elastic waistband.

"Oh my." Her eyes widened at the sight of his erection. "Oh my, my, my."

"This is what you do to me." Marco groaned as she wrapped her hand around him.

She fumbled with the condom, so he took it from her and made quick work of covering himself. He knelt between her legs, placing his hands beneath her thighs, he lifted her hips for easier access.

She gasped as he slid inside. She was tight, almost too tight. He withdrew, and then pushed again. Slowly, carefully, he eased into her.

"Please don't tell me you're a virgin." He laughed, hoping like hell that he wasn't hurting her.

"No." She shifted her hips, drawing him deeper. "It's just been a while."

He relaxed. *Thank God.* He thrust a little harder. Once, twice, a third time. He was just starting to find his rhythm.

"Oh hell no!" He pulled out suddenly. "I'm sorry. It broke."

He pulled the remains of the condom off, swearing in a combination of English and Spanish. "I think we're still okay. I didn't . . . I wasn't close."

"Relax, Marco." Her face softened into a smile. "I'm on the pill."

"Oh. Okay." He breathed a small sigh of relief. "And I'm . . . You don't have to worry about anything else."

"I know. I trust you." She wrapped her arms around his neck, pulling him back toward the bed. "Now. Where were we?"

She trusted him. Even now. She'd come to him tonight because she believed in him. She knew what he needed and she'd given it to him. He grabbed another condom. If only to keep the sensation down. He was a lot closer to losing control than he'd like to admit.

He shifted his weight, centering himself over her. She wrapped her legs around him and he entered her slowly. He didn't want to hurt her. He only wanted to please her. To prove to her that he was worth her trust, her faith in him.

He wanted to take his time. To make this last. But she was making it so damn difficult to hold on to his control.

She bucked beneath him, digging her nails into his shoulders. It was coming. He could feel her inner muscles spasm. She wrapped her legs around him even tighter, squeezing his hips with her thighs, drawing him deeper, deeper into her as her climax built.

She gripped him tighter, her hands, thighs, and inner muscles all tightening at once as she called out his name. It was all it took for him to plunge over the edge. He thrust once more, shuddering his release. Filling her with everything he had.

"Wow." She let go of his shoulders, sliding her hands down his arms.

"Yeah. Wow." He was pretty sure he had bruises where her fingers had dug into his flesh. And he'd never felt better.

Chapter 7

"Ms. Collins, you have a delivery." Hunter's receptionist buzzed shortly after lunch. "Can I send her back?"

"Thank you," she replied to the intercom. "That would be fine."

A small quiver of anticipation bloomed in her belly. She wondered what Marco had sent. Flowers? Chocolate? She hoped it wasn't too embarrassing, like a singing telegram.

An attractive brunette appeared with a large shopping bag. Bright pink stripes and the Victoria's Secret logo gave her a clue as to what was in the bag.

"I didn't know your store delivered." Hunter's cheeks flushed.

"Normally, we don't." The brunette smiled. "But your boyfriend is very charming."

Boyfriend? They'd slept together once. She was his boss. Okay, the boyfriend label kept things simpler.

"Yes. He is quite charming." Hunter's blush deepened.

"He wanted me to make sure it fits." The brunette handed over the bag and waited.

"Have a seat." Hunter offered one of the guest chairs. "I'll be back in a few minutes."

Hunter took the bag into the private restroom adjacent to her office. She peeked inside. Underneath the pink tissue paper she found more pink, in satin and lace.

She held up the camisole. It was pretty. Delicate. Feminine. Everything Hunter wasn't.

She shrugged out of her blouse and bra, slipping the lingerie over her head.

Unexpected tears sprang to her eyes as she realized Marco already saw her this way. As a woman. A feminine, sexy woman.

Hunter quickly took it off, stuffed it back into the bag, and put her plain white bra and ivory blouse back on.

"It fits. Thank you." Hunter returned to the woman waiting in her office.

"Good. I'm glad. Most men have a hard time judging sizes. He took his time, carefully selecting just the right thing." The other woman smiled. "He didn't even flirt. Some guys do, you know. Like we would be impressed with a guy who says he's getting something for his sister or mother."

"Men really do that?" Hunter couldn't imagine.

"Yeah. But not your man. He just wanted to pick out something special. For the special woman in his life." She sighed, impressed by Marco's charm. Maybe a little envious that it was wasted on someone like Hunter. "He wanted to buy you a lot more, but since he didn't know your exact size, I suggested I have you come in for a bra fitting."

"A bra fitting?"

"Yes. We do them in the store all the time. You'd be surprised at how many women wear the wrong size," the woman told her. "And your man convinced me to deliver the camisole and do a fitting while I was here."

"You want to do a fitting? Really?" She didn't want to take off her shirt here in the office.

"I can do it right over your blouse. It'll just take a minute." The woman withdrew a tape measure from her pocket and smiled. "He had several items picked out. I just need to confirm your measurements and then I'll deliver those too."

"Wow." A lump rose in Hunter's throat. A lot of guys would have just sent flowers. There were rumors that one baseball player left autographed baseballs as a souvenir for his one night stands.

The salesclerk took Hunter's measurements, and noted the figure on two cards. She handed one to Hunter and slipped the other in her pocket along with the measuring tape. She thanked Hunter, even though she was the one performing a service. A very personalized service.

Hunter glanced at the clock. Still five hours until game time.

Marco stepped up to the plate. He cast a quick glance at the seats behind home plate. Hunter was there, in her typical suit, but the blush on her cheeks was nearly as pink as the camisole set he'd had delivered to her office. The salesgirl had called, verifying the purchase for the remaining items. She'd told him that Hunter was willing to pick up the items at the store, but he thought it would be much more fun to deliver one piece at a time.

That way he would know what she was wearing each night when he stepped to the plate.

Tonight, she was in pink. Hot pink. Very hot pink.

And he was the only one who knew it.

Marco smiled as he settled into the batter's box. He noted the smug look on the pitcher's face. No doubt his opponent thought he had his number. He'd probably studied his last several at bats. He looked pretty confident as he went into his windup.

Marco took the first pitch. He even went so far as to shake his head as if he'd known he couldn't have hit it anyway. He asked for time. Stepped away from the plate, and closed his eyes. Oh yeah, he could picture Hunter sitting on the edge of her seat, wondering if nothing had changed.

Everything had changed. He'd show her. And everyone else in the ballpark.

Marco stepped in. He watched the pitcher nod to his catcher then wind up and throw it a little low on the outside corner. Right to his sweet spot.

Marco stroked a double down the left field line.

Damn, that felt good.

Almost as good as having Hunter in his bed.

He stood on second base, giving a nod in her direction.

That was for you.

He watched Hunter as she bent over her scorebook. She tucked an errant wisp of hair behind her ear. She had no idea how beautiful she was.

The next batter hit a slow ground ball to first base. Marco advanced to third on the sacrifice. With two outs, Hunter moved to the edge of her seat. She wanted him to score. To break up the tie. She wanted him to come home.

The pitcher dropped a curveball that squirted through the catcher's legs. Marco made a dash for home. Sliding just under the tag, he heard the umpire yell, "Safe!"

Marco stood, dusted off his pants and tipped his cap in Hunter's direction. Forty thousand fans erupted into cheers. But he had done it just for her.

He finished the night with three hits including a home run, a double and four RBIs. Not bad. Not bad at all. Especially when the Goliaths took the win to even the series. Tomorrow would be the third game. A game he felt a lot more confident about now.

"So Marco, I think this is the kind of game we were all expecting when you joined the Goliaths." Rachel Parker caught up with him after the game. She met him at the top of the dugout, with her microphone and her friendly smile.

"I hope it's just the beginning." Marco didn't want to spend too much time talking. Not when he had a lingerie inspection to conduct as soon as he could get Hunter alone.

"You looked a lot more comfortable at the plate tonight." Rachel had noticed. "Any change in your routine?"

"I think I was putting too much pressure on myself." Marco wasn't about to tell her the reason he was so relaxed. "I tried to let up a little, not take myself so seriously. I just hope I can continue to help the team."

"You looked pretty good in the outfield tonight, too."

"I pride myself on playing solid defense. If it's in the park, it's my responsibility to make the play. If I can't get to it, then I've let my pitcher down. I've let my team down."

"Well, tonight you lifted your team up. That's one of the longest home runs I've seen at this park."

"Really? I know it felt good coming off the bat, but I didn't see where it landed." Marco had long ago given up trying to figure out why one hit was a home run and another sailed directly into the defender's glove. A lot of it was luck. Timing. Hitting the ball in the exact right spot. If it was possible to do it every time, this game wouldn't be any fun anymore.

And he could admit that this game was a lot more fun when he was hitting. Home runs, doubles it didn't matter, RBIs were the stats he took the most pride in—the number of runs batted in that made the difference in a game.

"Congratulations on a great game." Rachel turned from him toward the camera. "This is Rachel Parker, signing off after another Goliaths' win, thanks in part to Marco Santiago's monster home run."

Marco made his way back to the clubhouse. He was greeted with high fives and back slaps, making him feel more a part of the team than ever.

Bryce came up to Marco after they'd both had a chance to shower and change. "So, you got a dugout interview with Rachel Parker, huh?"

"Yeah. I finally had something to talk about."

"Watch out for that one. She may look sweet, but she's not afraid to bust your balls."

"I'll keep that in mind." Sounded like Bryce had some experience with her.

"So, you coming out with us tonight?" Bryce leaned against the locker next to Marco's. "Celebrate a little?"

Marco was just about to make his excuses, when Hunter walked up to them, with a congratulatory smile on her face.

"Sounds like fun. You boys have a good time." She gave Marco a small nod. "Just make sure you're in bed by midnight."

She tapped Bryce on the shoulder, causing Marco's gut to tighten in jealousy. But she gave him a sultry glance as she walked away.

He was following Bryce to the parking lot when his cell phone chimed with a text from Hunter.

My bed. Midnight. Don't be late.

Not a chance.

Marco joined Bryce and a couple of other players who'd been picked up at the trade deadline. They had drinks. The two younger guys hooked up with a couple of women they met at the bar. Bryce asked Marco if he wanted to share a cab, but Marco had someplace to be. And he'd better hurry if he was going to get there before midnight.

* * *

"You're late." Hunter opened the door just before midnight. She stood in the doorway in a gray flannel robe, her arms folded across her chest. Her hair was contained in a low, loose ponytail, and Marco itched to bury his fingers in its silky strands.

"I still have three minutes." Marco didn't wait for an invitation to enter. He followed her inside and as soon as the front door was closed, he pressed her against it. He kissed her. Hard. Hurried. Hungry.

"We haven't made it to my bed, yet." Hunter squirmed, as he trailed kisses from her lips, to her neck, to that delicate spot just behind her ear.

"Lead the way." Marco reluctantly took his mouth off her skin.

"Upstairs." She tugged on his arm and he followed until she pushed open the first door on the right.

He moved her toward the bed. Pulled at the tie around her waist. The robe fell open, revealing the hot pink lingerie he'd had delivered.

"Oh, yeah. That's more like it." Marco uttered his appreciation. "Damn. You're beautiful. So, so, beautiful."

Hunter's cheeks stained to match her underwear.

Marco lowered his head to take her nipple into his mouth through the silky fabric. She moaned as he suckled. God, she was so responsive. Her taut nipples jutted against the damp cloth. He slipped his hand around her waist, pulling her closer. Closer. But not close enough.

As lovely as her sexy new underwear were, they were in his way.

Marco shoved the robe off her shoulders. He slid his hands beneath the satin top. Moving the material out of his way, he returned his mouth to her breasts, savoring each perfect mound. Her little groans of pleasure encouraged him to move faster.

He hooked his thumbs into the waistband of the little shorts that matched the top and slid them down her hips. His pulse rate skyrocketed at the sight of her luscious, naked body.

"Hunter." His voice was thick, almost inaudible. "Damn, woman. You are so sexy."

"Marco." Her skin flushed, not just her cheeks. "Please."

She tasted so good. Felt so good. How could she not know how hot she was? How hot she made him?

She tugged at his jeans, fumbled with the button, before sliding the zipper down. *Oh yeah.* Her touch was nearly enough to send him over the edge. She snaked her fingers down below the elastic of his boxer-briefs and he groaned.

He still hadn't made it to her bed. He'd have to fix that.

Together they tumbled to the mattress.

Marco lifted his hand to the back of her head and loosened the rubber band, setting her hair free. Long, silky strands of brown and gold and copper shimmered in the lamplight.

"So beautiful," he whispered, marveling at the goddess before him, with her hair down, flowing across the pillow, and her luscious curves spread out before him. "You're the most beautiful thing I've ever seen."

She laughed. A nervous titter, showing her insecurity. "You don't have to flatter me. I'm already yours."

"Yes. You are mine." He kissed her, claiming her with his mouth. "All mine."

He trailed kisses down her body, lingering at her breasts for a while before making his way down. She moaned in appreciation as he savored her soft silky skin.

Until he dipped his head between her thighs.

She whimpered, and then tensed as he dropped a delicate kiss on her inner thigh.

"Marco." She grasped his hair, holding him back. "Please."

The desperate plea was not an encouragement.

"You don't have to do that." She squirmed, uncomfortable with the direction he was heading.

"You don't want me to kiss you there?" He couldn't quite understand her hesitation. Her insecurity.

"It's just too . . . much." She shifted, moving her body away from him. She was uncomfortable.

"Tell me what you want." He slid his body so they could talk, face to face. Eye to eye. "Tell me what you need."

"Just, kiss me." Her voice quivered with uncertainty. "On the mouth."

"You're the boss." Marco placed a gentle kiss on her lips. He followed her lead. And when she parted her lips, he plunged his tongue into her mouth. He kissed her until her hesitation dissolved. Kissed her until her need overpowered her insecurity.

He slipped his hand between her thighs, stroking her gently, taking cues from her. When she bucked against his fingers, he plunged deeper inside her. Drawing her out of her inhibitions.

He stroked harder, faster, deeper, bringing her closer and closer to the edge.

"Come for me, sweetheart."

Her breath quickened, the little sounds escaping her throat telling him she was close.

"That's my girl," he coaxed her into a climax.

"Marco. Please." She moaned. "*Please.*"

He positioned himself over her. She reached for him, demanding.

"Is this what you want?" He teased her opening with just the tip of his penis. Her insistent grunt told him plenty.

He pushed inside, just a little and she bucked toward him. Greedy. Needy.

He pulled out and she whimpered. Then she grabbed his ass.

"Oh, you really want it?" Marco eased inside slowly, before withdrawing again. "You're going to have to beg."

"Marco . . ." Her voice was desperate. "Please."

He couldn't deny her any longer. He plunged deep, deeper than he thought possible. He moved with her.

He could feel another orgasm building. Her breath coming faster. Her moans becoming more insistent. Her inner muscles tightening. Gripping him. Holding on to him. Taking him to the point of no return. Finally she cried out his name. Her whole body shook with her climax and he followed almost immediately after.

He lay there, still inside her, aftershocks pulsing around him. Marco felt a seismic shift in his heart. He wanted this. What he had right here. Right now. Hunter. In his arms. In his life.

He looked around the room, the realization that this had been her childhood bedroom hitting him as he took in the whitewashed window seat with stuffed animals lined up at the corners. The bookcases filled with a mix of hardcover and paperback books, handmade ceramic figurines and baseball memorabilia from the last twenty years or so.

A twinge of envy swept over him. She had grown up here, in this very room of this very house. She'd gone from a girl, to a teenager, to a woman right here.

He felt the urge to protect the girl this room revealed. The woman who tried so hard to keep herself hidden from the rest of the world.

"Hunter." He stroked her hair and dropped delicate kisses along her neck. "My sweet, sweet Hunter."

Marco felt a sense of gratitude at being let in. At being one of the few who saw her like this. Vulnerable. Naked. Stripped of all her armor. He understood that her gray suits, her masculine clothing were nothing more than a shield against the world.

And she'd allowed him to break through her defense.

"So tell me, have you had many boys sneak into your room?" Marco asked playfully. Hoping he already knew the answer.

"Boys?" She shifted beneath him, pulling away. Putting up her defenses. "No boys."

"Okay, so how many men?" he teased, pretty confident he was in elite company.

"Just one. Just you."

"I thought you said you weren't a virgin." A slight worry tickled his chest.

"I wasn't. I went to college." She tried to sound so worldly. But she wasn't fooling him.

"Stanford, right?"

"Yes. I know, didn't exactly travel far from home." She laughed, as if she had settled somehow. "How did you know where I went to school?"

"I met your father when I was still in college. He came out on a recruiting trip." Marco tried not to think about what would have happened if Texas hadn't had the higher draft pick. Would the Goliaths have drafted him in that round? Signed him to a long-term deal?

"I didn't know you'd met him." Hunter's voice held a note of sadness. "I knew he always thought highly of you, but . . . Did he really talk to you about me?"

"Yes. He bragged about you to anyone who'd listen." Marco propped himself up on one elbow. "He talked about how smart you were. And how you knew more about the game than the commissioner himself."

"He did not." Her cheeks flushed. But she looked . . . happy. A little surprised, but overall, it was a positive thing to talk about her father in that way.

"He did. He bragged about you to the point that most of us couldn't help but think you were . . ." Oh, hell, how did he describe the image that he'd conjured up in his mind? Basically a younger, female version of the commissioner of baseball. Certainly not this beautiful, sexy, sensuous woman who was passionate about baseball, and passionate about him.

"I was what? A tomboy? Just one of the guys?" She rolled over onto her side, her lush breasts heaving with indignation.

"No, Hunter. You're more woman that most men can handle." Marco gave her one last kiss before falling into a blissful, worn out state of slumber.

Hunter woke to find Marco still in her bed. He hadn't snuck out at dawn like she'd done the day before. He looked so peaceful as he slept. Content. Gorgeous. His dark hair mussed from sex and sleep. His whiskers rough against his jaw. His skin was flawless, so smooth stretched across the muscles of his back, the color of salted caramel. She wanted to eat him up.

Hunter settled for tasting him. A flick of her tongue on his neck, a press of her body against his skin. Yum.

Marco roused from his slumber. He turned over and opened his electric blue eyes. A slow smile spread across his face. He wrapped his arms around her, pulling her against him.

"You just can't get enough of me, can you?" He groaned as she stretched out on top of him. "You're addicted to me."

"Shhh." She covered his mouth with hers and positioned herself over him. "Seems I'm not the only one who's ready for more."

"More." He moaned as she eased down over his morning erection. He tried to pull back, but she had him right where she wanted him. She brought her knees up so that she straddled him. She was in control. Except she wasn't. Not really. He drove into her, sending her spiraling out of control.

"Marco."

He held her hips, keeping her in place as he thrust. Again and again. Then he stilled. She was so close, tottering at the edge of insanity. Slowly, ever so slowly, he began to move again. He let go of her hips, and she started to pick up the pace.

Hunter moved her hands across his chest. Down, down lower, caressing his abs. He groaned, grabbing her wrists and guiding her to the spot where they were joined.

"Show me." His voice was rough, barely more than a whisper. "Show me how you want to be touched."

But she already had what she wanted. She clenched around him and he dropped her hands. Clutching her hips, he thrust hard one more time. An explosion of color and sensation and ecstasy clouded her mind.

She collapsed on top of him, still thrumming in pure satisfaction. But he wasn't finished yet. His breath quickened, and he thrust again. His whole body tensed and then she could feel his release deep inside her. He relaxed beneath her, his heart beating steady and strong. He wrapped his arms around her, gently stroking her back. Not letting her go.

"Don't move." Marco held her in place. His voice sexy. Commanding. "Ever."

"Ever?" She'd never had a lover who made her feel so desired. So cherished. So tempted to see just how many days they could go without ever leaving the bed.

"I could stay with you like this forever." Marco's voice softened into a contented sigh.

"I think eventually we would need food. Water. Maybe a shower." She snuggled tighter against his chest, secure in the bliss of the moment, wishing that it could go on forever. "One cannot live by sex alone."

"No. But two of us can." Marco ran his fingers through her hair. "Oh, Hunter. You are so lovely. I don't think I can tear myself away from you."

"Well, you do have a game tonight," she reminded him. "I need you on the field."

"You're the boss." Marco's relaxed manner disappeared in an instant. "And I guess this is just a side job, huh?"

He chuckled, moving away from her, the magic gone.

"Would you mind if I took a shower? Maybe you could call me a cab and I'll be out of your hair." He eased to the edge of the bed, swung his legs around, and sat up, his back toward her.

"Go ahead and get in the shower. But I can drive you home."

Hunter tried not to feel the sting of his sudden change of mood. "I'll even make breakfast."

"I think I should take a cab. If someone sees your car in front of my apartment, it might look suspicious."

"Yes. I suppose we should keep this discreet."

"Discreet would be good." He raked his hand through his hair. "I don't think it would do either of us any good if people find out we are sleeping together."

"Right." Hunter felt a small glimmer of hope at his choice of "are" instead of "were."

"Look, Hunter . . ." He turned around, his eyes stormy with emotion. Uncertainty. "I don't know what I'm doing here."

"It's just sex," she lied. "A way to loosen you up. You had a great game last night. If sleeping with me helps, then great. We can keep this going."

"So if I have a good game tonight, you'll invite me back into your bed?" Marco made a show of searching the floor for his clothes. Acting like it was no big deal one way or the other. "But if I go O for four?"

"You won't. I know you'll have a great night." She hoped. Because, yeah, she wanted to invite him back to her bed. She didn't have any idea what she was doing here, either. But she didn't want to stop until she figured it out.

"I'm going to hit the shower." Marco carried his clothes with him to her bathroom. She watched him walk away, admiring his sexy backside. Damn, she was so tempted to follow him into the shower. But maybe they both needed a little space, before he ended up on the disabled list.

Or she ended up falling in love with him.

Chapter 8

Marco and the Goliaths finished the home stand with four straight wins. He ended up going nine for seventeen, with four home runs, two doubles, a triple and eleven RBI's. He was on one hell of a hot streak. And as every ballplayer knows, you don't mess with a winning streak.

Hunter knew it too, because she made sure he followed his nightly ritual. Sometimes at her place. Sometimes at his. Either way, they barely made it through the front door before tearing each other's clothes off.

She wore the lingerie he'd sent her. That was part of the ritual too. He entered the game knowing exactly what color underwear she wore under her gray suits. She sat in her usual spot, scorebook in her lap. To the forty thousand people surrounding her, nothing had changed. Only Marco noticed the slight transformation taking place behind home plate.

It started with her hair. She wore it looser, softer, still pulled back and up, but instead of a severe bun she had it in a soft twist with a few loose strands tickling the sides of her neck. She kept up her professional image, until he got her behind closed doors. He had mastered the art of kissing her senseless while letting her hair down.

Hunter had also added a hint of color to her wardrobe. Tonight she wore a soft, pink blouse. Over a red-hot bustier if she wore today's special delivery. Her cheeks were rosier, and when he dared glance in her direction, she looked happier, more relaxed than when they'd first met.

She came into the clubhouse after the game, like she did after every game. She congratulated several of the players and gave him a silent signal as to where their postgame action would take place. A tap on the shoulder meant she would meet him at his place. A firm handshake signaled she would drive them both to her house.

Tonight, he wasn't surprised to get a pat on the shoulder. Marco and the team would fly out in the morning to San Diego before continuing on to L.A. He'd already packed, but he was glad he would be able to leave directly from his apartment.

Marco hurried home. At least he didn't have to make excuses for not hanging with the guys. He'd have plenty of time for after-hours socializing on the upcoming road trip. Too much time.

But tonight? Tonight was for Hunter. She'd been his good luck charm and he wanted to take as much of that luck with him as possible.

Who was he kidding? It wasn't about luck. Not just about luck, anyway. He tried to back off when he felt like they were getting too hot, too fast. But baseball players were a superstitious breed. When things were going good, they kept up the routine. If it meant wearing the same socks or not shaving or eating a certain pregame meal, it was important to stick with the ritual. Marco didn't have lucky underwear— unless he counted the lingerie he bought for Hunter—but he had been getting lucky both on and off the field.

Neither one of them wanted to end the winning streak.

And they both insisted that it was just that. Good baseball and even better sex. The two were intertwined. By an unspoken agreement, they would keep up the ritual until it stopped working. Personally. Professionally. Marco wasn't about to let something as complicated as emotions interfere with a good thing.

"Good game." Hunter was waiting for him in the lobby. She had a parking pass, but he was afraid he'd jinx it if he gave her a key to his apartment. "I knew you had it in you."

"Yeah. I guess I just needed to find my groove." Marco hit the call button for the elevator. They were both playing a game, trying to keep it casual, trying to keep their affair a secret. So far, no one had confronted him, but that didn't mean they hadn't caught on.

As soon as they were alone inside the elevator, Hunter slipped her arms around his waist. She rose on her tiptoes, demanding a kiss.

Marco was more than willing to give it to her. He would give her everything he had, on the field and in her bed.

The chime warned them the doors would open, and they broke apart. No one was on the other side, but they couldn't be too careful.

Marco led her silently to his apartment door. He slid the key into the lock and tugged her inside. He kicked the door closed, flipping the deadbolt and dragging Hunter back to his bedroom. The ritual remained: clothes falling by the wayside, blankets thrown from the bed, thirty seconds of admiring her lingerie before discarding the satin and lace along with the wool pantsuits and patent leather pumps.

"God, you're beautiful." Marco marveled at just how good it was. Making love to Hunter was like nothing he'd experienced before. "More beautiful than anyone I've ever known."

"Stop it." She laughed, the sound going straight to his chest. "We both know that's not true."

"What do you mean?" He lifted his head off her chest, looking into her deep brown eyes. "You are beautiful."

Only the word was too small to really describe what he meant.

"Please. How many supermodels have you been with?" She turned her head, breaking eye contact.

"What does that have to do with anything?" Deep down Marco had always known that someday his years of playing the field would come back to bite him in the ass. "So I dated a few models. But they weren't real."

Shit. That made him sound like a superficial jerk.

"No? They didn't have feelings? Or dreams? Or insecurities?" God, he loved when she got passionate about something. Even if it was pointing out that he'd been a first class shallow ass.

"Oh, they had plenty of insecurities," Marco acknowledged. "But I guess that's what all the makeup and clothes and airbrushing was for."

"So they could fulfill your fantasy?"

"No." Marco cupped her cheek. "You're my fantasy."

And his obsession.

"Marco. Please." She blushed, unable to accept the compliment.

"Come with me to San Diego," he pleaded. "I need you. To keep the streak going."

"You'll be fine." She reached up and stroked his hair. "Believe it or not, I didn't bring you here for my personal pleasure."

"No?" He didn't like the reminder that she owned him professionally.

"I know you can be a five tool player." She propped herself up on one elbow. "You've got speed, power, a good glove. You can hit for average. And you've got one hell of an arm."

"Not to mention good hands." Now it was his turn to not take a compliment for what it was.

"Very good hands." Hunter blushed. "But the point I was trying to make is that I wanted you because of what you bring to the team. Not what you can do for me . . . or to me."

"That's just a bonus?" Marco kept trying to tell himself that this was just about getting lucky. The sex happened to coincide with the winning streak so they would keep it going. But he wondered what would end first. The lucky streak or the relationship?

"Yeah, a bonus." She rolled over on her back and closed her eyes. Playtime was over for now. He knew he would eventually lose. He'd even walk away from the game someday. But he didn't like the thought of someday walking away from Hunter.

Hunter made herself at home in Marco's kitchen. She whipped up a quick breakfast before he had to leave for the airport. She wasn't too worried he'd think she was trying to get too domestic on him. He had no trouble washing her dishes or flipping burgers on her grill, so there was a good chance he'd think that an omelet was just an omelet.

"Mmm. Smells delicious." Marco snuck up on her, wrapping his arms around her waist. "And you made breakfast, too."

"Yes. I was hungry." She leaned into him, savoring the little kisses he placed on her neck and shoulder. "And I figured I might as well make enough for two."

"Come to San Diego with me," he murmured, sending chills down her spine. "Please."

The need in his voice would have been a lot more flattering if she knew it had more to do with him wanting her rather than wanting to keep his hitting streak going.

"You'll be fine without me." Hunter moved from his grasp, plating the omelets and crossing over to the fridge. She poured two glasses of orange juice and carried them to the table. Marco had already taken the dishes to the table, and set out the silverware and napkins.

"Maybe." Marco held out her chair and waited for her to sit before taking the seat next to her. "But you should come down, just in case."

"I have work to do. Besides, you're in a groove. You've got your timing back, and more importantly, your confidence."

"I've got confidence because of you." He looked up at her with those impossible to resist blue eyes. So not fair. She needed this break from him. Six days on the road should be enough time to settle her emotions. To remind herself that this was just sex, nothing more.

She couldn't afford to get her heart tangled up in this.

Especially since she had a bet to win. The division title. And if Marco kept playing like he had been these last few days, they could win it all.

She had to keep her goal in mind. She couldn't just succumb to his every request. She was in charge here.

"Marco, you will go on this road trip with your teammates. You will continue to hit and hit well."

"You're the boss." He smiled as he dug into the eggs.

"Yes. And you will behave yourself after hours." She wasn't going to get her heart involved, but she also wasn't going to share him with anyone else.

"It would be a lot easier to do if you were with me," he teased. "Otherwise . . ."

"No other women. Are we clear?"

"Yes, ma'am." Marco saluted and took a drink of his juice. "But that rule goes both ways. If Baxter gets into a slump or Garcia can't find his fastball, you're not going to help them out are you?"

"Of course not. This is a unique situation." One she wasn't sure how she'd gotten herself into. "I've never slept with a ballplayer before. Or any kind of athlete."

"I've never slept with a team owner before," Marco said with that irresistible smile of his.

"Just their wives?"

"Hey, that was a long time ago. And she's got nothing on you." He lifted his gaze, heat lingered. "Hunter, you outshine every woman

I've ever known. You do not have to worry about me even looking at another woman. Not on the road. Not ever."

His sincerity warmed her, but made her even more determined to put some space between them. This was getting too hot too fast.

"I'll clean up. You'd better get moving so you don't miss your flight."

Marco made his flight, settled into his hotel room and went to the ballpark with the rest of his team. He took his turn in the batting cage, making solid contact on most of his reps. He felt good. Not great, but good. Maybe Hunter was right, he had confidence going into the last few games, he should approach the plate tonight with the same attitude.

He was a professional, a good hitter, good enough that Hunter had wanted him. Wanted him enough to trade a hot pitching prospect and a couple of guys who could be pretty solid players if given a chance.

Hunter had gone against her partner's wishes to bring him to San Francisco. And now that he knew he could be the player she'd expected, Marco would do anything to keep it going.

He tried not to think about the sex. It was fantastic in every way, but it wasn't the reason he'd come out of the slump. Sure, he'd relaxed because of it, because of her. Hunter gave him confidence on a deep level. She believed in him.

That confidence carried him through the first game of the road trip. He went two for three with a single, a double and a sacrifice, knocking in two runs in their win. Not bad, considering his heart was still in San Francisco.

After the game, he went to the hotel bar, trying to keep from calling her. To keep from missing her to the point of losing the concentration he'd finally recovered.

Bryce snuck up on him and patted him on the back.

"Buy you a beer?" he asked, but his offer lacked his usual enthusiasm.

"Sure." Bryce had been responsible for one of the other runs of the game, a solo home run to tack on to their lead in the ninth.

"Good game." Marco waited until their beers had been delivered before hitting the small talk. They both knew that Los Angeles had won their game tonight as well. The race was tight. The Goliaths were just two games out of first place. Their five game winning streak kept them alive while L.A. had won six of their last seven games.

"Yeah. We're still in it. Let's just hope we don't lose any ground before we have to face them in their yard." Bryce was usually the most upbeat player on the team. The rah-rah guy, who could spin just about anything into something positive. But he wasn't his usual cheerful self, tonight.

"All we can do is play our game. Put ourselves in a position to be in the race come September." Marco knew there was a fine line between taking a realistic look at their chances and jinxing the whole damn thing. He wasn't about to screw things up by getting too cocky. But he needed to maintain a certain level of confidence. And make sure his teammates felt it too.

"So, it seems you've been able to elevate your game a little in the last few days." Bryce took a long pull on his lager. "You getting laid or something?"

The way he said it, and the way he avoided eye contact made Marco wonder if the other man was fishing for information. More information than Marco was willing to share.

"Not tonight, that's for sure." Marco tried to make a joke out of it. "I mean, you're the best prospect I've seen all night."

Bryce laughed, but he didn't really mean it.

"Just tell me the truth." He looked Marco straight in the eye. "Have you slept with Rachel Parker?"

Who?

It took a minute for Marco to remember who Bryce was talking about. The reporter. The perky redhead from Bay Area Sports Net who conducted the postgame interviews.

"No." Marco shook his head and placed a reassuring hand on his teammate's shoulder.

"You can tell me." Bryce kept his gaze steady, but he was bracing for the worst. "You wouldn't be the first guy to fall under her spell."

"No. I've only talked to her on camera." Marco didn't envy the man. Not when he seemed so into a woman he didn't trust.

"You sure?" Bryce leaned forward, resting his elbows on the bar. "There's got to be some reason for your transformation at the plate."

There was. But he wasn't going to share it with Bryce Baxter or anyone else, not when the reason was their boss.

"I think I'd remember something like that." Marco tried to keep his tone light.

"Sorry man." Bryce flipped some kind of switch in his head and turned into Mr. Happy-go-lucky all over again. "It's just that we were supposed to hook up, you know after that game where you broke out of your slump. But then she canceled on me, not long after you left the bar. What was I supposed to think?"

"Maybe something came up." Marco was hardly in the position of handing out advice on women. He was only sitting there to avoid calling Hunter and begging her once again to come down there.

"You sure it wasn't you?" Bryce shook his head, as if he was disappointed in himself. "I don't know what my problem is. It's just that your turnaround came at about the same time she started pulling back."

Marco wished he had some sort of wisdom to share with the other man, but he didn't. Instead, he started worrying about Hunter slipping away from him. He had a feeling he'd be in worse shape than Bryce.

Two long-legged women walked into the bar, smiled at Marco and Bryce, and took a seat across from them. Close enough to let them know they were interested, but far enough away they could keep their options open.

"Maybe it's time I move on." Bryce swallowed the last of his beer. "What do you think? Want to join me?"

"Nah. I think I'm going to call it a night after this one." Marco still had half a glass. "I've been in a good rhythm. Don't want to do anything to get me off my game."

"Suit yourself. I think I need to head over there." Bryce tossed a few bills on the bar for a tip. "They look like they could help me with my hand-eye coordination."

He grinned and then strode around the bar with a big, cocky grin on his face. The blonde looked over at Marco, but when Bryce shook his head she shrugged and turned her full attention on the shortstop.

Marco finished his drink, added to the tip, and headed up to his room. He knew better than to call Hunter. Hearing her voice would tie him up in knots. But he knew he wouldn't sleep without letting her know he'd been a good boy.

He cleaned up and got ready for bed. He slipped between the sheets and sent her a text.

I'm in bed. Alone. Wish you were here.

He set his phone on the nightstand and tried to close his eyes. Images of Hunter—naked, moving over him, under him—filled his mind, moving him in ways he never expected.

The phone buzzed and he grabbed it.

It'll do you good to miss me. Make you realize what you've got.

Marco propped the pillows behind his head, and leaned back.

I've got one hell of a woman.

And one hell of an ache.

Don't you forget it.

Don't you forget me.

Impossible.

He could deal with the pain in his groin. It was the one in his chest that was starting to concern him.

Chapter 9

"Does the offer for a girls shopping trip still stand?" Hunter had called Annabelle, hoping that the other woman hadn't merely been trying to be polite the last time they spoke.

"Of course. I was hoping we could get together soon." Annabelle's cheery voice helped Hunter relax a little. She'd never had girlfriends to hang out with. Let alone one who'd been a supermodel.

"So, I think I need a makeover," Hunter confessed. She wanted to be the woman Marco thought she was.

"Are you free this afternoon? Clayton's taking the girls for a father-daughter day. You know, princess movie, tea party and I'm thinking there will be some playing dress up."

"Wow. My father-daughter days consisted of baseball games, hot dogs, and locker rooms full of half-naked jocks." Hunter smiled at the bittersweet memory. Grief had a way of sneaking up on her at the most unexpected times.

"Oh my." Annabelle giggled. "Clayton would never allow our girls around naked athletes. In fact, he didn't like the idea of having the players and their families over. He's very protective of our girls."

"Maybe he's protective of you, too." Hunter remembered his jealousy over Annabelle's past relationship with Marco. Finally, something she had in common with her business partner. Jealousy was a much easier emotion to deal with than grief.

"Oh, that's just an act. He trusts me." The lightness in her tone slipped. She wasn't telling the whole truth. "But he's determined to keep our girls innocent until they're thirty."

"Maybe he should follow my father's plan, then. I didn't date until I went off to college." But Hunter had never felt like she was missing anything, not even prom. The idea of getting so worked up over a dress seemed silly. Until now.

They made arrangements to meet at Neiman Marcus. They'd start there, grab some lunch, and hopefully improve Hunter's wardrobe and their friendship in the process.

"I think we should hit the lingerie department first." Annabelle grabbed Hunter's hand like they were a couple of schoolgirls.

"Actually, that part of my wardrobe is covered." A blush crept across her cheeks. "It's what goes over that I need help with."

"Oh, really?" Annabelle threaded her arm through Hunter's. "Who is he? And when do I get to meet him?"

"We're keeping a low profile right now." Maybe this was a bad idea. By inviting Annabelle shopping, Hunter had also invited her into her personal life. The last thing she needed was for her relationship with Marco to become public. She especially couldn't let Clayton find out about it.

"Oooh. A secret love affair. How exciting," Annabelle practically squealed. "And is there a particular occasion we're dressing you for? A super-secret hot date?"

"No. No occasion. Just everyday stuff." Hunter smoothed the front of her suit jacket. She wished the pockets were real, so she had somewhere to put her hands. "Something I can wear to the office, and then over to the ballgame afterward."

"And after that?" Annabelle was making way too much of this.

"Let's just say I want to soften my appearance, but remain professional." Hunter hoped she wasn't asking for too much. "Some of the dinosaurs I work with have a hard enough time with me being a woman in a man's business. I don't want to throw it in their faces."

Much.

"Not your husband, of course." Hunter had almost forgotten who she was talking to.

"No. He's not a dinosaur. Just a Neanderthal." The other woman let out a frustrated sigh. "I want to apologize again for the scene he made at the barbecue. I should have known better than to throw myself at Marco like that. Clayton would have flipped out if I'd greeted my cousin that way. But a former lover? What was I thinking?"

That Marco Santiago was hot? That she wished she'd never let him go?

"See, that's another reason I'm glad you called. I want to be more involved with the team. Not that I want to be involved with any of the players, of course." Annabelle laughed, her cheeks coloring. "But I think if I showed more of an interest in my husband's business, well . . ." Her voice trailed off with some unspoken disappointment.

Hunter wondered what she could offer to the conversation. She'd never been good at small talk. Especially the kind that didn't revolve around baseball.

"Do you know much about the game?" Hunter knew plenty of owners, not to mention their wives, who didn't know the difference between a force and fly out. Let alone the infield fly rule.

"Oh, I know the basics. You know, there's a pitcher and a batter. The object of the game is to reach all four bases and score a run. But I get a little confused on what the difference between an earned run and a not-earned run. How do they determine an error and what the heck is the difference between a dinger and a tater? Is there a baseball lingo cheat sheet or something?"

"The best way to pick it up is to watch the game, listen to it on the radio."

"Should I follow a fantasy league?" Annabelle asked on the escalators up to the women's career wear department. "Clayton spends a lot of time on the Internet checking out different player's stats."

"I guess, but there's more to a player than just his stats."

"Like his abs and lats?" Anabelle gave her a knowing grin.

"Trust me, after twenty years in the locker room, one well-toned body is pretty much the same as the next."

Liar. But she didn't need to tell the other woman about Marco's assets. They already had that knowledge in common.

"Oh, that's a nice suit." Hunter tried to change the subject by approaching the mannequin showing a designer suit very similar to the one she was wearing.

"I thought you wanted to upgrade." Annabelle dragged her away from her usual section, over to another display. This one a lot more trendy. "How about this?"

Annabelle fingered the sleeve of an orange blazer.

"No. Too bright."

"You could use a little more color in your wardrobe, though. Let's keep looking."

Two hours later, Hunter sat in the department store's café, surrounded by shopping bags full of new clothes. She'd updated her black and gray staples with a pale blue blazer and a coordinating blue and ivory silk blouse. She'd traded her boxy jackets for more form-fitting styles and somehow Annabelle had talked her into an electric blue trench coat. She added two pair of dark denim jeans and a few silk T-shirts in basic black, white, and soft pink that she could wear with her suits or jeans.

"Next stop, the makeup counter," Annabelle said enthusiastically after they'd paid for their lunch.

"I think I've taken enough of your time." Hunter wasn't sure she'd be able to keep up with a fancy makeup routine, anyway.

"Nonsense. This has been fun. Really." Annabelle's eyes shone with sincerity. And maybe a little bit of loneliness. "I've enjoyed spending the day with you. Even if you haven't spilled anything about this mystery man."

Hunter's cheeks flamed. Part of her really wished she could share, but it wasn't a good idea. Maybe someday, but certainly not during the season, and not with her partner's wife.

"You're thinking about him right now, aren't you?" Annabelle sounded almost giddy. "Are you going to see him tonight?"

"No. Not tonight. He's . . . He's working. But when I do see him again, I think I would like to look pretty for him."

"Oh, you're gorgeous. The only thing you lack is confidence." Annabelle shook her head. "Come on, let's go spend a small fortune on powdered confidence. And a little lipstick."

After leading off the second inning with a single to right, Marco didn't do shit at the plate that night. He kept looking behind the backstop and when he didn't find Hunter sitting there, scorebook in hand, lace bra hidden beneath her suit jacket, he couldn't quite get his head back in the game. Not good considering it was only the second game of a six game road trip.

They lost a close game, putting them two games behind L.A., the team they would face next before heading back to San Francisco to finish the month of August. Then they would hit the road again. It would be his first trip back to St. Louis since the trade. He had to get this figured out before heading back to the town that had embraced him and set him free in less than a season.

Damn. He missed her. Missed touching her, holding her. He missed the post-workout conversations. When he was naked and satisfied and relaxed, he was more open to hearing how he was dropping his shoulder on his swing, or if he pulled his head on the inside fastball. He wondered if she'd seen the game. Had she caught an error in his mechanics? Or was his problem mental?

He grabbed a bite to eat from the clubhouse and headed straight to his room. A lot of the guys didn't feel like going out after a loss. Marco just wanted to go straight to bed. Too bad he was alone.

He wasn't going to call her. But he found his fingers pulling up Hunter's number.

"Hey." He closed his eyes, trying to picture what color bra she'd be wearing today. Had she put on the red one? Or the leopard print? Or had she gone back to the white cotton? They all got his heart racing, his blood pumping and his thoughts heading in the opposite direction of where he needed them.

"Hey yourself." Her voice was sexier than he remembered.

"Come down here." He hadn't meant to ask her that. He wasn't desperate. He just wanted her. Desperately.

"I have work to do."

"It's the weekend. Can't you take a couple of days off?" He might just have to beg.

"You'll be leaving by the time I could get down there." She had a teasing note in her voice, like maybe she'd consider it.

"We have an evening game. Five o'clock start. It's an hour and a half flight."

"You really want me to fly down there so we could spend a couple of hours together before your game?"

"Yes. Come on, you know I'm worth it," Marco teased.

"Oh really?"

"I miss you." He stretched out, wishing the bed wasn't so big. "I wish you were here with me right now."

"What would you do if I was?"

"What wouldn't I do?" Marco groaned. "I'd like to think I'd have enough restraint to get you up to my room before ravishing you."

"Ravishing me?" Her teasing tone got under his skin, right behind the letters of his uniform.

"Yes. I'd press you against the door. Kissing you breathless before taking you into my arms and carrying you to the bed."

"Oh my." She let out a soft sigh.

"I'd help you let your hair down, running my fingers through the silky strands. Burying my face in the sweet smell of you."

"Marco, please." Oh, how he loved the way she said those two little words. And all the various ways she said it.

"And I'd kiss you some more. On the lips. The soft skin behind your ear. Your breasts, belly and . . . everywhere."

"Everywhere?" Her voice caught with apprehension, and arousal.

"Everywhere. I want to taste all of you. I want to show you pleasure like you've never known before."

"Why?" she asked simply. "Why me?"

"Because." He was on the verge of telling her he was falling for her. Falling hard. But damn it. That wasn't something he could do over the phone. It wasn't something he could do even in person. "Because you're the sexiest, most amazing woman I've ever known."

"I had lunch with Annabelle today."

"I guess that's nice." Not exactly the direction he wanted the conversation to go.

"We went shopping. She helped me spruce up my wardrobe."

"Really?" He wondered why she was changing the subject. They had been this close to phone sex, but maybe he'd end up more frustrated than before.

"Yeah. Kind of like one of those makeover things that girls do."

"Honey, you don't need a makeover." Marco resisted the urge to relieve the pressure in his groin. "You're perfect just the way you are."

"Oh, so I should send all that lingerie back? If I don't need it?"

"No. Don't do that." She was killing him.

"So you do want to see me looking like a girl," she teased.

"Not a girl." He was going to need a very cold shower when he got off the phone. "A woman. Pure, sexy, one hundred percent woman."

"How do you do it?" She had a slight quiver in her voice. "How do you see me as something I'm not? Something I didn't ever know I wanted to be?"

"What do you want to be?"

"Yours." Her voice was barely audible. "I want to be the sexy, strong, confident woman you seem to think I am."

"I don't think, I know." Marco wished he could reach through the phone, and show her just how strong, sexy, and amazing she was. "Please, I'm begging you. Come down here. Hunter, I need you."

"You need me? Why, because you won four games in a row after sleeping with me? So I must be your good luck charm?"

Something like that.

"Forget it." Marco pretended he wasn't hurt. She was brushing him off, downplaying their relationship as if it was just a pregame ritual. "Hey, what's the worst that could happen? We lose tomorrow and head into L.A. three games back. If they sweep, we'll be six out, but there's always the wild card."

"Not good enough."

Fear of flying had never been an issue for Hunter before. Neither had motion sickness. So the feeling that she just might need to gather up all the little paper bags on this flight to San Diego for her personal use must have something to do with the fact that she couldn't turn down Marco's plea to come down here.

She could turn around. Fly back to San Francisco and pretend she wasn't afraid of losing the two things that had come to mean the most to her. Her team. And Marco Santiago.

Why had she made that stupid bet? Or why couldn't she have bet something other than control of the team? Money would have been more logical. But then logic and Marco didn't seem to exist together.

Just look at her. She was sitting on an airplane, waiting to land in San Diego so she could hook up with one of her players before he took the field tonight. She was wearing jeans and heels for goodness sake, not to mention a red lace bra and matching panties.

When had she become this impulsive, daring woman who would take off at a moment's notice just for a little hanky-panky? When she met Marco. Just thinking of his strong hands, his soft yet-masculine mouth, and his blistering blue eyes sent a little shiver down her spine.

When the plane finally landed, she couldn't wait to get to his hotel room and surprise him. She grabbed her carry-on bag, the one packed with mostly lingerie, and made her way to the car waiting outside the terminal.

She walked into the hotel lobby just as Marco was coming out of the elevators. He walked right passed her, but then stopped, turned around, and grabbed her bag. He led her back to the bank of elevators.

"Checking in?" he asked. His gaze took in her low cut tank top, snug fitting jeans, and high heels. His smile spread wide when he got to her face. "I think they're completely booked."

"I guess I'll just have to share a room, then." Hunter had never had another man look at her with such desire, such blatant need.

The elevator doors slid open and he held his hand over the opening as she stepped inside. Other people on board kept them from attacking each other before they could get to the room.

"I was just trying to kill time by walking around the city before batting practice." Marco slid the keycard into the slot of his room. "But I guess I'll stick around."

"I think we can find some way of keeping you occupied until the game." She entered the room ahead of him and waited until she heard him slide the deadbolt before jumping into his arms.

He lifted her and carried her to the bed. He loosened the ponytail she'd brushed her hair into and buried his face into her long tresses.

"I missed you." His words were another caress. It wasn't enough that he touched her with his hands, his mouth. His voice penetrated deep inside her. "Are you wearing jeans?"

"Yes. I went shopping."

"For me?" His voice deepened as he dropped his head to examine her new clothes more closely. "You bought these sexy jeans just for me?"

"Yes." Her heart fluttered as he slowly undid the button and slid the zipper down.

"That's too bad." He chuckled as he pulled them down her hips. "What a waste of fabric."

She giggled when he got to her feet. Marco slipped off the wedge heels and traced his hands up her calves. He kissed her just below the knee. His blue eyes blazed with desire as he moved ever so carefully up her leg, brushing his lips across the delicate skin of her inner thigh. Closer and closer to her most intimate place.

"Marco. Please." She squirmed with anticipation.

"Please what?" He lifted his head to gaze into her eyes. "Please stop?"

A whimper escaped her throat. She shook her head and scooted her hips closer to him.

"You want me to kiss you?" His voice, eyes, and mouth all quivered together.

"Yes Marco, please."

He just barely brushed his lips against her center, the sensation almost too much to bear. The rough stubble on his jaw contrasted with the smoothness of his lips. The tip of his tongue barely traced her edges. Then he dipped inside. Flickering. Swirling. Sucking.

She drove her fingers through his hair, bucked against him, and cried out his name. It was too much. It wasn't enough.

"Marco. Please. Please . . ." She wanted him inside her. All of him.

"Please stop? Or please more?" He laughed, knowing damn well what she wanted.

"*Please.*" She didn't want to beg. She already felt exposed enough. But she couldn't quite put into words what she needed from him.

He grinned, they both knew she was at his mercy. Yet he undressed quickly, positioning himself over her. He thrust slowly, teasing her once again. Yet somehow, he knew just what she wanted. What she needed. What she couldn't resist.

Marco rolled off Hunter and flopped on the mattress next to her.

"Well, this was a nice surprise." He could barely form words, let alone a complete sentence.

"A surprise?" She leaned over him, her hair tickling his chest. A satisfied smile lit her face. "You begged me to come down here."

"Begged? I merely suggested you might want to come down here. The weather is nice."

"Nice weather, huh?" She pressed her breasts against his chest. "It's a little hot for my tastes."

Marco swallowed, his throat dry. It was pretty hot. But they could be in Antarctica and she'd make it this hot.

"Whatever the reason, I'm glad you came." And came and came

again. He'd never known a woman who was so easily satisfied and so greedy at the same time. The more he gave her, the more she demanded. The more she demanded, the more he wanted to be the one to give it to her.

"So, what now?" She rested her cheek on his chest and sighed. Content at last. Or at least for now.

"I have to go to work." Marco wished he could put it off, but he did need to get some batting practice in. And probably some fluids.

"Yes. You do." She kissed his chest, lightly. Making him ache in the spot just below his ribcage.

"You can stay as long as you like." He had a late checkout due to the Sunday evening game.

"I think I'll take a little nap, then maybe catch a ballgame this evening." She snuggled even closer, making it damn near impossible to get out of bed.

"Maybe it will get rained out." He could be so lucky. But the closest thing to rain would be the cold shower he'd need if he spent another five seconds next to Hunter.

"Hey . . ." She released him and rolled over on her side, her head propped up on her elbow. "Have a good game out there tonight."

"I will," he promised. "We'll win this series. And the next. I'm going to make sure we win this division."

"And then what?" Her hair fell around her face, framing her big brown eyes, her satisfied grin.

"I'm going to get you that ring." He reached up and brushed her hair back. "The World Series ring."

"Oh, that ring." Her smiled slipped, but she replaced it with a bigger, brighter, if less genuine one. "And after that? What are you going to do?"

"I wish I knew." He rolled over on his back, staring straight up at the ceiling. "I'll be a free agent, so I have no idea where I'll end up."

He couldn't look at her. Didn't want to take the chance that she wouldn't want him to stay.

"Do you want to stay in San Francisco?" Her voice was hesitant. Was she afraid he'd say no or more afraid he'd say yes?

"More than anything. I'd like to finish my career here." He decided to go with the truth. His agent would kill him, but then he'd probably kill him anyway if he found out about his relationship with

Hunter. "But I'm a realist. Yeah, if I finish strong, I'd like to think you'll keep me around. But I know the odds are against it."

"Why do you say that?"

"Your partner isn't exactly in love with me."

Maybe not the best choice of words.

"Well, we'll just have to make him fall in love with you. Make him believe he can't live without you." Her nervous laugh told him she didn't believe it was possible.

Yeah. Clayton Barry wasn't going to change his mind about him.

"He already doesn't like me." Marco sat up. "I don't know what kind of numbers I'd have to put up to make him forget I once dated his wife."

"And you're sleeping with his partner." She forced a smile. "If he finds out about us, he could make trouble for you."

"I know." Marco wondered how far the man's influence would reach. "But it could be more trouble for you."

"True. And yet, here we are." She was scared. He could hear it in her voice. "So why are you here with me?"

"Because I can't not be with you." He dropped a kiss on her forehead before sliding out of bed. "I can't resist you any more than a rookie can lay off a high fastball."

She laughed again. But this time it was for real. They were both in this together.

"I can't seem to resist you either."

"So, I guess we just let this play out." Marco wanted to make some kind of statement, to let her know that they were a team. But he was scared. Terrified that he'd somehow jinx what they had. He couldn't talk about a possible future with Hunter any more than he would talk about a potential no-hitter to a starting pitcher. Not until the last out was recorded.

"Yes. We'll see where we end up come October." She settled against the pillow and closed her eyes. But Marco could swear he saw moisture leaking from the corners.

He was going to end up hurting her. Hell, hurting them both.

One thing he knew for sure. He was going to go down swinging. He wasn't going to give up on her or the division title without giving it everything he had.

Chapter 10

Hunter watched from behind the visitor's dugout as Marco strode up to the plate. He had a swagger in his step, a confidence that radiated off him. Why not? She'd flown down there at his request. Couldn't help herself. She couldn't resist him even though they both knew their relationship would only cause complications should her partners, his teammates, or the sports media find out.

With two outs, the pitcher walked Baxter, thinking the hot and cold Santiago would be an easier out. But Hunter knew he'd give her everything he had, just like he did in bed. Marco stroked a triple down the right field line. He stood on third base, found her in the crowd and removed his batting helmet to shake his head. He was letting her know she hadn't made a mistake in bringing him to San Francisco. She hadn't made a mistake in bringing him to her bed. Hopefully, she hadn't made a mistaking in letting him into her heart.

Marco finished the game with a triple, a home run and two doubles. The Goliaths won by a wide margin and since Los Angeles had lost earlier, they would face their division rivals only one game out of first place. Hunter was starting to feel it. The sense that this could be the season where they accomplished everything they'd set out to do. All the work that went into building the team might finally pay off.

If only her father was here to see it. In the twenty years he'd owned the team, they'd come close, but never won it all. Hunter would love to give him this last gift.

One good thing about being an owner, Hunter was able to have Marco's room moved to a different floor of the hotel, away from his teammates. Conveniently, it was right next to her room. They were able to spend the night together while arriving and leaving the hotel separately.

They met for an early lunch before Marco had to head over to the ballpark for his workout. In a city of nearly four million people, they figured they were safe going out together in public.

They ordered a hearty meal and were just settling into a relaxed conversation when Annabelle walked past their table. She stopped, turned around, and approached the two of them.

"Hunter, what are you doing down here?" She gave her a friendly smile before noticing Marco. "Oh? Oh. Well, I'm sorry to interrupt."

"No. It's okay. Are you meeting Clayton here?" Hunter tried to keep her voice steady. She didn't know the other woman well enough to know if she should panic or not.

"Clayton? No." She gripped the back of the chair between them. "He doesn't know I'm here, actually. I'm meeting with an agent. You know, just to see if there are any opportunities. I'm thinking of getting back into modeling. You know, part time. Just for fun, really."

"That's great. I hope things go well for you," Hunter said, hoping Annabelle would continue on to her meeting.

"I don't know." Annabelle let out a sigh and sat down in the empty chair. "It's just the girls will be starting school soon, and I feel so . . . insignificant."

"I'm sure you'll be plenty busy," Hunter offered. "Maybe you can help in their classroom or something."

"Yeah. But I just feel like . . ." She glanced over at Marco, as if he was the intruder here. "Clayton's off to Florida again. Though I have no idea why. Is there a minor league team there he needs to scout or something like that?"

"We have a single A team in Augusta, Georgia, but nothing in Florida." Hunter hated to be the bearer of bad news.

"That's what I thought." Annabelle pasted a brave smile on her face, but her eyes glistened. "Well, I'll let you two get back to your . . . lunch. Marco, it was nice seeing you."

She stood, but hesitated to leave.

"So, let me know when you want to go shopping again. I had fun." Annabelle leaned close to whisper in Hunter's ear. "Don't worry, I'll keep your secret. If you'll keep mine."

Marco rose to his feet, while Annabelle made her exit.

"Well, I certainly didn't expect to run into her here." Hunter tried to brush if off like it was no big deal, but she was rattled. "Small world, huh?"

"Yeah. You okay?" Marco sat in the chair closer to Hunter. Genuine concern laced his tone.

"Sure. I guess the one person I didn't want finding out about us will know soon enough." Her stomach knotted thinking about the bet and how Clayton would have a field day with this knowledge. If she won the bet, he'd accuse her of sleeping with Marco just to win. And if she lost, he'd have the power to ruin Marco's career.

"Who will find out soon enough?"

"Clayton Barry. We don't exactly see eye to eye most of the time." Hunter cringed.

"I don't think Annabelle will tell him she saw us together." Marco turned to watch her greet her agent. "She doesn't trust her husband."

"You know her that well?" Hunter tried not to read anything into it. So he'd dated another woman. He'd probably dated several.

"No. I just recognize a woman who's been let down by a man she depends on." Marco leaned forward to take her hand. "I hope I never see that kind of disappointment in your eyes."

He gave her his full stadium-light grin, the one that lit her up from the very beginning. The heat from his touch blazed through her entire body. Hunter needed to get control over herself.

"I'm sure you won't disappoint me. The team is on a roll. Keep playing like you're playing and we'll go deep into October."

"Yes, ma'am. You're the boss." He withdrew his hand and Hunter felt like she could breathe again. But in the spot where her heart had felt like it was getting too big for her chest, she now felt an emptiness.

Their food arrived, giving them a chance to focus on something other than each other.

* * *

Marco took a cab to the stadium. He didn't want to ride over with Hunter and it wasn't just because he didn't want anyone else catching them together. He was falling for her and she was in love with his talent.

He'd give her talent. Then, when they won the division, he'd give her a reason to keep him around. He'd give her a real good reason to keep him around. Like the fact that she was falling for him, too. She just didn't know it yet.

He was early. He could take a few extra swings in the batting cage or spend some time in the weight room working out the kinks. Except he didn't have any kinks to work out. No physical ones, anyway.

"Hey, Marco, got a minute?" Annabelle had somehow snuck into the clubhouse. No real surprise there, she could probably get in anywhere she wanted.

"Yeah. Sure." He took in her appearance: her carefully arranged hair, flawless makeup, and stylish clothes. The low-cut blouse and tight jeans could convince any man to give her what she wanted. Unless she wanted Marco to make her husband jealous. Then she'd have to look elsewhere.

He led her to one of the training rooms, so they could have a little privacy. But he left the door open. That way he could hear if anyone approached.

"Thank you." She glanced down at her hands, the bright purple polish matched her blouse. She began fiddling with the rather large diamond ring on her left hand. "I know we don't know each other all that well, but you're the only one I feel like I can trust."

Marco crossed his arms and leaned back against the table. Surely she had to have at least one person she trusted more than a guy she had a brief affair with almost a decade ago.

"Hunter and I are becoming friends, but I don't think I can burden her with this." She twisted the ring around her finger as she spoke. "I want to hire a private investigator. I need to know what my husband is up to."

"I have many talents, but I'm afraid spying isn't one of them." Marco dropped his arms to his sides. "Besides, I'm a little busy with this baseball thing."

"Oh, I don't expect you to follow him yourself." She smiled weakly. "I need someone to make the contact. To make the payments.

I'll pay you back, but Clayton tracks everything I spend. He gives me free reign for things like shopping, spa treatments, hell, I could buy a new car and he wouldn't flinch, but if he saw a payment to a PI, he'd freak."

"And he wouldn't freak if you wrote a check to your ex-lover?" Marco wondered if she was trying to set him up. But then he saw the fear in her eyes. The desperation. "You won't pay me until we know what he's been up to."

"You trust me enough to . . . to . . ." She fumbled through her purse for a tissue to wipe her eyes, carefully, so as not to disturb her makeup.

"Yes, Annabelle. I trust you. And I guess you remember that I can't resist a damsel in distress." Marco no longer had feelings for Annabelle, but he couldn't stand to see a man treat a woman with so little respect.

"Yet, you're with Hunter." She patted his shoulder. "She's hardly a woman in need of rescuing."

"Maybe she'll rescue me." Or she might destroy him. Either way, it was worth the ride.

"But I do have to ask you Annabelle," Marco said. "Are you sure you want to know the truth? If Clayton is cheating on you, are you prepared to learn the details?"

"Yes." She held her shoulders back. Her chin up.

"What if he's not up to anything? What if he's down there secretly building a theme park for you and the girls?" He tried to offer an alternative. A positive reason for her husband to be running off to Florida several times a year.

"That would be something." She let out a little laugh. "But I don't think so. I think he is up to something and I have a bad feeling it's no good. But I need to know for sure. So I can do what's best for my daughters. And myself."

"Okay. If you're absolutely certain." Marco took her hand. "We'll meet when I get back to San Francisco. Bring me as much information as you can to help the investigator. Recent photos, copy of his driver's license, passport, maybe even bank statements. Clubs he belongs to, even social media presence. Is he on Twitter, Facebook, LinkedIn?"

"I'll have everything you need." Annabelle gripped his hand and then let go. "I'll be in touch. And Marco . . . thank you."

Chapter 11

Marco was still unpacking when Annabelle called to set up a meeting. She was serious about investigating her husband's activities in Florida. She would be at his apartment in half an hour.

Great. What had he gotten himself into? Life would be simpler if he could say no to a woman. He understood exactly why he couldn't say no to Hunter. She held his contract, sure, but she also had his number. She owned him on a personal level. Whatever she wanted in bed, he'd been more than willing to give to her. Not that he was this all self-sacrificing fool. Oh no, he got plenty out of their arrangement.

His game had improved for one thing. He felt better than he had in months, physically and mentally. He was relaxed, focused, and he had a hitting streak that coincided with the length of their affair.

Marco also enjoyed getting to know Hunter. Discovering her playful side. She liked to drive fast, with the top down, for instance. That was the real reason she wore her hair pulled back, to keep it from flying around in the wind.

She was also very passionate about her team. She did know more about the game than the rest of the league combined. She knew more about every player on the Goliaths' roster than the manager. She just didn't yet have the confidence to approach him when she saw something that he didn't in a player's mechanics, or off-field distractions.

He wanted to help her find that confidence, wanted to empower her to let her hair down and be the force behind the team he believed she could be.

He also wanted to help Annabelle. Not because he had any remaining feelings for her, but because he had once cared enough about her to want to help if he could. He just hoped that investigating her husband was the right thing. For Annabelle, and also for Hunter. If her partner was up to something, she needed to know. A divorce could cause disruptions for the team. A nasty divorce could mean financial entanglements that she'd need to prepare for.

Annabelle arrived right on time.

"I can't thank you enough for helping me with this, Marco." She clutched her oversized purse as if it held the last bit of hope in her marriage.

"I haven't done anything yet." Marco wished she was just being paranoid, but he had a feeling if she was desperate enough to ask for help, she had enough evidence to support her fears.

"Still, not many guys would go out of their way for an old girlfriend. Especially if it meant calling another man on his behavior."

"We don't know what your husband is up to." Marco just hoped they weren't asking for trouble by looking into it. On the other hand, if Clayton Barry was up to no good, there were two women Marco wanted to protect.

"I know he's hiding something." Annabelle dropped her purse on the counter and started rifling through it. She pulled out a thick folder. "Everything you'll need . . . I mean, everything an investigator will need is in here. Copies of his driver's license, passport, credit report. The dates of his visits to Florida in the last year. Our last tax return."

She sank onto the barstool at the end of the counter.

"Have you looked through everything yourself?" Marco didn't want to go through her personal stuff. But as usual, he'd said yes to a woman before he could think.

"Yes. But I know there is something missing." Annabelle shook her head. Her eyes were weary, despite the carefully applied makeup. "I'm no accountant, but you'd think he would report his business expenses if he was traveling for business."

"You would think." He had a bad feeling about all of this.

"But I guess he'd rather pay more in taxes than admit to a mistress, right?"

"I really don't know the man all that well." And what he'd seen so far had not impressed him in the least.

"Apparently I don't either." Her voice held a note of regret. "But, I guess I shouldn't have married him on the rebound, huh?"

"It's really none of my business."

"Oh, come on, Marco, you know you broke my heart. So I just married the next man who walked into my life."

"We weren't serious, you knew that." He started to squirm a little.

"No. We weren't. But you were worried there for a second, weren't you?" Her playful smile told him she was only joking with him. "You always were too good to be true."

Marco felt a blush creep up his neck. He'd heard similar responses. *Too nice of a guy. So sweet. Such a good friend.* All reasons why his relationships never lasted.

Annabelle wasn't the only woman to break it off with him only to end up with some asshole like Clayton Barry. What was it with bad boys that women found so attractive?

"So tell me"—Annabelle reached for his hand—"how are things with you and Hunter?"

The change of subject caught him by surprise, but the genuine interest in her tone made him think that she really did care.

"Good." Still, he wasn't comfortable discussing his current lover with his ex.

"I like Hunter. I really do." Annabelle's smile seemed sincere enough. "I think you're good for each other."

"Thanks." Marco figured the less he said, the better.

"And I could totally see the sparks flying between you two at the restaurant. I hope things work out between you."

"Yeah." He hoped so, too.

"Don't worry, your secret is safe with me. I suppose you'll want to keep it a secret. Especially since you don't have a long-term contract, right?"

Marco just nodded.

"Wow. I didn't think about that when I asked you to help me." She sounded a little worried now. "I suppose Clayton would have to agree to any deals, right? Along with Marvin Dempsey, too. Hunter could want to keep you here, but if her partners don't agree, you could end up somewhere else, right?"

"That would be entirely possible." Marco didn't want to think about that happening. But he knew the reality of the situation.

"So your relationship with Hunter could hurt your career?"

Marco shrugged. Yeah. It could kill it. Right when he was in his prime playing years.

"Oh Marco." She slid off the barstool and came around to where he was standing. She started to put her arms around him, but when he stiffened, she stepped back.

"What about Hunter? What would happen if the other owners found out about your relationship?"

"You tell me. What would your husband do?"

"He finds her very presence in the owner's box a blow to his masculinity." Annabelle's voice held just enough contempt for Marco to feel better about snooping into the man's personal life. "He hates that she knows more about the game, the players, and the business of baseball than he does. So I could totally see him getting nasty if he finds out she has a relationship with one of her players."

"Nasty, huh?" The lump in the pit of his stomach started to grow.

"He won't find out from me." She patted him on the shoulder. "Besides, if we find out what I think we're going to find out, he'll be too busy trying to cover his own ass."

"You really think he's cheating on you?"

She simply nodded.

"And you need proof." He wondered if there was a prenuptial agreement that would make it difficult for her to just walk away.

"I need proof."

"Okay then. I'll get the proof you need."

Marco called the last person he had expected to talk to after he left Miami. He'd been this close to proposing to Vanessa when he was traded to St. Louis. She'd made it clear she wouldn't be willing to accompany him to his new city. He'd been more relieved than hurt. At least he hadn't popped the question before finding that out.

They'd parted amicably enough, but he hated to call her for a favor.

"Marco, how nice to hear from you." Vanessa sounded genuinely happy to speak to him. "It's been ages."

"It has been a while. How have you been?"

"Good. Not as good as you, though." Her tone was polite, almost friendly. "You've been on a hot streak."

"I've had a few balls drop in for me."

"I'm happy for you. Truly."

"Thank you." He switched the phone from one ear to the other. They chatted for a few minutes, catching up on her family and everything going on in her life.

"What about your cousin Antonio?" He might as well get right to the point. "Is he still working for that private investigator?"

"Tony?" she asked. "He bought out the company. He's keeping pretty busy these days."

"I might have a job for him."

"So who is she?" Vanessa asked, her tone not so friendly.

"Why would you assume this is about a woman?"

"You're in the middle of a hot streak. You're not going to call me up out of the blue, pretend to care about my life, my family, and oh-by-the-way I need to hire Antonio, if it wasn't for a woman."

"I'm just trying to help an old friend." Marco sighed. "And I do care about you and your family."

"But you've met someone. She must be pretty special." She had just a little note of jealousy in her voice. "Is she willing to follow you anywhere your career takes you?"

"That's not possible." Marco's gut twisted at the thought of changing teams once again. And of losing Hunter in the process.

"That's too bad," Vanessa said. "You deserve a woman who would follow you to the ends of the earth. Japan, the Dominican Republic, or even St. Louis."

"And you deserve someone who can give you the kind of family life you need. A man who comes home every night, changes diapers, and never misses a school play or family dinner."

Her silence spoke volumes about the regret that neither of them could be what the other needed.

"I'll let Antonio know to expect your call." Marco was relieved when she ended the awkward pause in conversation. "And I hope things work out for you."

"Appreciate it." He also regretted that there hadn't been enough between them to make the sacrifice.

Hunter was back in her office, pouring over the minor league stats from the past several weeks. She couldn't believe that instead of scouting the Triple A affiliate she'd spent the last few days with Marco. Sure, she already had a good idea of who she wanted for September call-ups, she just needed the data to back up her choices.

She opened the spreadsheet to update the statistics on her top twenty prospects. The top ten were easy to rank. Four relievers were slated to join the club and provide depth in the bullpen. By this time of year even the sturdiest pitchers had some arm fatigue. Having the extra players would lighten the load and eat up innings to save their regular pitchers for the postseason.

She had two utility players who could play any spot in the infield, and provide late inning replacements, a third catcher to provide insurance at that position, and that left three spots for outfielders.

There wasn't as much depth in the outfield as she would like. One of their top prospects had been injured and their best minor league outfielder had gone over to St. Louis in the trade for Marco Santiago.

Marco. He had given her more that she'd expected on the field. His defense had been nearly flawless, and in recent weeks, he'd put up the kind of offensive numbers that would have him in the running for player of the month.

And what he did for her off the field . . .

Hunter pushed away from her desk, her concentration now shot. Last night had been the first night she'd spent in her own bed, alone, and she missed him. Actually ached for him. The whole flight home, she contemplated all the reasons she should cool things off with him. The close call with Annabelle had her stomach twisting and turning like Lombard Street. But who was she kidding?

She couldn't stay away from him any more than seagulls could resist the bleachers after the game.

Damn. She grabbed her cell, texted a message, and was on her way to his apartment a half hour later. She'd picked up some Chinese takeout, since they couldn't share a meal together in public.

She'd barely set the cartons of garlic beef and Kung Pao chicken on the kitchen counter before Marco led her down the hall to the bedroom. They tumbled into bed starving for each other.

They satisfied one need and Marco brought the takeout to the bedroom, where they had a naked indoor picnic.

Hunter set the empty carton on the bedside table and reached for the two fortune cookies. She handed one to Marco and cracked hers open.

"Your greatest desire is within reach." She read her fortune aloud and Marco pulled her closer.

"Yes. I am." He nuzzled her neck, scattering kisses along her skin. Two seconds ago she had been completely satiated, but now desire flooded her and she could devour him again.

"So what is your greatest desire?" She pulled away, needing to put some space between them.

"Besides you?" He leaned back against the headboard. "I want what we all want. The World Series. I want to get you that ring I promised."

His answer didn't surprise her, it was the answer they'd both expected him to give. But she sensed that it wasn't the whole truth. There was something he wanted more than a championship. Something he was afraid to ask for.

"What do you really want, Marco?" Their eyes locked and she had the feeling that she was hovering far above the earth, held up solely by his gaze. She knew that the instant either of them blinked she'd fall, harder and faster than she ever imagined.

Hunter closed her eyes, realizing it was too late. She'd already fallen for this man. This beautiful, sexy, talented man had stolen her heart the moment he stepped into her car.

"I want my next contract to be my last." This time she had no doubt about his sincerity. "I want to finish my playing career with a team that would be interested in keeping me around on the coaching staff."

"You want to coach?" She was surprised, considering he was still in the prime of his career, that he was thinking about his next step.

"Sure. Even if it means starting all over again in the minors." He folded his hands behind his head, staring straight up at the ceiling. "I want to give back to the game that has given me so much."

"Does that mean you're no longer upset about being traded here?"

She snuggled up against him, almost giddy at the thought of keeping him in San Francisco for the long term.

"I never had a problem with the team. It's just that I have been on so many different ball clubs. Never quite sticking around for long. It was the same as when I was kid. We were always moving, every time my mom would get a new job, we'd move somewhere else. Sometimes not far, but most of the time I'd have to change schools. I got real tired of being the new kid in town."

"I can't even imagine." Hunter rested her head on his chest, listening to his heartbeat. "Other than college, I've always lived in the same house. I was going to look for my own place when I graduated, but then my dad got sick. He needed me home."

"Home." Marco sighed. "For me, home means crossing the plate. So I guess you need me to come home as often as possible."

She kissed his chest, wanting more than anything to promise him long term stability.

He put his arms around her, pulling her against him. He kissed her thoroughly before moving to the delicate skin behind her ear. He dropped kisses down her neck before turning her over and taking her breast into his mouth.

"Mmm." She moaned. "Keep doing what you're doing and I'll see what I can do about keeping you around."

"Around your bed?"

"That too."

"You want to keep me with the team?"

"Of course I do." She reached up to stroke his cheek, the rough stubble sending shivers straight to her lower abdomen. "I brought you here for a reason."

"Instant gratification?"

"No. Although you do have quick hands." She smiled. "I also want something that lasts. I want to build a team with staying power."

"I do have stamina," Marco teased. There were many nights when they'd gone extra innings.

"I wish I could promise you a long term deal." She might as well be honest. About wanting him for the team. "Keep doing what you're doing, and I'll do my best to convince my partners to re-sign you."

"Keep doing this?" He kissed her again. He moved down her body with his mouth. His hands. "And this?"

He dipped his tongue in the hollow of her navel, brushed his lips across her belly, spread her legs apart, and dropped tiny little kisses along the inside of her thigh.

"Marco, please." She threw her head back in anticipation of the pleasure he was going to give her. "Just don't do this with my partners. Or their wives."

He stopped. Lifted his head.

"Oh, Hunter." He shook his head. "What would it take to convince you that you are the only woman I want? The only woman I've ever wanted this much?"

Without waiting for her answer he drove into her, convincing her with each thrust.

Chapter 12

Marco sat in front of his locker after another Goliaths' win. He was starting to feel like his dream was within reach. He'd always been on teams that were good, but not good enough. But this one was different. The vibe in the clubhouse was different. Almost electric.

They were winning. Everyone was a part of it, too. There wasn't one guy who couldn't be counted on when the game was on the line. From the manager on down to the clubhouse attendant, there wasn't one single person who wasn't giving it their best. Every. Single. Day.

The clubhouse doors opened and Marco didn't need to look up to know Hunter had entered the room. He felt it, deep down in his every nerve ending.

Javier was joking with the catcher when he stopped laughing, looked up, and smiled at Hunter.

An unwelcome, and completely uncalled for, jolt of jealousy hit Marco in the chest. He reminded himself that none of them would be in this position if it wasn't for the work she'd done to get them there.

His manager looked a little too happy to see her.

"Finally." Javier strode toward her. "She's come out of it."

Marco made a noise, something of a grunt, and Javier stopped in front of him.

"She was in mourning far too long. But look at her." He nodded and Marco dared glance in her direction.

She looked fantastic. Radiant, even. A look he'd become accustomed to, but only in the privacy of the bedroom. Tonight she looked like herself. Her true self, with her hair down, pulled back into a simple barrette at the base of her neck. It took every ounce of his control for Marco to resist going up to her, in front of everyone, and running his hands through those silky strands.

Her skin glowed, with color on her cheeks and lips, and he realized she was wearing makeup. Eye shadow and a dark liner that accentuated her deep amber eyes. And lip gloss, pink and shiny, that drew his attention to her lips. Not to mention everyone else's.

"She looks like she's here on a mission." Marco recognized the determined look in her eyes and he hoped her mission was to drag him out of here and have her way with him.

"Yeah. She's got her list."

"Her list?" Marco wasn't sure what kind of list his manager was talking about.

"September call-ups. She said she wanted to meet with me, make sure we're on the same page." It took him a while, but Marco finally realized it was admiration in Javier's voice, nothing more. "I'll bet we have very similar lists. But she'll have a surprise or two. She was right about you, wasn't she?"

"I hope so."

"You know, a lot of people counted her out. Thought she wasn't up to the job." Javier didn't always have a lot to say, but when he got on a roll, the man could talk your ear off. "They figured this season would be somewhat of a wash. We'd be lucky if we didn't finish in the cellar with all the distractions. First Cooper's suspension before the season even started, then losing Henry Collins."

"Either one of those things could have an effect on a lot of teams," Marco agreed.

"Not to mention having a woman take over the team." Javier put his hand on Marco's shoulder. "But she's not just a woman."

Marco tensed, wondering what direction this conversation was going to take.

"She's been a part of this team since she was a little girl," Javier said. "And she's had her hand in running things since she finished college. But she kept it quiet. I think she's been the real brains behind this team for some time."

"No. She's the heart of this team." Marco watched her greet each of the players on her way to Javier's office. She smiled and looked each man in the eye. She wasn't like some owners who smiled and shook hands with their players only on signing day.

Javier acknowledged Marco's comment with a small nod and moved toward her and their impending meeting.

"Good game tonight, Santiago." She never used his first name in public. "You, too, Luis."

"Thanks," both players said at the same time.

"Damn," Luis said as Hunter and Javier walked away to the manager's office. "I never realized how hot she is."

Marco gritted his teeth to keep from saying something he'd regret. Or slamming his catcher into a wall.

"But who am I kidding? Not like either of us would stand a chance."

"You're married." Marco didn't think he'd need to point that out.

"Yeah, but even if I wasn't"—Luis shook his head, making little noises of appreciation and disappointment—"she'd never end up with guys like us. We're just players. Latino players. Nah. She'll end up marrying some rich, white bastard."

Marco qualified on two out of the three. He could be considered rich, an eleven and a half million dollar contract was nothing to sneeze at. And since his father had abandoned his mother, leaving her pregnant and alone . . . He was indeed a bastard.

"So what do you think she's worth? Probably billions," Luis kept talking. And Marco was doing his damnedest to stay neutral.

"Her billions pay our salary." He didn't want to think about how much money she had. Not when it reminded him he wasn't good enough for her. Not really. Yeah, she saw his worth as a player. But he wondered, not for the first time, what she was doing with him off the field.

Slumming? Flirting with her wild side before settling down with someone her daddy would have approved of? Maybe even arranged for her. He thought of Annabelle and her filthy rich husband. She'd been perfectly happy to sleep with a guy like Marco, but she'd never in a million years stoop to marry someone like him.

Was Hunter the same way? She'd grown up in that mansion on the hill. Instead of a pony, her daddy had bought her a baseball team. Was the team just a plaything? Something to keep her from getting bored while her interest compounded? Was he just a plaything?

No. He looked around the locker room. At the guys who remained, just hanging out, bullshitting with each other. They were more than just a collection of millionaires. They were a family. And Luis was acting like an obnoxious cousin, trying to goad Marco into giving something away, trying to push his buttons until he admitted that yeah, he was hopelessly in love with Hunter.

"No use buying her a diamond necklace, she probably got one for her seventh birthday." Luis kept at it, putting Marco in the uncomfortable position of wanting to defend the woman he was secretly sleeping with and keeping the clubhouse chemistry intact.

"You wanna know how Miss Collins celebrated her seventh birthday?" Sully, the clubhouse manager, had overheard their conversation and decided to butt in. "She got a front row seat at her mother's funeral, then she was picked up in a limo to go live with a man she barely knew. A man who was too busy making money to even attend his ex-wife's funeral."

That finally shut Luis up.

"Henry Collins didn't have the first clue how to deal with a little girl," Sully continued his story. "Until he took her to a baseball game. He was entertaining clients and brought her along. She loved it. And the two of them finally found some common ground."

"Baseball does have a way of bringing people together." It had brought Marco and Hunter together. But would it be enough?

"All it took was one smile on that little girl's face, and Henry knew he'd do anything to keep making her smile," Sully kept talking. "He bought the team for her a year later. It worked out for all of us, huh? They were thinking of moving to Florida. He saved the Goliaths, but more importantly, he saved his relationship with his daughter."

"Excuse me." Luis had a little catch in his voice. "I gotta go . . . I gotta call my little girl. Let her know that Daddy misses her. And her Mama, too."

The catcher was pulling his phone out of his pocket on his way out the door.

"I've been with this team since 1962. I've seen it all." Sully wasn't finished with Marco yet. "I've watched that little girl grow up in this clubhouse. She's more than family to me."

Marco waited, sure there was more.

"I've never seen her so happy."

"Her team is playing well." Marco didn't want to let the other man see him sweat. "She's worked hard for this."

"It's not the team's record that has her glowing." The older man placed a hand on Marco's shoulder. He knew. "I hope you're not taking advantage of her."

"No sir." Marco felt sixteen, getting *the talk* from his date's father before he could take her to the movies.

"Hunter may know more about baseball than you and me combined"—Sully's voice held fatherly concern—"but when other girls her age were going to clubs and dating, she was taking care of her father and this team. Secretly running this organization while covering for Henry."

"She's been in charge all along?" Marco's respect for her grew.

"Since she graduated from Stanford," Sully told him. "Henry didn't want anyone to know about his condition. He thought he could beat the cancer."

"I can see why this season means so much to her." Marco wished he could go to her right now. Take her in his arms and just hold her. "Believe me when I tell you I will give her everything I've got. On and off the field."

"This is the list of players I'm bringing up September first." Hunter pushed the piece of paper toward Javier. They'd been having a heated discussion for over an hour. Her temples throbbed, her back ached, and her cramps were killing her. All the more reason to stand her ground. "Your job is to get the most out of the guys I'm giving you."

"You really think Davis is a better choice than Swift?" Javier tapped the list, toward the bottom. They had been in agreement over the top seven names. They were just at odds over one player.

"Yes. I do. On paper, Swift is a more obvious choice." Hunter wasn't going to back down. She had faith in her manager, but she wasn't going to let him bully her into giving in. "But he's not ready.

Bringing him up too soon will mess with development. Besides, Davis is more versatile. Plus, he's been here before."

"He does have some serious speed." Javier was letting up. "And if you think he can help the team, I'll find a way to use him. Besides, you were certainly right about Santiago."

"You had doubts about him, too?"

"Not at first. I was excited when you brought him here. He'd always played well in this park. Kicked our ass a time or two. But then he got off to a slow start."

"I think he was putting too much pressure on himself." Hunter hoped she could keep her feelings for Marco from her manager. "He just needed to settle in and relax a little."

"I think he had some help." Had Javier discovered their relationship? It was probably only a matter of time before it came out. "Baxter's on one hell of a streak. Scottsdale and the rest of the pitching staff have kept the games close. Santiago figured out he didn't have to hit three run homers every at bat."

"Let's hope they can keep it up through September." Hunter kept her focus on the team. "I think I've selected the right guys to help that happen."

"I think you're right," Javier finally conceded. "You know more than you give yourself credit for."

"'Than I give myself credit for?'" Her defenses were up. "I've never had any doubt about my knowledge of the game."

"Really?" Javier leaned forward, as if he was going to reveal a great secret. "If you're so sure of yourself, why did you spend an hour and a half trying to convince me you were right? Why didn't you just tell me that this was who you were bringing up, and if I didn't like it I could look for a new job?"

"Because I want everyone on this team to buy into what we're trying to accomplish. If I'd told you to take this team or shove it, you'd fight me. You'd set Davis up to fail, even if you didn't realize it." Hunter leaned forward, knowing that if she backed down now, if she showed any sign of weakness, she could forget about leading this team anywhere. "If I didn't at least ask for your opinion, even if I didn't accept it, you would fight me even when you knew I was right."

Javier gave a deep, from the heart, belly laugh.

"Woman, you are wise beyond your years." He shook his head, beaming with pride. "I am honored to work for such a smart cookie."

He extended a hand and she gave him her firmest handshake.

She watched him walk out of his office, still shaking his head, and muttering to himself.

As soon he was out of the clubhouse she let herself sink back against his desk.

She'd proven herself to her manager. He was old school. A throwback to the way things had always been done. Having his support meant a lot.

Now if she could convince her partners that she knew what she was doing. As soon as the season ended, she would have the difficult task of re-signing free agents, including Marco. She knew she wanted him back, but the line between professional and personal reasons had become quite blurry.

His numbers were right where she'd want them to be. His batting average was up, his RBI totals were good, and he was currently on a fourteen game hitting streak. Plus, he roamed the outfield with a single determination to catch every ball hit within the same zip code.

If he remained healthy, there was no reason to believe he wouldn't put up the same kind of numbers next year. The only uncertainty was how she'd be able to deal with seeing him in a Goliaths' uniform once he grew tired of having her in his bed. She was pretty confident he'd keep her around for the rest of the season. A player on a hot streak was reluctant to change anything about his routine.

It was almost midnight when she made it out of the ballpark. She could slip across the street, pull into the parking garage, and take the elevator up to Marco's apartment. But she was exhausted. Besides, she'd gotten her period that morning. The birth control pills were doing their job.

And she had to do her job. Marco wasn't the only free agent she hoped to re-sign. Johnny Scottsdale had a one-year deal, but she'd heard rumors he wanted to retire at the end of the season. Bryce Baxter had one more year on his contract, so she'd have to think about extending it. And then there were the flashy free agents coming on the market that Clayton was drooling over. He wanted the power hitter who would be asking for a huge contract. A gamble Hunter wasn't willing to take.

Nor did she feel it a necessary risk. She had enough pop in her lineup to contend. And she had depth in the farm system to fill holes. She just needed to plug in the numbers to make a spreadsheet kind of guy like Barry take notice.

Then again, when she won the bet, he'd have to comply.

The Goliaths would enter September with at least a tie for first place. Best case scenario, they'd have a three game lead. Then they'd start looking at the postseason. They were four wins away from at least a wild card berth. But she wanted the division. And she felt strongly that it was within reach.

Marco was a big reason they were in the position they were in. And keeping him was going to be her first priority.

She just had to make sure she didn't lose her heart in the process.

Chapter 13

On the last game of the home stand, Marco went hitless and he was caught stealing. To make matters worse, he'd blown a play in the outfield that cost them the game. The official scorer ruled it a double, but he should have caught that damn ball. If he hadn't been thinking of Hunter at the time.

She hadn't come by after her meeting with the manager. It was late, and she'd sent a quick text saying she was too tired. But because of her absence, he didn't get much sleep. And he'd let it interfere with his performance.

After the game he texted Hunter, asking her to stop by the clubhouse before he left for the airport. He needed to see her. To talk to her and assure her that he would come through for her.

"I'm sorry I let you down." Marco had been about to give up on seeing her when she walked into the nearly empty clubhouse.

"It was one game." Her voice was calm. Reassuring. "You'll bounce back."

"I should have made that catch." He was still beating himself up over the momentary lapse of focus.

"It was a difficult play." He could feel the tension between them, but he wasn't sure if it was because she wanted to touch him and couldn't or if she was just saying what she thought he wanted to hear. "You just make it look easy most days."

"How can you have such faith in me?" He looked up at her, not caring anymore about hiding his feelings.

"How can I not?" She smiled at him, looking as proud as if he'd hit for the cycle. She leaned close to whisper in his ear. "Besides, it's my fault you had an off game. I should have let you known earlier I wouldn't be coming over last night."

The fact that Sully wasn't the only one left in the locker room was the only thing keeping Marco from pulling her onto his lap.

"Come with me on this road trip." He kept his voice low. "Please, Hunter."

"I can't." She shook her head, regret showing in her eyes. "I have too much work to do here. I can't take off for a ten day road trip."

"Meet me in St. Louis then." He missed her already. "I kept my apartment there. We'd have plenty of privacy and I could show you around."

"You still have a lot of fans there." Her voice softened, as if she might consider it. "Aren't you worried about being recognized?"

"No." He knew they couldn't keep their relationship a secret forever, not when he was falling in love with her. "I don't think that will be a problem."

Marco had never been in a relationship with a woman where he'd wanted her along on a road trip. He usually saw his traveling as a much-needed break. A chance to cool things off before they got messy. Not that his relationships had ever been too complicated. Even with Vanessa, he'd never had much more than a friends with benefits kind of thing. And when the benefits ran out, he remained friends with most of the women he'd been involved with.

Which explained his upcoming meeting with his ex-lover's cousin who was investigating another ex's husband. Maybe it was a good thing Hunter couldn't make it to Miami. She didn't need to get mixed up in all this, even though she had business ties with Clayton Barry. He just hoped that whatever he found wasn't going to hurt her, too.

"You know you don't need me at every game. Today was just an aberration." She flashed a playful smile after first checking that no one was close enough to overhear their conversation.

"Oh, I need you." Marco took her hands in his. Only Sully was left in the room, and there was no point in trying to put anything past the man. "I need you, but it's not just about luck. Or sex."

She trembled in his grasp.

"That's good, because I'm temporarily on the disabled list." Her voice shook almost as much as her hands. "But the good news is, I'm not pregnant."

"So that's why you didn't come to me last night?" He was a little disappointed that she didn't trust him to want to be with her even if sex was off the table, or floor, or bed.

"I was tired, too."

"Hunter. You don't have to make excuses. If you don't want to be with me, just say so. I'm a big boy. I can handle the truth." He did pull her on his lap this time. He stroked her cheek in a gentle caress. "I don't know what kind of men you've gone out with before, but I don't need to make love to you to . . . to enjoy spending time with you."

He'd almost said he didn't need to make love to her to love her, but he had a strong sense that she wasn't ready to hear that.

"You want to just spend time with me?" She pulled away from his touch, but didn't get off his lap.

"Yes. I do. I want you to come to St. Louis with me. I want to take you to my favorite restaurants and show you around. I want to hear about your childhood. Your college years." He wanted to know more about what drove her. What made her the woman she was.

"So you are tired of having me in your bed." She tossed that idea out with a self-deprecating laugh.

"Not at all." He kissed her then, in case she was serious. Kissed her with everything he had, letting her know that he still wanted her, wanted her more than ever.

Hunter gave in to his kiss at first, but she eventually pulled away.

"Marco, we need to be more careful." She stood up and tugged at her sweater. The soft fabric clung to her curves. He'd noticed the change in her wardrobe. It seemed to be a reflection of her change in attitude. She'd become more sure of herself and her place with the team. If only she would be as confident about her place in his life.

"Don't worry, only Sully is still here, and he already knows about us."

"Still, I think maybe we should . . ." She smoothed her hair, twisting one long strand. "Maybe we should cool things off a bit."

"No." Marco was on his feet. He tilted her chin so he could look her right in the eyes. "No. I don't want to cool things off, and I don't think you do either."

"How am I supposed to enter negotiations for your next contract if everyone knows we're sleeping together?" She folded her arms across her chest. "I'm sure it violates some part of the Player's Association Agreement."

"I wouldn't worry about the union," Marco spoke softly.

"Easy for you to say," Hunter said. "You're not the only female owner and team president in the league."

"No. I'm not a woman." He squeezed her hands. "But I do know a thing or two about having to be twice as talented and work three times as hard and still be considered inferior."

"There's nothing inferior—" Marco placed a finger over her lips.

"Believe in yourself," he told her, "like you believe in me. I know you've done more for this team than most people give you credit for. Especially your younger partner."

"What makes you say that?"

"I pay attention." Marco didn't want her to know he'd researched her, even before they started sleeping together. He'd been hoping to find reasons to stay away from her. Instead he'd found a woman he admired and wanted more than any woman he'd ever known. "I know you've built this team, piece by piece to be a winner. Each season has brought you closer to your goal. And this year, this team will finally pay off for you."

"Don't you have a plane to catch?" Hunter trembled beneath his touch, beneath his praise.

"Only if you promise to meet me in St. Louis." Marco leaned his forehead against hers. "I will do my part, but I need you there. I need to know you're waiting for me after the game."

"Marco, I . . ." She tried to resist, but he wouldn't let her. He kissed her, just a soft brush of his lips on hers. But he felt her surrender.

"Promise me," he whispered. "Please."

"I'll meet you." She closed her eyes and he pulled her close, breathing her in, taking as much of her as he could carry in his heart.

Hunter collapsed on the leather sofa provided for player comfort.

"Oh, Daddy . . ." she cried out to the heavens. "What have I done?"

Marco had promised her victory. But what if it wasn't enough? She could lose everything. Control of her team. Her self-respect. And worst of all, she could lose Marco.

"Are you okay, Miss Collins?" Sully startled her.

"Shouldn't you be on the plane to Miami?" She sat up straight and tall. Thank goodness she hadn't let herself cry right there in the empty clubhouse.

"They won't leave without me." Sully's laughter rang through the empty locker room, bringing back so many warm memories of a childhood spent in his clubhouse. "Or their equipment. I was just making sure no one left behind a lucky bat."

"It takes a lot more than luck." Hunter knew how hard the remaining weeks would be. As much as they wanted to win, their opponents wanted it too, even the teams who were already out of contention. They would play for the satisfaction of beating a better team, of possibly ruining their chances at the postseason.

"You've built a fine team here, young lady." Sully had scared her when she was a little girl. He was a great big Irishman, with a booming voice and no tolerance for disorder in his clubhouse. Managers and players had come and gone, but Sully had been the one constant all these years. He was here even before her father. And he remained. He would probably last longer than she would. "I think this might be our year."

"You say that every season."

"Yes. But this year I truly believe it." He came over and placed a gentle hand on her shoulder. "Your father would be very proud of you. He always was."

Would he be proud of her getting involved with one of her players? She had her doubts.

"He would want you to be happy."

"I know he would. And I'll be happy. As soon as we win this division." They had to win the division. She had to win the bet against Clayton. And she had to somehow convince her partners to re-sign Marco to a long term contract. He was the future of the Goliaths.

Even if he couldn't be her future.

The Goliaths took the first game in Miami. Barely. They won on Baxter's home run in the eleventh that broke up a six inning tie. Marco had contributed with an RBI single, a walk, and run scored. His defense was back on track and he felt pretty good about his game overall.

He had a brief phone conversation with Hunter, but she had been distracted by the last minute details of September call-ups. Instead of twenty-five players, teams could expand their roster up to forty players. This allowed teams to rest the regulars, provide fresh legs in late innings, and give the younger players a chance to make their mark on the big stage.

He'd been one of those guys. He'd never forget his first big league game. He swore the grass was greener, the chalk lines whiter, and the sky was bluer than any field he'd ever played on. It was almost like stepping into a cathedral, making him feel awed and humbled at the same time.

He'd arranged a meeting with Antonio Velez, Vanessa's cousin and a private investigator. They would meet for an early lunch before Marco headed over to the ballpark for that evening's game.

Arriving at the restaurant fifteen minutes early, Marco sat at the bar drinking a diet soda and wondering if he was doing the right thing. But he'd given his word, and he really did want to help if he could.

Finally Antonio showed up and Marco stood, ready to get on with it.

"Thank you for meeting with me." Marco shook the other man's hand.

"Thank you for the work. It's an interesting case." Antonio led Marco to a back room of the restaurant, where they would have plenty of privacy. "Not at all what I expected."

"So the son of a bitch isn't cheating?" Marco was relieved, for Annabelle's sake.

"I don't know if I'd go that far." Antonio waited for Marco to take a seat before joining him. "But he hasn't committed adultery, as far as I can tell."

"What can you tell me?" Marco was now more curious than ever.

"How do you know this man?" Antonio held a thick folder on the table in front of him. "He is the husband of someone you care about?"

"He's married to an old friend." Marco was getting a bad feeling about this. Had he poked a hornet's nest? And would Hunter be the one to get stung? "He's also one of the owners of the San Francisco Goliaths."

"Oh, this is not good." Antonio shook his head. "You're playing for the Goliaths, right?"

"Yes. I was traded to them at the end of July."

"You like it there?"

"Very much. But I'm not too sure of Clayton Barry." Marco hated to admit his unease. "He seems like a slime-ball, and that's not just because he tried to start a fight with me once he found out I used to know his wife."

"He is a slime-ball." Antonio fisted his hands. "He's been coming to Miami a lot the past couple of years. Not for a woman, though, like you thought."

"So what's he up to?"

"Performance enhancing drugs." Antonio leaned forward. "Steroids, HGH, testosterone, if it's on the banned substance list, he's into it."

"You're sure about this?"

"There's a company called FITNatural, that sells itself as a total fitness and nutrition solution." Antonio opened the folder, spreading flyers, brochures, and a stack of printouts on the table. "They promote personalized nutritional programs, such as paleo, gluten-free, or vegan diets and then suggest certain supplements. Some are legitimate, such as adding calcium to those on a dairy-free diet, and protein powders for vegetarians. But then they have a whole regiment of additional supplements, which are of course illegal. Not to mention dangerous."

"And Barry's involved?" Marco was steamed. "You have proof?"

"He's definitely involved." Antonio pulled out another file. "As for the proof, that's where it gets murky. He's backing them financially. That, I know I can prove. But as far as how much he's involved with the PEDs?" The other man threw his hands up, as if to admit it could go either way.

"The thing that gets me . . ." He leaned forward, confidentially. "They prey on our guys. You know, the Latinos. Guys who maybe don't speak such good English. Or maybe it's just that where they come from, the risk is worth too much to pass up. You know, even half a season's salary will provide for their whole family back home. Of the two dozen names on this client list, over three-fourths of them are Spanish names."

"Son of a bitch." Marco took a deep breath, trying to control his anger for his fellow ballplayers, Latinos, and most of all Hunter. "You say you can prove his financial ties, but nothing more?"

"Yes. I have proof he's an investor, and I'll find out how much he knows." Antonio cracked his knuckles, as if he wanted to hurt the man.

"No." Marco leaned back against the chair. "This might be better. We know he's involved in a company that is bad for baseball. But we don't have any proof of criminal activity, is that correct?"

"Right." Antonio nodded toward the waitress approaching with their drinks. She took their lunch order and retreated, leaving them alone again. "But I can get more, I just need a little time. And some additional resources."

"Sure. Whatever you need. But hold off for a bit." Marco was formulating a plan. "I wonder if he'd be willing to make a deal. If he would sell his share of the team . . ."

Marco shook his head. Frustration welled up, ready to overtake him. He could think of only one time he'd felt this much anger toward one man. The day his father dared show his face at the Texas ballpark when Marco made his first start. Just because his family's company owned the naming rights to the stadium, didn't give him the right to claim Marco.

There was too much money in this game. It tainted it. Money took something good and pure and turned it into something else.

"Is there any way to protect his partners from all this?" Marco was scared for Hunter. He knew how much the team meant to her. "His baseball partners. The team."

"So this partner? A woman?" Antonio didn't quite answer his question.

Marco nodded.

"A special woman?"

"I can't let her get hurt by this," Marco said.

"And you're sure she's not also involved?"

"Absolutely."

"If she's not involved, she's got nothing to worry about." Antonio almost sounded convincing. "So what are you going to do?"

"Whatever it takes." Marco needed to decide how far he was willing to go to stop Clayton Barry. And to protect Hunter, the Goliaths, and Annabelle. If he confronted the man, it could cost Marco his career. If Barry wasn't guilty, he could easily have him blackballed from baseball. But if he was guilty, he could ruin Hunter. And everything she'd worked for.

Chapter 14

Marco was the first player to arrive in the visitors' clubhouse. He took advantage of the peace and quiet to get his head right for the game. He let go of all his outside distractions: the failures of his last game, adjusting to a new city, a new time zone, a new bed. He wouldn't think about his meeting with Antonio. He couldn't think about what he'd learned. Or how he was going to tell Annabelle that her husband was a scoundrel, but not the kind she'd suspected.

He wasn't even going to worry about his next stop. Packing the few things he'd left behind in St. Louis. Facing the apartment he'd thought might finally be home for a while. And he certainly wasn't going to worry about whether or not Hunter would join him there. She'd said she would, but he couldn't be too sure about anything anymore.

No. He couldn't think about the possibility of losing her.

Time to start his pregame routine. He needed to forget about everything that happened or would happen off the field.

"You're here bright and early." A man's voice pierced Marco's concentration. A man he had very little respect for. Clayton Barry. "What? No late nights with the local ladies?"

"No late nights. No ladies."

"You're saving yourself for someone special?" The contempt in the other man's voice was unmistakable.

Marco busied himself with getting ready for the game. What this man was paying him for.

"You know she's using you." Barry propped a well-polished shoe on the bench next to him. "To win a bet."

When Marco didn't acknowledge his comments, Barry continued.

"See, she bet me that you could help the Goliaths win the National League." He chuckled, like it was some sucker bet. "That's why she's sleeping with you."

He must have thought Marco should be insulted. A beautiful woman wanted to have sex with him, and she had enough faith in his on-field abilities that she'd put money on him. He should just go jump in the Atlantic right now.

"So how much did she bet?" Marco couldn't help but be curious. "Must have been a lot, for her to stoop so low as to fall into my bed."

"Ten percent."

"Ten percent of the postseason revenue?" Marco was impressed. Pretty ballsy of her.

"No. Ten percent of the Goliaths." The smug look on the man's face told Marco that he had no idea how much she'd risked. Or how much she believed in her team. In him. Barry thought Marco would be insulted. Instead he was incredibly humbled. And even more determined to protect her from this creep.

"Maybe you should up the bet." Marco stood, facing the man. "What do you say to giving up your full share if we win it all?"

"Yeah, right." Barry laughed. "You expect me to just give away my share?"

"Or you could sell it. Walk away with no questions asked."

"And why the hell would I do that?" Barry narrowed his gaze, but there was a hint of fear in his eyes. "You've got a lot of balls for someone whose contract is up at the end of the season. When everyone finds out you've been sleeping with Hunter Collins, I don't see a whole lot of offers coming your way."

"You tell anyone about Hunter"—Marco stepped closer, towering over the other man by a good six or seven inches—"and I'll tell Annabelle about why you're here in Miami. Then I'll make sure everyone knows about what FITNatural is really selling. The Player's Association, Major League Baseball. The press."

The color drained from Barry's face. He trembled as he stepped back.

"I'm giving you a chance to get out before you're forced out." Marco kept his tone friendly, but gave him a look that let him know he meant business. "Annabelle was a friend of mine. She doesn't deserve to be dragged through a major scandal. Neither do your daughters."

At the mention of his daughters, the other man deflated. He dropped his head into his hands, covering his eyes and then raking his fingers through his hair.

"You stay away from my wife and children." The threat contained no real force. Just defeat, as the man turned to leave.

Marco had faced his opponent. He was ahead in the count. Now it was a matter of time before he'd find out what Clayton Barry would do next. Would he challenge him? Or would he do the right thing and take the walk?

Marco couldn't control what the other man did. He couldn't control what his teammates did. He could only control what he did. He would do his part to win for his teammates, his fans, and most of all for Hunter.

A soft tap on her office door interrupted Hunter's focus. She was making the final travel arrangements for her minor league players so they could get to the ballpark in time for the game on Tuesday. She'd already booked her flight to St. Louis. If anyone asked, she was going along to make sure the rookies settled in okay.

"Oh, you're busy." Annabelle took her sunglasses off the top of her head and twirled them by the earpiece. "I won't bother you."

"No, that's okay. I'm just being neurotic, making sure every detail I can control is, well, under control."

"So what details are you working on now?" Annabelle sat down in what was becoming her usual chair. "If you don't mind my asking."

"Just getting the September call-ups to the big club." Hunter wondered if she needed to explain what that meant. She sometimes forgot that not everyone ate, slept, and breathed baseball.

"I've been watching the games. Hoping to learn more about baseball." Annabelle sounded proud of herself. "I know that you're allowed to bring up extra players for the last month of the season. That's what you mean by September call-ups."

"Yes. We're bringing up seven guys. And I'm sure they'll all make their flights. I just hate it when the team is away. I get so nervous. Like something could go wrong and I won't be there to fix it."

"That's how I feel when I'm away from my girls." Annabelle gave a knowing smile. "But I suspect you're missing Marco, too."

Hunter felt heat creep into her cheeks. Yeah. She missed him. But she wasn't going to admit it. Not out loud.

"Here I was thinking you'd be sitting back, relaxed, waiting for the team to win just a few more games before celebrating making the playoffs." Annabelle's smile faded a little. "But I guess there's still plenty to do."

"Sure. And I haven't been putting in as many hours in the evenings as I would normally." They both knew Marco was the reason her nights were full.

"Is there anything I can do to help?" Annabelle surprised her with the request. "I can make plane or hotel reservations. I can order equipment or the cute little hats that say 'National League Champion.' That's kind of like shopping."

"You wanted to go shopping?" Hunter was pretty pleased with her wardrobe. Marco had been even more pleased by her new look.

"No. I want to learn the business side of baseball." Annabelle's tone took a very serious turn. "I started watching the games, so I could learn. Okay, and to see a little bit of Marco in action. He's good, isn't he? Like, really good."

"Yes, he is a very good player." Hunter kept her jealousy in check.

"I thought maybe if I showed more of an interest in the game, and yes, even in Marco, then maybe Clayton would show more of an interest in me." Her voice was tinged with sadness now, but with an undercurrent of resolve. "But I think we're beyond that. I think I need to learn the game—and the business—so that if I do divorce Clayton, I won't be in the way. So I'll be able to help keep the team successful."

"You're thinking of divorcing Clayton?"

"He spends more time in Florida than in California." Annabelle twirled her sunglasses almost furiously. "That must be where his heart is."

"Oh, Annabelle, I'm so sorry."

"He can have Florida. He can have everything. I only want the house. The girls. And the Goliaths."

"You want the team?" Hunter couldn't have been more surprised if she'd said she wanted Marco back.

"My fair share. I don't want to push anyone out of the way. But I do want something I can build for my girls." She reached into her purse for a tissue and blotted at her eyes. "So I can show them that a woman can have it all. A career. A passion. A man who truly loves her."

Hunter was a little confused. One minute Annabelle was telling her she was considering divorce. Then she was talking about true love the next.

"You're my hero, you know."

"Me?"

"Yes. You're the real force behind this team. Obviously Clayton doesn't know what he's doing. He's got his head so far up his ass he doesn't even realize what an idiot he is. He thought he could push you out, make you give up control of the team. But we can't let that happen, can we?"

Did Annabelle know about the bet?

"You're the brains of the entire Goliaths organization. And I have a feeling you have been for a long time."

"I've always had certain instincts."

"Like signing Johnny Scottsdale and Bryce Baxter. And trading for Marco."

"I knew each of them could be a huge factor in our run for the postseason."

"Tell me, truthfully, did you have your eye on Marco for more than just his defense?"

"No. I mean, I knew he could contribute at the plate."

"But you didn't bring him to San Francisco to bring him into your bed?"

"No, of course not." Even if she'd wanted to, she never would have believed he'd have been interested.

"Well, that's good. Because I can tell he's pretty smitten."

"He's *smitten* with winning." Hunter hadn't had enough girl-friends to know if this was normal girl talk or if Annabelle was teasing her.

"No. That man is head over cleats in love with you."

"He is not. We're not serious. In fact, the only reason we're still seeing each other is because we're still winning."

"No. I see the way he looks at you."

"That's just part of his charm. His irresistibility." Hunter was becoming more and more uncomfortable with this conversation. "I'm sure he looked at you the same way. You just don't remember."

"No. He never looked at me like that." Annabelle sounded wistful. Envious, even. "Sure he *looked* at me. Maybe he even liked what he saw."

She made a motion to draw attention to her face, her body, her cover-model looks.

"But he only saw the packaging." Annabelle sighed. "He only saw what I presented to the world."

Hunter looked at this gorgeous woman sitting in front of her. The woman she'd been jealous of so many times. But now she felt a little sorry for her.

"When Marco looks at you, he sees beyond the surface. He sees the whole you." Annabelle wiped her eyes, this time with the back of her hand. "I saw it at the barbecue. He looked at you like you were the only woman in the world."

"Are we talking about the same barbecue? You wore that emerald green top that dipped almost to your waist. Every man there was drooling over you. Including Marco."

"No. He was just being friendly. But he couldn't take his eyes off you."

"Right. Because I was so enticing in my baggy pants and plain T-shirt."

"You were. You captured his heart. And yeah, I was jealous. Still am, if you want to know the truth."

"You're jealous of me?" Hunter stood up, shaking her head. "That's ridiculous."

Hunter laughed. What a joke. The supermodel was jealous of the tomboy. The woman who'd been named one of the most glamorous woman in the world before she was even old enough to drink.

But Annabelle wasn't laughing. She was crying. Hunter was at her side, putting her arm around her friend.

"Annabelle, I don't know what to say."

"Promise you won't hurt him. Marco's a good man. A really good man." She tried to laugh. "I keep telling myself I let him go, but he was never really mine."

"He's not really mine, either." Hunter hoped she could be the kind of friend to Annabelle that she would need in a few weeks or months when she'd need a friend herself.

"Don't sit there and tell me he's just playing you like he plays left field." Annabelle gripped her hands. "You have something special. Don't let it slip away. Fight for it. Fight for it the way you'd fight for your team."

Chapter 15

The Goliaths swept the series in Miami. Marco went five for thirteen with four RBIs. They were on a hot streak going into September and their closest opponent in the division had dropped three of their last four. They needed one win to clinch at least a wild card berth. Then, even if Los Angeles got hot the last few weeks, they were guaranteed a spot in the postseason.

But Hunter wasn't going to be satisfied with a wild card. She had her sights set on the division title, and she was going to do whatever it took to help them get there. She'd picked the minor league players she thought were the most likely to contribute down the stretch, and she was personally going to welcome them into the clubhouse when they arrived in St. Louis.

She wouldn't be available if they had problems with the hotel, however. She was staying with Marco. Her flight arrived just minutes before the team's charter was scheduled to take off. That would give her a few hours to gather her luggage, grab dinner, and arrange for a car to take her to his apartment where she would shower, change into something not-so-comfortable, and await her lover.

She laughed when she let herself into his apartment. It was almost an exact replica of his place in San Francisco. The same leather sofa, big screen TV, and masculine—if not boring—black and silver bookcases. It was as if there was a bachelor pad catalog that catered to ballplayers who spent more time in a hotel room than their own place.

The only difference was the kitchen was on opposite sides of the apartment. In San Francisco, the living room faced west. Here it overlooked the city to the east. And back home, Marco had a view of the ballpark. When she looked out the window here she could catch a glimpse of the Gateway Arch.

Finally, she heard Marco's key in the lock. She tried to hide her anticipation, but it was difficult when she was perched on his sofa in nothing but a bustier and matching red panties.

Marco dropped his suitcase, kicked the door shut, and fell to his knees in front of her.

"I've missed you." He devoured her with kisses, stripping off his shirt when he came up for air.

"Really? I couldn't tell." Hunter grabbed at his zipper, tugging off his pants. Yeah, he'd missed her. The evidence was irrefutable.

"Did you miss me?" His mouth was magic, awakening her senses as he explored her body from her earlobes to her ankles.

She couldn't answer, didn't need to answer, her body responded for her.

"Marco. Please." Her head fell back and she moaned as he slid inside her.

Marco drove into Hunter. God she was good. Too good. A part of him wondered if he hadn't fallen asleep on the plane, and was only dreaming of her. Dreaming of this perfection.

He'd arranged for her to meet him at his apartment. That way she could make herself comfortable in case the game went late or their flight was delayed.

She'd made herself comfortable, all right. She was dressed in the sexiest of her sexy lingerie, just waiting for him to come home.

He'd planned on taking it slow, being smooth and romantic. Instead, he'd taken her right there on the couch. Right where he'd found her.

The minute she'd said "please" he was a goner.

"I love you," he said the words at the exact moment that she cried out his name. Spiraling out of control, they surrendered to an earth-shattering climax. He had no idea if she'd heard his confession. She just held on as the aftershocks ripped through them both.

"Does that answer your question?" She fumbled around for her panties, but wouldn't look him in the eye. "I guess I did miss you."

She slipped the tiny scrap of satin over her hips and wriggled off the couch.

Yeah, she'd heard him. Heard him and was terrified by his confession.

He dropped back on his heels and watched her escape to the bathroom.

With a sigh, he pulled his pants on and wandered into the kitchen. He'd made sure the cleaning service had come that morning to change the sheets and air out the place. But he hadn't thought to have them stock the refrigerator.

He stood there staring at the empty fridge, feeling sorry for himself until he heard the shower.

He tapped on the door before entering with an extra towel.

"Just wanted to make sure you had everything you need." Yeah, that was a lame excuse to barge right on in.

"I found everything easily enough." Hunter laughed as the warm water sluiced down her body. "Once I figured out everything was a mirror image of your place in San Francisco. I'm starting to think that having identical apartments near every ballpark is part of the collective bargaining agreement."

"An apartment's an apartment." Marco tossed the towel on the counter and started to back out of the bathroom. "One place is the same as the next."

"And why is that?" She lathered herself up, turning to rinse. "Why don't you care about where you live?"

"I don't know. I guess I moved around enough as a kid, I never got attached to any one place." He stood there, watching her make herself at home in his shower.

"Why did you move so much?"

"My mom was a hard worker." He leaned against the bathroom counter, his past opening up like his pores in the heavy steam. "She had a good job. Worked for a wealthy family. Until their son came home from college."

He'd never told anyone his story. It was too painful. Too shameful. But he wanted Hunter to know where he'd come from.

"He seduced my mother and when she got pregnant, he went back to college and she was out of a job."

"Oh Marco. That's so unfair." She opened the shower door, inviting him in.

"Yeah." Marco slipped out of his clothes, and joined her in the shower. "It was. But she never gave up. Even if it meant packing up and moving to a new town, wherever the jobs were. She kept a roof over our head. Food on the table. She made sure I got an education. And that I could play ball."

"Sounds like your mother and my father would have been good friends, if they'd had a chance to meet." Hunter stepped aside so he could rinse off.

When she wrapped her arms around him, Marco felt like he'd finally found a home.

Hunter woke before Marco. She eased out from under his embrace, wanting to escape, but unable to tear herself away. So she propped herself up on the pillow and watched him sleep. He was gorgeous. Even in slumber, his muscles flexed, revealing his power. Not a scratch, or blemish, or spot of ink marred his perfectly smooth skin. Just a sprinkling of dark hair, in all the right places, inviting her to sample the fine tastes and textures and pleasure she'd grown to love.

Love. It hit her like a ninety-seven-mile-an-hour fastball. It was powerful and frightening and intoxicating at the same time, especially when it came with amazing sex. The kind of mind-blowing, earth-shattering, and all that other cliché inducing stuff she'd thought only existed in the movies.

He'd told her he loved her. True, he'd said it as he was plunging deep inside her and sending her over the edge. She'd been unable to respond, at least not verbally. But then he pulled away. Maybe he was just caught up in the moment. Or maybe he was as frightened by the thought as she was.

Watching him now, she felt butterflies in her stomach. No, more like a thousand hairy spiders. Still, she couldn't tear herself away. She brushed a kiss across his forehead. His eyes fluttered open and a warm smile spread across his face.

"Good morning gorgeous." Marco pulled her against him.

"Please, I'm a mess." Hunter attempted to smooth her hair back.

"That's what makes you even more beautiful." He snuggled even closer. "Your hair is tousled from me running my hands through it. Your lips are swollen from my kisses. Your cheeks are pink from my whiskers."

He kissed the top of her head before lifting her chin to meet her gaze.

"I'm the only one who sees you like this."

Her stomach growled, ruining the moment.

"I guess I should have had some food delivered. I'm afraid I have nothing more than a bottle of hot sauce in my refrigerator."

"You have an unopened jar of salsa and a box of stone wheat crackers in the pantry."

"Good thing there's a diner just down the street." Marco sat up. "Let's get dressed, grab some breakfast and go explore the city."

They showered, dressed, and walked hand in hand to the family diner down the block.

"Marco Santiago!" The waitress set the coffee pot back on the burner before throwing her arms around him. "Aren't you a sight for sore eyes."

"It's good to see you again, Kelly." Marco gave her a quick hug. "Any chance you have my table ready for me?"

"For you, Marco, anything." She beamed at him, a neon flashing smile, and led them to his table.

"Does that mean I can get my favorite omelet?" He slid into the booth.

"It's been added to our list of specials. 'The Marco' is one of our most popular menu items." The woman was flirting with him. Shamelessly.

"Well, I guess I'll have the special." Marco flashed his dimples at the waitress before acknowledging Hunter was there. "Do you need to see the menu?"

"No. I'll have French toast with a side of bacon." Hunter wasn't very hungry now. "And a glass of orange juice."

"Coffee?" The waitress barely glanced at Hunter while she wrote down her order.

"Please. With cream and sugar." Hunter assumed the waitress already knew that Marco drank his coffee black.

Marco was still grinning when the waitress left to put in their orders. He picked up the silverware packet and unrolled the napkin.

"Can you believe they named a special after me?" His dimples deepened and his cheeks flushed.

"You must have spent a lot of time here." Hunter carefully placed her napkin in her lap. "You've certainly made quite the impression."

"I guess I ate here too often. It's a good thing my omelet is made with half egg whites and is stuffed full of veggies." Marco leaned back into the vinyl booth and patted his rock hard abs. "Otherwise I would have gotten fat."

"You manage to stay in pretty good shape." Unfortunately Hunter wasn't the only one who'd noticed.

The waitress returned with their coffee, and a smile for Marco. She chattered on and on about how much they missed him in St. Louis, how the team just wasn't the same without him. He was irreplaceable.

Hunter ate her meal, the French toast sitting in a lump in her stomach. No amount of cream and sugar could reduce the bitterness of her jealousy. Marco had obviously had a relationship with their waitress. And like with Annabelle, he was still on friendly terms with her.

Marco left a generous tip and they walked back toward his apartment.

"Do you mind walking some more, or should I get my car?" he asked as they approached his building. "The arch is just a few blocks more, but we could drive if you want to."

"I'd rather walk." Hunter could use the fresh air and the time to think. She couldn't imagine remaining friends with Marco after their relationship ended. Couldn't see him with another woman and still manage to smile.

"Okay, that way I can show you places along the way." He slipped his hand in hers and led her down the city streets. He stopped to point out local landmarks, places he'd been, and people he'd met.

Marco still had a lot of fans in St. Louis and he was recognized a few times on the street. He signed about half a dozen autographs on the forty minute stroll from the diner to the Gateway Arch.

He approached an attractive woman at the ticket window. "I'd like two tickets for the next tour."

"The next one we have available is at four o'clock." She smiled at Marco, like every other woman he'd met.

"No. That's no good." He glanced at her name tag and turned on his charm full blast. "See, Tricia, I have to go to work at four o'clock. Are you sure you don't have anything earlier?"

"Oh. It's you. I almost didn't recognize you out of uniform." The woman blushed. "Let me see what I can do for you, Mr. Santiago."

She started clicking away at her computer.

"Please, call me Marco." He leaned on the counter, grinning his impossible to resist grin.

"Oh, here we go, Marco." The woman looked up briefly. "I can squeeze you in on the next tour. But you'll have to hurry."

"Thank you, Tricia. I appreciate it." He slid his debit card to the woman and she melted under his charm.

"Just don't be too hard on us tonight." She handed him the tickets and his receipt.

"I'll do my best." He gave a humble shrug.

"That's what I'm afraid of." She shook her head, but was smiling the whole time.

They rode the tram to the top of the arch. Marco pointed out landmarks, both famous and personal. They could see his apartment building from there. And the stadium he'd played in before she swooped him up. As he showed her more and more of the city, it became increasingly clear that he'd belonged here. He could have made a home here.

Marco had the game of his life. He went four for four with a walk. He either knocked in or scored six of the Goliaths' nine runs during the rout. His defense was flawless, it was like he had a magnet in his glove, pulling in every ball hit to the left side of the outfield.

With the victory and the fact that L.A. trailed seven to three in the eighth inning against Chicago, they were almost certain to lock up a playoff berth. Life was looking pretty good as Marco hit the showers.

Hunter entered the clubhouse just as the final out was recorded in Chicago. The whole place erupted in cheers. They were headed to the postseason. They still had a lot of work to do. The magic number was now six—the combination of wins for the Goliaths and losses for Los Angeles—and the division was theirs.

He couldn't help it, Marco swept Hunter into his arms, spun her around, and gave her a big kiss, right there in front of everyone.

"Marco! Please." Hunter wriggled out of his grasp, a look of horror on her face.

He leaned in and whispered in her ear. "I think we should wait until we get back to my place."

He knew she was embarrassed by his public display of affection, but he was feeling so good he wasn't going to apologize. He slipped his hand in hers, but she tried to pull away.

"Everyone is staring at us," she said through a clenched jaw.

"Is there anyone here who didn't already know I'm crazy about this woman?" Marco only made matters worse by his question. No one stepped forward, of course. Not even the seven players just called up from the minor leagues. No, everyone just smiled, and nodded, and pretended their teammate wasn't making a complete fool of himself.

"I need to go home." Hunter was pissed at him.

"Fine, we'll go back to my place." Marco's good mood faded. Until he thought about getting her naked.

"No. I think I should go back to San Francisco." Hunter turned and walked out of the locker room.

Marco followed, a sense of panic rising in his chest.

"Look, Hunter, I'm sorry if I embarrassed you back there. But, come on, it's going to come out sooner or later that we're together." Marco reached for her arm, but she shook him off.

"That's not it." She quickened her step.

"Then what? What has you so upset with me? Why are you pulling away from me?" They reached the doors leading to the player's lot. She pushed them open with a bang. If he didn't stop her, she could easily get a cab that would take her to the airport.

"Hunter, wait." He grabbed her hand, not letting go this time.

"I need to go."

"No. No, you don't." Marco pulled her closer to him. "We have something here. Something pretty special."

"You're just excited about winning." She struggled to get away from him, but he picked up her other hand, held on gently but firmly.

"Tell me you don't love me," he dared her. "Look me in the eye and tell me you're only with me to win a bet."

"You know about the bet?" That disarmed her. She quit fighting him.

"Yes. And I have to say, I'm flattered." He smiled, hoping to pull her in with his charm. "That you believed in me enough to risk your team, your legacy . . ."

"It wasn't much of a gamble." Her voice trembled. "I knew you'd come through."

"You had faith in me, and that means a lot." Marco squeezed her hands. "So why can't you have faith in us?"

She looked up at him, her eyes glistening with uncertainty, fear, and hope.

"Marco Santiago!" A woman's voice sounded from just outside the gate. "I love you, Marco! Come back to St. Louis."

Hunter stepped back. She shook her head.

"I can't do this." She retreated even more. "I can't handle all the women who fall at your feet. They find tickets that don't exist. They throw their arms around you and name an omelet after you."

"They're just fans." Marco was floored by the sudden jealousy.

"Like that waitress. I'm sure she was just a fan."

"Kelly? She's a friend."

"Like Annabelle is just a friend."

"Annabelle is just a friend. And I thought she was your friend, too."

"So you did sleep with that waitress?"

"No, Hunter, I did not." He shoved his hands in his pockets. He knew he was screwed. "But yeah, I have had lovers before you. I can't change that. Just like I can't change the fact that half of my fans are women. What do you want from me?"

"I want . . ." She glanced over at the crowd of fans. The ones screaming his name, not caring that he was with someone. "I want to believe in you, but . . . but you tell me you love me then you flirt with every woman in St. Louis."

"I do love you, Hunter." He dragged her over to one of the waiting cabs, away from the crowd. "I've never said that to anyone before. This is a whole new ballgame for me. I know I'm going to make a lot of rookie mistakes, but we make a pretty good team. Don't give up on us."

He kissed her then, desperate to show her everything he was feeling.

"Marco." She sighed and he hoped that meant she was going to give him a chance to prove himself. "Please."

He closed the space between them. He would do whatever it took to win her trust. He'd already earned it on the field. After a rocky start, he'd come through for her enough that they were guaranteed at least a wild card spot in the playoffs.

Now he just had to make her trust him off the field. He would still be courteous to the fans, even the female ones, but he'd make sure Hunter knew she was number one in his heart.

Chapter 16

With one swing of the bat, Marco had given the Goliaths a three run lead in the bottom of the eighth inning. If the score held up, they would clinch the National League West Division title. As he rounded third base, he looked up into the stands only to find Clayton Barry sitting next to Hunter. What the hell was that slimy bastard doing there with his woman?

He hadn't crossed paths with the man since their little discussion in Miami, but Marco had passed on the information he'd gathered to Annabelle. He didn't want to know, but he was pretty sure she'd started divorce proceedings. The man's personal life was in shambles and Marco was hoping Antonio could come up with more leverage to get Barry to sell his share of the team.

Marco didn't like keeping what he'd discovered from Hunter, but he didn't want to put her in any more of an awkward position. He figured the less she knew about her partner's activities the better. At least until he was out of the picture.

Besides, they were so close to everything they'd worked for. He didn't want to do anything to mess it up. Like forget to step on home plate before he returned to the dugout. Marco tapped the plate with his toe and barreled down the steps to his spot on the bench. His teammates were busy congratulating him, but he didn't hear a word they were saying. He was worried about Hunter. About what she would do when she found out her business partner had been supplying performance enhancing drugs to major league players.

Marco tried to keep his spirits up and get swept up in the excitement in the dugout. He tried to focus on getting through one more inning so he could see Hunter after the game and make sure she was okay, and that Barry wasn't trying to pull anything with her. He tried to keep his head in the game but his heart was with Hunter.

"Wow, that was quite a shot." Clayton had joined Hunter behind home plate during the seventh inning stretch. "Looks like your boy toy has turned out to be a wise investment after all."

She knew he was trying to goad her, but she chose to ignore him, instead focusing on the excitement of the game. Yes, they were winning what could be the clinching game. She wondered if he was going to try to get out of the bet.

"If you don't mind, I'm trying to watch the game." Hunter filled in the scorebook, smiling to herself at just how impressive that home run was. Her instincts about Marco had been spot on. He'd been the spark this team needed to become a champion. Oh, sure they still had a lot of work ahead of them, with nine games left in the regular season. They would play a best of five game divisional series, and would need to take four of seven in the championship series in order to win the National League Pennant.

"So what do you say to double or nothing?" Clayton leaned forward, as if he was actually watching the game. "If they win the pennant, I'll give you twenty percent."

"And if they don't?"

"Then we keep what we had at the beginning of the season." It sounded like he didn't care for that alternative.

"Not to sound too overconfident, but you do know we've got a really good chance of winning." Hunter hoped she didn't just jinx everything.

"Yeah. I think you're right. But I still want to make the bet." Clayton stared straight ahead, focusing on the field. "A man needs a chance to keep his pride."

There was something in his voice that made Hunter think he was hiding something. Maybe Annabelle had asked for a divorce. Was he trying to lose on purpose, just so he wouldn't have to give up his share in court?

"Why don't we just drop the whole thing?" She'd only made the bet because she wanted to prove to herself that she could put together a team better than he could. "It was just a friendly wager."

She looked at him and saw a man who looked like he hadn't slept in days. A man who was on the verge of losing everything.

"I need you to make the bet." Desperation shone in his eyes. "Can we head up to the suite and talk about this. Please?"

The last out was recorded and the ballpark went crazy. The Goliaths had won their division. The party started on the field as the bench players poured out of the dugout, surrounding their closer and jumping up and down on the mound. Marco joined in with the celebration. And the champagne began to flow even before they could get off the field.

Rachel Parker was the first to interview him.

"How does it feel to hit the game winning home run and clinch the division?" She practically had to shout her question above the noise of the crowd.

"It feels pretty good." He tried to blink enough to keep the champagne from stinging his eyes. But it was worth it.

"And just think, two months ago, you weren't even a Goliath." She shrieked as someone dumped a bottle of bubbly over her head.

"A lot's changed in those two months." He shook his head, trying to clear his vision. He couldn't see Hunter in the stands. He wanted to be the first to congratulate her, but it looked like she'd already headed into the clubhouse. "So much has changed. But I'm truly happy to be here. I can't even begin to tell you how grateful I am to be a part of this team. The fans here—"

The stadium erupted, drowning out his words. They were going wild. He'd been embraced by the fans from the moment he stepped onto the field after the trade. He didn't even have a uniform, and they'd welcomed him, taken him in as one of their own. He felt the love of the crowd, forty thousand of them, chanting his name.

"Marco. Marco. Marco."

Oh yeah, he felt the love. But it was nothing compared to the love he felt for Hunter.

* * *

"So do you want to tell me what's going on?" Hunter followed Clayton up the elevators into the private suite. "Why are you so adamant about upping the bet?"

"I screwed up. Big time." Clayton collapsed into a plush leather chair. "I need you to take the other twenty percent of the team, I don't care what you do with it. Sell it to Dempsey, give it to Marco Santiago as a bonus. I don't give a fuck."

"Excuse me?" It wasn't the first time she'd heard that word, but she was a little offended all the same.

"Look. I need to dump my share. And quick. But I can't sell it. It'll just make me look desperate. I can't give it to Annabelle, either... community property and all that bullshit."

"Clayton, you're starting to scare me. What the hell is going on?"

"I'm in real trouble here. I made some bad investments and it's coming back to bite me in the ass." He ran his fingers through what was left of his hair.

"So why not just sell your share?" She had the cash.

"I can't sell. I can't... *Fuck*." He stood up and staggered over to the bar, poured himself a stiff drink, drank it down and poured another before catching a glimpse of himself in the mirror. After setting the glass down, he turned to face Hunter. "Please take the bet. Just promise me you'll look after Annabelle and the girls."

"Clayton, what have you done?" She had a feeling she already knew, but she wanted to hear it from him that he'd been a cheating bastard.

"Ever hear of FITNatural?"

When she only stared blankly back at him, Clayton continued.

"You will. I hope to have severed all ties with the team by then. Taking this bet will help us both."

"What is FITNatural and what does that have to do with the team?" Hunter held her breath.

"A nutritional supplement and fitness company I'd invested in." Clayton sunk back into the chair. "I thought they were legit. An old friend from college hit me up a few years ago. He wanted to start a fitness company, one that was different than anything else out there. He wanted to focus on eating right and conditioning. He had the best nutritionists and personal trainers all lined up. He just needed the cash to get it up and running."

"And you invested." Hunter sat down across from him with a knot in the pit of her stomach.

"Heavily. And they were so successful that I turned a blind eye to what made them so profitable." Clayton shook his head wearily. "It wasn't until Nathan Cooper's suspension that I even had a clue."

"Was Cooper a client of FITNatural?"

"He was."

Shit.

"So I've been going back to Florida, trying to figure out how to get untangled from this mess, but it's big. Real big. And it's only going to get bigger."

It took every ounce of strength she had not to throttle the man sitting in front of her. She got up and walked to the window. The ballpark was still full, but not because the game was still going. They were celebrating. A huge victory. A step in the direction of everything she'd been working for.

And it could all come crashing down. Because of Clayton Barry's greed.

"So who else knows about this?" Surely the media would have splashed the story all over the place if it had gone public. "Who else knows about your involvement?"

"Besides your boyfriend? Just my attorney, and the Commissioner's office." He followed her to the balcony. "I've cut a deal. I'll tell them everything I know, including players involved, in exchange for amnesty. I can't go to jail. I can't do that to my family."

She wasn't sure what shocked her more, the fact that he was going to testify or that Marco somehow knew about this.

"How is Marco involved?" She needed to know if he was taking steroids. She couldn't believe he would risk it, but there was so much at stake.

"He's the one who called me on it. I don't know how he knew, but I figure it's only a matter of time before the whole world finds out." He sounded defeated. "Please, Hunter. Take this bet. Let me walk away with what's left of my dignity. Let me do the right thing."

"The right thing?" She turned and walked back inside the suite. "You wouldn't know the right thing if it crawled into your lap."

"That's where you're wrong. The only two things I've ever done right crawl into my lap. Or at least they used to." He followed her. "Take the team off my hands, and look after my girls for me. I need to know they have someone like you to look up to."

"Someone like me?" Hunter laughed. "Yeah. I'm such a role model. I gamble with my team. I sleep with my players."

She smoothed back her hair, trying to put everything back in place.

"I can't take your bet." Hunter was furious. With Clayton. With herself. "Oh my God. I bet on baseball. The cardinal sin. Where was my head?"

"In Marco Santiago's bed?" Clayton wasn't so defeated that he couldn't throw one last jab at her and Marco.

"I had no intention of sleeping with Marco when I made the stupid bet." Hunter felt ill. "It was my pride, not my hormones that made me take that bet."

"Your pride?"

"Yes. I wanted to prove to you . . . No I wanted to prove to myself that I could get this team to the postseason." And she'd done that. It had been six years since they'd made it to the playoffs. Six long years in which they'd come close, sometimes only a game or two out.

"You did get them to the playoffs. And I really do think they have a good shot at going all the way." For the first time, Clayton sounded sincere.

"It doesn't matter. I've screwed up. Big time. Gambling. Steroids. Sex. What more can I do to ruin my reputation with the league?"

"You could give up." Clayton brought her a drink and she took it. "You could back down. But I don't think you will. I mean it when I say that I want my girls to look up to you. I've always admired your determination. Your grit."

"My grit? Stupidity is more like it." She swallowed the aged whiskey. It burned, but felt pretty damn good going down. "I never should have let you push me into making the bet in the first place."

"And sleeping with Marco Santiago. Do you regret that?" Clayton looked at her in such a way that she got chills down her spine. Like she could have had him instead.

"My personal life is private." She couldn't regret what she had with Marco. Even now, as she realized she couldn't have it all. She couldn't continue her relationship with Marco, remain president of the Goliaths, and sign him to a long term contract. "But with your involvement in FITNatural, when the scandal does break, nothing will be private anymore."

It would all come out. Instead of focusing on Marco's production in the playoffs, reporters would be wondering about his performance in her bedroom. There wasn't anything prohibiting a personal relationship between an owner and an active player, but there was some language that could be interpreted as "negotiations outside the structure of organized baseball."

"Sell to Marvin Dempsey." Hunter finished her drink. "Work out all the details with him, but do it quickly and quietly. We still have a lot of season left, and we don't need any more distractions than we already have."

"You trust Dempsey?"

"Yeah. I do. He'll do what's right for this team." She just hoped he was strong enough to survive getting dragged through the mud with her and Clayton.

"I'll sell to Dempsey." Clayton sounded truly remorseful.

"What about Annabelle?"

"She's filed for divorce." He hung his head.

"She thought you were cheating on her."

"In a way I was. I was cheating in so many ways. Just not with other women. You have to believe that. You have to make her believe that."

"Why?" Hunter knew too much about their personal lives already. "Why would you think I could convince her of that?"

"Because you're friends. She respects you and admires you and she wishes she were more like you."

"Please."

"Just look out there." Clayton pointed to the still rocking ballpark. The game had ended some time ago, yet no one wanted to leave. They were all enjoying the moment. They were winners. They were a part of something special. Something that doesn't happen every year. This could be the year. Everyone hoped. Believed. And no one wanted to give up that feeling.

Hunter didn't want to give up on that feeling. The team had come too far to let her mistakes ruin everything they'd worked for.

Chapter 17

Hunter walked into the clubhouse with the postgame celebration well underway. They had an off-day tomorrow and an afternoon flight to Phoenix, so they might as well enjoy the moment.

She gave a few congratulatory handshakes and pats on the back before finding Marco holding court in the center of the clubhouse. He was surrounded by several of his teammates, Bryce Baxter, Johnny Scottsdale, Roberto Luis, and Diego Garcia were among the players laughing and celebrating with the man who'd hit the game winning home run.

Hunter was pleased with the way the team had come together over the last few months. In some clubhouses the Latino players kept to themselves, separated by language and cultural barriers. The veterans stayed away from the rookies, and vice versa. The players who'd been brought up in the farm system felt threatened by the guys acquired through trades or free agency. But not here. They all seemed to be united with one common goal. Hunter thought Marco had something to do with the way the team had come together but maybe she was a little biased. It could just as easily have been Johnny Scottsdale who'd gotten Bryce Baxter and Roberto Luis to act like brothers instead of a couple of guys who had nothing in common except their jobs.

Before she could think too much about it, Marco spotted her. He handed his champagne bottle off to Garcia and started toward her. His blue eyes shone with excitement and desire as he swept her up, twirled her around and kissed her right in the middle of the clubhouse.

She should protest, but he kissed her long and hard and with his erection pressing against her she couldn't think about why she would want him to stop. She couldn't think about scandal or steroids or that stupid bet. She couldn't even think about baseball at the moment.

The room erupted into whistles and cat calls and someone dumped champagne over the two of them. Marco interrupted the kiss only long enough to warn her to keep her eyes closed. So she did.

Finally when they came up for air, Marco pulled her up to a bench and drew everyone's attention to them, as if they weren't all watching them already.

"Gentlemen, do you see this lovely lady here?" He held her up on a makeshift pedestal. "She's the reason we're celebrating together tonight. She brought us all here. Each and every one of us. Okay, maybe not you, Sully, you came over with the gold rush. But the rest of us are here because she had the foresight to make sure we were drafted, signed, or traded for."

They laughed at his remark about Sully, but a lot of the guys simply nodded when he spoke of how they'd come to be part of the team. Marco looked up at Hunter, smiling that sweet, sexy, so-hard-to-resist smile.

"And I, for one, am not going to let this lady down." He turned to face the crowd, his teammates, coaches and trainers, their families, and the reporters who were recording his little speech. "I know this is just the beginning. And it's not going to be easy. But nothing worth fighting for ever is."

He could be talking about the team, or he could be talking about their relationship. Probably both.

"So I'm ready to fight. I'm ready to give everything I've got to get to the next level." He pulled Hunter closer. "Are you with me?"

The clubhouse erupted in shouts and "Yeah. Let's do it. We're with you. All the way."

Hunter's eyes filled with tears, overcome with emotions she couldn't keep under control. They flowed down her cheeks and the second Marco noticed, he whisked her into his arms.

"Let's go," he whispered. He led her to a cab. There were too many fans still lingering around the ballpark to walk to his apartment. He gave the driver the address to her place. Hopefully they'd have privacy for one more night, at least.

"What's wrong, baby?" Marco wiped her tears and dropped tiny little kisses on her face, neck, and head. "Did I go too far?"

"No. That's not . . . It's . . . It's everything." Where should she start? "My father . . ."

She broke into more sobs and Marco just pulled her against him, holding her, loving her.

"Your father would be very proud of you."

"No. He'd be proud of the team, but not of me."

"We wouldn't be here if it wasn't for you."

The cab pulled up in front of her house. Hunter reached for her purse, to pay the driver, but Marco put his hand on hers.

He pulled out his wallet, paid the fare, and exited the cab with her.

"Hunter, I know something is bothering you. More than just people finding out about us." He followed her to her front porch. Her hands shook as she unlocked the door.

"I bet on baseball. I got involved with a player, I . . . I've ruined everything."

"You haven't ruined anything." He locked the deadbolt behind them.

"I should have known better." She shook her head.

"So you regret being with me?"

"No. No, that is the one thing I don't regret. But, Marco, even if we win, it will be tainted."

"Because we slept together?" He sounded angry. Hurt.

"No. Because I bet on baseball with a partner who's involved with selling performance enhancing drugs to ballplayers. And you knew about it." She tried to put more distance between them. "You knew Clayton Barry was involved, but I don't know how or why you found out."

"Annabelle asked me to have him investigated." He leaned back against the door. "I only agreed because I thought it would hurt you, if he was cheating on her. I wanted to protect you. I had no idea what he was into."

"Annabelle asked you. And you couldn't say no." She waited for the familiar stab of jealousy to hit her, but she was too exhausted, too heartbroken to care.

"I'm not the bad guy here." Marco raked his hands through his hair. "I should have told you as soon as I found out, but I thought I could convince him to get out before all this came down."

"He's selling his share." She might as well tell him that part of it. "To Marvin Dempsey."

"He was supposed to sell it to you." Marco looked like he wanted to hit something. Not her, but she feared for the plaster in her hallway.

"That wouldn't do any good." Hunter dropped her purse on the bench just inside the door. She was exhausted. If she was alone, she'd be tempted to just curl up on the rug in the foyer. "I slept with a player. I bet on baseball. I broke the rules. They'll ban me for life. Like the 1919 White Sox."

"No. They can't do that. I won't let them." Marco leaned against the wall, balling his fists in frustration.

"What can you do?" Her heart was breaking. Everything she'd worked for her entire life was within reach and she was going to lose it all. Not only that, but Marco could go down with her. "No. You need to stay out of it. I think . . . I think we should stop seeing each other."

"No." He stood over her, his hands on her shoulders. "I'm not going to just walk away from you. From us."

"Marco, do you realize what you have to lose?" She couldn't let him give up his career trying to fight the system. There was a reason there weren't any women high up in the baseball ranks. It was an old boys' club, and she'd been fool enough to think she could use her brains to get into it. Her knowledge and love of the game weren't enough. Her business skills were one thing on paper, but when it had come down to it, she wasn't ready to take over.

"Yes. Yes, I do." He reached for her hand, but she pulled away.

"Maybe you should go." She went to retrieve her phone. "I'll call you a cab."

"No. I'm not leaving." Marco took the phone from her. He took her face in his hands. "I'm not going anywhere. Not tonight. Not ever."

Marco looked into Hunter's eyes. He saw a world of emotions swirling in their depths. Fear, despair, hope, and unless it was his feelings shining back at him, he even caught a glimmer of love. He couldn't let her go through all that alone.

He lowered his mouth to hers and kissed her. He kissed her until he felt her soften. She went limp as his kiss deepened. He'd like to think it was because she was surrendering to his undeniable charm and prowess as a lover. But he had a sinking feeling she was just giving up.

Still, he swept her in his arms and carried her up the stairs to the master bathroom. They were both covered with champagne and maybe, just maybe, he could wash some of her troubles down the drain.

He turned on the hot water, testing the temperature before he carefully and tenderly started to remove their clothes. Hunter was first. She stepped mindlessly into the large marble shower and Marco followed behind her. This wasn't about sex. Not for him, although his body was more than willing to go along with it.

He poured shampoo into his palm and began to lather up her hair. He massaged her scalp and he could feel the tension slowly slide away along with the suds that swirled down the drain.

Hunter moaned beneath his touch. Her eyes were closed and what was left of her mascara ran down her cheeks. He couldn't help it, he turned her toward him, kissing away the traces of her tears.

"I wish I could tell you everything is going to be okay." He wanted to reassure her, but she placed her finger over his lips.

"Shh. Don't talk. I'm done talking for the night." She opened her eyes and all he saw was raw desire. "Just hold me, Marco. Please."

He never could resist her "please."

Marco took the handheld sprayer and rinsed her hair. He rinsed her body, wishing he could wash away her pain. He adjusted the nozzle to the massage setting, and ran it across her back and shoulders. She rolled her neck from side to side, allowing him to give her this.

He moved the shower head down her back, concentrating the pulsing jets on her lower back. She moaned in pleasure and he moved her so she could lean on the marble wall. He nudged her feet wider and he aimed the water lower, between her thighs.

With a whimper, she let him know he'd found another spot that needed attention. She squirmed and writhed and he knew she was getting close to losing her mind.

She bucked and moaned and he brought his hand around to stroke her, and hold her up.

"Turn around," he commanded. She obeyed. "Grab onto my shoulders."

It took a little maneuvering, but they found a position where he could finish blowing her mind. He wanted to give her this. Needed to give her this.

She dug her nails into his muscles. The onslaught of pleasure overtaking her.

"Marco." She shuddered, gripping him even tighter. "Pleeeeee—"

He dropped the shower head as she wrapped her legs around him. He thrust deep inside her, could feel her pulsing around him. He pressed her against the wall hoping like hell he could stay on his feet as he drove into her. Hotter, wilder and more intense than he'd ever had.

The water nozzle danced around at their feet, spraying in all directions.

His emotions were dancing around in all directions, too.

Finally, she cried out, digging her nails so deep into his flesh she drew blood. He pumped again. Once. Twice. That was all it took. He exploded.

No way in hell was he going to let this go.

Hunter loosened her grip on him, sliding her legs down until her feet hit the floor of the shower. Marco dropped to his knees. His legs could no longer hold him up.

Hunter picked up the shower head and adjusted it to a fine spray. She rinsed his shoulders and Marco winced as the water stung his cuts.

"I'm sorry, I didn't mean to . . ."

"You don't have to apologize to me." Marco clenched his jaw, hoping she wouldn't notice his pain. "Not for that."

She slid down beside him, kissing the wounds she'd caused.

"I never meant to hurt you." She sounded like she was crying again. Shit.

"I'm tough. I can take it." The water started to run cool.

"Let's go to bed." He got to his feet, took the shower sprayer, replaced it in the bracket, and turned the water off. "It's been a long day."

She nodded and let him wrap her in a big fluffy towel. He dried off quickly and they tumbled together into the nearest bed.

Chapter 18

Hunter had been too exhausted to kick Marco out of her bed last night. At least that's what she told herself to keep from thinking about how she was only delaying the inevitable. It was only a matter of time before everything blew up around her.

She'd set up a meeting with Marvin Dempsey for later that afternoon. The team was safely in the air and she had several loose ends to wrap up. Cleaning out her office was only part of it. She couldn't quite bring herself to take down all the photos and team memorabilia. She still had enough superstition in her to think that she needed to keep everything in place throughout the postseason.

But she'd started cleaning out the old files. Organizing the business records for the sale. She wanted to make sure this was a clean transaction. She also wanted to be able to prove that she had no ties to Clayton Barry's investments with FITNatural.

"I'm sorry, Miss Collins, I tried to stop him." Her secretary tried to block the door, but the up and coming reporter burst through. His cameraman was right behind him.

"What can I do for you, Rex?" Hunter tried to maintain her dignity. "If you're here to congratulate the team on their division title, you'll need to detour to Phoenix. They're down there for a three game series before coming home for their final home stand."

"Congratulations." The reporter flashed her a smile that was a phony as those black and white striped "prisoner outfits" they sold as Alcatraz souvenirs. "It's been an interesting road to get there."

"Yes, it has been difficult." She stood, not letting him intimidate her by his height. Although he was several inches shorter than Marco, he thought he was big stuff. "My father would have liked to have been able to celebrate last night's victory with us, but . . ."

She let her voice trail off, noticing the cameraman shifted uncomfortably but continued to film the conversation.

"Would he have liked your trade for Marco Santiago?" Rex had a nasty little smirk on his face when he asked this question.

"Absolutely. He'd tried to get him last year, but couldn't make the deal." She gave him an innocent look. Or as innocent a look as she could give after spending last night naked with the player in question. "My father and I always discussed team business. Even when I was younger, he'd always ask my thoughts on a player or direction the team should go. While other kids went to summer camps, I went to spring training camps. My classmates went to Disneyland and rode the Pirates of the Caribbean. I went to the Caribbean League and learned how to scout raw talent. My father raised me on baseball. He trusted me one hundred percent."

"A daddy's girl through and through." Rex kind of mumbled that last statement. Good. She was making him feel at least a little small for trying to get to the real story he was after.

"I guess you could say I was a daddy's girl. But more than that, I've always been a Goliaths' girl." She smiled sweetly. "This team means the world to me, especially now, when it's all I have left of my father's legacy."

The tears that formed now were not for the camera. They weren't to keep Rex Knight from pursuing his scoop. They were genuine tears of real regret. Because once she sold the team to Dempsey, she'd put the house on the market as well. She'd need to get away from San Francisco and all the memories that came with it. And she planned on going somewhere they didn't even have baseball.

"You seem to have the admiration of your team." Rex cleared his throat, as the words sounded a little muffled. "One player in particular."

"Oh that." She tried to fake a smile. To make it sound like it was no big deal. That Marco was simply caught up in the moment when he kissed her during the postgame celebration.

"Yes. How long have you been having an affair with Marco Santiago?" Rex finally got to the point.

"An affair? Ooh, you make it sound so sordid." She laughed, but inside she wanted to shrivel up and lie on the floor crying. "We met for the first time when he flew in after the trade."

"So is that the reason you traded for him? So you could get him into your bed?"

"Now really?" Hunter crossed her arms. "Do you honestly think I'd need to spend millions of dollars and send away my hottest prospect just to get a date?"

Rex stood there speechless for a moment.

"I know I'm no supermodel, but I haven't cracked the lens on your camera, either." She laughed like it was no big deal to be insulted by this jerk.

"I didn't mean . . ."

"When I traded for Marco Santiago"—she looked Rex straight in the eye before turning to the camera—"I had every intention of putting together the best team I could get. The factors I considered were the very factors that helped win the division title. Marco Santiago is a player with speed and power, who can hit for average, cover a lot of ground on the outfield, and he's got an amazing arm. I will not apologize for acquiring a player I knew would give us the best chance of becoming a champion."

Rex glanced down at the carpet for a brief instant.

"So your personal relationship?" He gave her a nasty grin.

"Is personal." She kept her head held high even though what she really wanted to do was punch this jerk in his capped teeth.

"It looked pretty public last night in the clubhouse."

"We were caught up in the excitement of the moment." She wanted to be angry with Marco for outing them like that, but on the other hand, it only made it easier for her to come up with a plan. "I'm sure there were plenty of kisses exchanged all over San Francisco last night. If you'd been there, you might have been kissed, too."

"Are you denying your involvement with Marco Santiago?"

Damn reporters. Marco was almost glad he wasn't there when that son of a bitch Rex Knight stuck his nose in his and Hunter's business. Almost. He would have liked to put his fist through the asshole's teeth.

But he thought Hunter had handled the interview with class and a little bit of spunk, at least until he asked if she was going to deny their relationship.

The network had cut to commercial before she answered. Anything for ratings, damn it.

"Hey man, you coming out for batting practice or what?" Bryce had returned to the clubhouse and Marco had almost forgotten why he was there.

"Yeah. I'll be right there. I just need to . . ." What? Find out if she was going to deny them on national sports TV?

"Don't you want to talk about Johnny Scottsdale's one hit shutout or Bryce Baxter's run at MVP?" Hunter wasn't backing down, but she wasn't answering his question either. "Don't you have any baseball related questions you can ask? Like why we traded Nathan Cooper after he returned from his suspension? Surely that would be of much more interest to the real sports fans out there, than who I may or may not be dating."

Marco hoped he was the only one who noticed she got a brief look of panic when she brought up Cooper and his ties to PEDs.

Before he could respond, Hunter continued her speech.

"See, out here in San Francisco we care more about the game than the private lives of the people playing it. Sure, we want to be accessible to the fans. Most of our players have Facebook and Twitter accounts to encourage interaction. But there is no need to start poking into people's bedrooms. I would expect more from your network."

"Oh man, she told him." Bryce clapped Marco on the back.

"Not really." Marco felt like he'd been punched in the gut. All she had to do was tell the idiot reporter that she wasn't just sleeping with Marco. They were in love. Or was he alone in that department?

"Hey, I'm sure she was just covering her bases." Bryce must have picked up on Marco's dismay. "Sometimes the worst thing you can do is go public with a relationship. Especially if things don't end up working out."

"You think it's not going to work out?" Marco lashed out at his teammate, who'd done nothing other than be there at the wrong time.

"No. That's not what I'm saying at all." Bryce looked around the clubhouse, to make sure they were alone. "I mean, sometimes it's kind of risky to let the world know what you're doing behind closed doors. Especially when both of you are in the public eye. It's not like she's a waitress or a school teacher or an accountant. Then no one cares who you're sleeping with."

Bryce sounded like he knew what he was talking about. Maybe a little too well.

"Look, I can see that you're really into her. And I'm sure she's into you too. But she's got a lot at stake, here. If people think you two are just hooking up, well, it's sad to say but the lady's going to get the raw end of the deal."

"You're right. Man, I am an idiot." Marco was mad at himself now. "She tried to tell me to keep it quiet. That she had a lot of pressure from the league and the other owners. I'm a selfish bastard."

"Look, I know you care about her." Bryce tried to sound soothing. "You just got carried away. You were riding high after the win and you just wanted to share it with your woman. Who wouldn't?"

"I should have been more careful. Man, all that shit they say about love making you do crazy stuff . . ."

"You love her." Bryce simply nodded, like it was the logical conclusion.

"Yeah. And I've put her in a tough spot."

"She's even tougher." Bryce put his arm around Marco's shoulder. "You're a lucky man. Don't blow it."

"I just hope I haven't already." Shit. Marco should get out on the field but he couldn't take his eyes off the TV. While he was proud of the way Hunter handled herself with that gasbag, he couldn't help but think it was his fault she'd even been put in that position.

Finally, the station went back to the studio. A New York player had been spotted walking his dog in Central Park. The big news, he hadn't picked up after the pooch. Now that was important in the big scheme of things.

Sometimes he wished he was still playing in the schoolyard. When the only one watching him had been his mom and the kids waiting around for their game to start. Things were so much simpler then. But he never would have had a chance with someone like Hunter Collins if he wasn't a major league ballplayer.

Marco grabbed his glove to head out to the field when his cell phone rang. He had a bad feeling it wasn't Hunter calling to ask if he'd seen her interview.

Sure enough, the caller ID displayed his agent's name and number.

"Can't talk now, gotta go to work." Marco would have let the call go to voicemail, but he knew he deserved the earful. "I'll give you a call after the game."

"Yeah, sure. I'll just scratch San Francisco off our list of clubs you're interested in signing with next year."

"No. San Francisco is the only team on the list." Marco sank back in the padded folding chair in front of his locker. "I'm a Goliath or I don't play. End. Of. Story."

"Now Marco, have you been negotiating on your own?"

"What's the matter? Afraid you won't get your cut of my next contract?"

"You'll be lucky if I can get you a contract. What the hell were you thinking sleeping with an owner? An *owner*." He'd said the last word like it left a bad taste in his mouth. "I guess I shouldn't ask what you were thinking, but rather what you were thinking with."

"Look, I didn't plan on this. It happened. We'll deal with it. But right now I've got to get out on the field."

"Sure. Go hit for the cycle or something." His agent let out an exasperated sigh. "I'm on my way down there, so we'll talk later tonight. You don't have other plans do you? You're not hooking up with any lady umpires are you?"

"Go to hell." Marco hung up. He threw his phone in his locker and stormed out of the tunnel onto the field where he proceeded to have one of the worst games of his professional career. He committed two errors, struck out and grounded into two inning ending double plays.

"Thank you for meeting with me." Hunter waited for Dempsey in the conference room overlooking the empty ballpark. Even with the team on the road, she found her gaze constantly drawn to left field. Marco belonged there. Even more than she belonged up here. "I won't take up too much of your time."

"Not a problem. You know I'm always here for you." Dempsey settled into one of the plush leather chairs and waited expectantly for Hunter to tell him why she wanted to meet with him.

She took a deep, fortifying breath. "The thing is, I want to sell my share of the Goliaths. I've drawn up a contract. I think it's very fair, but of course I expect you to look it over carefully before you sign. Just keep it quiet until the season ends. And the postseason."

"I'm sorry, I must be getting senile or something. Did you say you want to sell the Goliaths?"

"Yes. I do." She had an explanation all worked out in her head, but the lump in her throat made it hard to say more than that.

"Oh, Hunter, you can't do that. Not when you've worked so hard to get to where we are."

"Yes. I have worked hard. And I . . . I think it's time for me to move on."

"What's really going on here?" Dempsey scooted his chair closer to her, he took her hand, and waited until she had the courage to look him in the eye. "First Clayton offers to sell, and now you. What are the two of you up to?"

"Clayton has his own reasons, I'm sure. But I just need to step away from the game. I only have one request before I step down as managing partner and president."

When he didn't ask what that request was, Hunter told him.

"I want you to offer Marco Santiago a minimum five years." She slid the proposed agreement across the table. "No contract for Santiago, no deal between us."

"I see." Dempsey leaned back in the chair. He looked her over carefully before breaking into a wide grin. "You love him that much?"

She flinched, hoping she wouldn't have to explain her relationship to a man who'd known her when she was missing her two front teeth.

"I know that the Goliaths need Santiago and he needs the Goliaths."

"What about what you need?"

"I need to know the team is in good hands." She would carry the memory of Marco's hands with her forever. Wherever she ended up.

"And you need to know that the man you love is taken care of." He reached over and patted her hand. "But what are you planning on doing?"

"I thought I'd travel for a while. Go someplace that doesn't have baseball. Paris maybe."

"Paris? You want to give up your team and go to Paris?"

"I hear they have art museums and culture and fine dining."

"You're running away." He shook his head. "You had one confrontation with a mean-spirited reporter and you're just going to run away?"

"It's more complicated than that."

"So explain it to me. I'm an old man, I don't understand you kids these days." He narrowed his gaze. "Back in my day when a man and a woman fell in love they found a way to be together. They didn't go running off to Paris when things got scary. They got married."

"Well, things were simpler back then. You didn't have to worry about how your career affected Helen's or vice versa. I know the odds were against me in the first place to truly be accepted in the league." Hunter blinked back the tears she couldn't afford to let fall. She couldn't tell him about the bet. Couldn't tell him how she'd almost ruined everything because of her stupid pride. "And rather than fight that, I'd prefer to walk away on my terms. Knowing that my team is going to thrive without me. I trust you to do the right thing. I trust you to continue the tradition my father started."

"But he started it for you."

"This is what I need." Hunter couldn't back down. "I need you to buy the Goliaths and I need to know that Marco will be in left field for the foreseeable future."

"And what does Marco want?"

"He wants a long-term deal. He wants to stop moving from team to team and finish his career with a sense of accomplishment. He fits in well here. The fans love him. He brings an energy and excitement to the game every time he steps onto the field. I think once he's settled, his numbers will only go up. You saw what happened when he got comfortable, his at-bats became much more productive."

"He started playing better when he started spending time with you."

"You knew?"

"Of course. I saw it at that barbecue. The sparks between the two of you were flying all over the place that day. It was only a matter of time before you two kids ended up together."

"Yes. It was inevitable. I just wish I'd had the foresight to sign him to a long term contract before it became a conflict of interest."

"So you're going to give up your team so he can sign with the club."

"It's the only way."

"So this trip to Paris, will it be a honeymoon?"

"No. I can't be with him until his contract is finalized. I'm leaving as soon as the final game is played. That way no one can accuse him of negotiating outside of the structure of organized baseball."

"Sounds like you've got it all figured out."

"Yes. So please, take this contract home, look it over. Show it to Helen and your attorneys and we'll get it signed and notarized. But I don't want to announce anything until after the playoffs. I don't want to cause any more disruption than I already have."

"Are you sure there isn't a way for you to keep the team and keep Marco?"

"There isn't any way I can keep either. But I can walk away knowing they'll both be okay." She picked up the contract and placed it in his hands. She patted her father's partner on the shoulder and left the conference room.

Marco wasn't surprised to see his agent waiting for him after the game. L.A. was just a short flight from Phoenix. He must have called from the airport.

"Marco we need to talk."

"Yeah. I know." He'd screwed up. He should have kept his relationship with Hunter private a little longer. Like until the season ended. But he couldn't help it. After all these years in the big leagues, he finally had something to celebrate and she was the person he wanted to celebrate with.

"You've made my job very difficult, you know that."

"I'm sure you can handle the challenge." Marco wasn't in the mood to be chewed out by his agent. Not when he hadn't done anything wrong. He'd fallen in love. It wasn't the end of the world.

"It is going to be one hell of a challenge, finding a team willing to sign you."

"I already told you, the only team I'm interested in is the Goliaths." He wasn't leaving San Francisco. He wasn't leaving Hunter.

"Not going to happen."

"Look, if you can't make the deal, then you can find yourself another client." Marco didn't know how else to make his position any more clear. "I'm staying in San Francisco."

"So you have been *negotiating* on your own." He said the word like it was something dirty. "And what exactly did she promise you during these *negotiations*?"

"We haven't discussed my contract. We've done nothing that goes against the current bargaining agreement. We haven't broken any rules." He'd reread his contract carefully. There was no explicit clause that stated a ballplayer couldn't have a personal relationship with an owner or anyone in the front office.

"Maybe not technically. But some would consider your conduct detrimental to the best interest of baseball."

"That's bullshit and you know it." Marco was furious now. "If baseball wanted to regulate players' sex lives, they would have gotten rid of groupies a hundred years ago."

"Sex with groupies isn't a problem. Sex with the woman who pays your salary is."

"Now there's something really wrong with that statement."

"That may be true, but the fact of the matter is, I can't negotiate a contract with someone you're sleeping with."

"Then I guess we're done here." Marco crossed his arms over his chest. "You can let yourself out."

"Look, I can make some phone calls, see if anyone's willing to bite, but you crossed a line here." His agent shook his head, like he thought Marco had brought shame upon the entire baseball world. It wasn't like he'd been involved with a married woman, or an underage girl. He hadn't hooked up with a drunk stranger who couldn't be sure about just how consensual the sex was.

"You don't get it, do you? I am not going to leave Hunter behind. I can't." Marco felt like he might as well be talking to the brick wall out in left field. "I love her. And I'm pretty sure she loves me."

Pretty sure. But he wasn't certain they would be able to work everything out. His agent acted like he'd screwed himself by getting involved with Hunter. Maybe he had, but he'd screwed Hunter even more. He knew it was wrong, but she'd be looked down upon by her fellow owners. Any future trades she'd make would be questioned. Maybe not to her face, but they'd nudge each other behind her back, wondering if she was getting a guy for his playing ability or his sex appeal.

He dropped his head against his locker. Let out a string of curses in English and Spanish. This should be the high point of his career. He was on the verge of his first run at the playoffs. They had a team that could go all the way. He wanted nothing more than to be able to celebrate the accomplishment with Hunter.

Instead he'd fired his agent, and was now wondering if this was going to be his last season as a professional baseball player.

Well, if it was going to be his last season, he'd better make the most of it.

Chapter 19

The Goliaths won four of their last six games. After dropping the first two games to Arizona, they came back to finish the season strong and ready for the playoffs. They won the division series in four games against Atlanta before beating Cincinnati in game six of the Championship Series.

They were heading for the World Series. The ballpark was rocking from the celebration. Champagne was sprayed everywhere, but the players had figured out to don ski goggles to protect their eyes from the stinging spray. Hopefully they'd have one more celebration, because Marco wasn't quite satisfied.

Hunter had stayed away from the clubhouse since the division clinching game. It killed him to think it was his fault she wasn't here to celebrate. It was as much her victory as any of the players. She watched the games from her usual spot, but as soon as the last pitch was thrown, she'd quietly exit the ballpark, avoiding reporters and fans.

They still met up after the games, but the closer they got to the big game, the more distant she'd become. They still made love, but she withdrew almost immediately after. He wanted to believe it was because as soon as the series ended, so would his contract. And she refused to talk about it, not wanting to violate any free agency rules.

A podium had been set up in the infield. League officials were getting ready to announce the series MVP award. It was between Marco and Bryce, but either way, Hunter should have been there to be a part of the ceremony. But as he scanned the crowed, Marco knew she'd already slipped away. The team's manager conferred with the suits from the commissioner's office and the crowd settled down in anticipation of the announcement.

"Ladies and gentlemen," the Fox reporter had stepped up to the podium and spoke to the now hushed ballpark. "Here to announce the winner of this year's National League Championship MVP, Mr. Allen Cambridge."

"I'm proud to present this award to a man who exemplifies what it means to be the most valuable player. Twelve hits, seven RBIs, and three home runs over the course of the series. Not to mention his outstanding glove work in an outfield he'd played in for only two months."

The crowd erupted into chants of "Marco! Marco! Marco!"

"As you've guessed, this year's MVP goes to Marco Santiago."

He approached the podium, accepted his award, and addressed the crowd.

"Thank you. Thank you very much, although I think you could have given this award to any of the other twenty-four guys on this team. Still, I'm honored." Since he couldn't be heard above the roar, he ended his speech and shook hands with the presenter, his manager, and after tipping his cap and holding his trophy up for the fans, he made his way back to the clubhouse.

He was trying to figure out a way to fit the darn thing in his locker when the Fox reporter approached him.

"You didn't have a lot to say up there." She smiled and thrust a microphone in his face. "Is there something you'd like to add?"

"Look, I appreciated the award, but our work isn't finished yet. We still have a tough opponent in Texas, and I want to turn my focus on winning the next series."

"I noticed that Hunter Collins was absent from the celebration." She smiled not-so-sweetly. "I've heard rumors there's a bit of a shake-up amongst the ownership group. Clayton Barry is out, and I was wondering if you had any inside information."

"Nope. This is the first I've heard of it." He wanted to tell her the reason Hunter wasn't there was because of people like her who couldn't keep their nose out of her personal business. But he kept his mouth shut.

"Come on, with your relationship with Miss Collins, surely you must know something."

"When I'm on the field, I'm focused on baseball. One hundred percent. Hunter takes her job just as seriously. When we're together, we don't discuss business. When I'm with her . . . Nothing else matters."

Marco gave a quick nod to the camera before turning and walking away.

He didn't even try to shower at the ballpark with all the champagne spraying still going on, so he grabbed a cab to Hunter's house. He let himself in with the key she'd given him weeks ago. But she didn't come rushing to the door like he'd hoped.

She wasn't in the family room, or the kitchen. He headed upstairs to the master bedroom, where they'd been sleeping for the past several weeks. Instead, he found her in her childhood room. Sitting cross-legged on the bed, with her arms wrapped around a well-loved, one-eyed teddy bear.

"Hunter." He pushed through the partially open door and put his arms around her. "Oh baby, what's the matter?"

"He should be here for this." She tried to wipe her tears but there were too many of them.

"Your father?" Marco held her, rocked her against him until the sobs subsided. "I'm sorry. So sorry he's not here for you. But he would have been so proud of you. You know that, don't you?"

"If he'd been here, maybe I wouldn't have . . ." She looked up at him, desperate agony in her eyes. "Maybe I wouldn't have made things so complicated."

"Oh baby, it's not as bad as it seems." He stroked her hair, that long gorgeous mane that had enticed him from the beginning. He didn't think her father would have been able to stop him from loving her. Nothing would have stopped him.

"I just miss him so much." She buried her face in Marco's chest and cried hot, silent tears that he was powerless to soothe. But he tried anyway.

"Of course you do. But I'm here, baby. I'll be here for you. Always."

She hadn't had the chance to grieve. She'd been so busy keeping the team going, and doing a hell of a job, that she hadn't let herself mourn the loss of her father. That was part of the business. The season must go on. Sure the league provided a few days bereavement, but a player still had to make his next start. Take his next at bat. And Hunter had to keep the team moving forward. She had to make roster moves, bringing up players as an injury replacement. Making the trade that brought them together.

He held her until she was all cried out. Picked her up and carried her to the master bathroom. He ran a bath for her and helped her undress. God she was beautiful. The most beautiful woman he'd ever seen, but he didn't bother telling her that. She still didn't believe him.

Oh, she believed in him on the field. And she'd been right, as his MVP award testified. If only she had as much faith in him off the field, in real life. If only she believed he could be the man to make all her non-baseball dreams come true.

"What do you need?" he asked as she settled into the tub. "Do you want company or would you rather I give you some privacy?"

"I don't know." She leaned back against the tub.

"I'll leave you alone then." He started to back out the door.

"No. Wait." She sat up, a look of panic on her face. "I'm just tired. That's all."

"Is that why you didn't stick around for the awards? The team trophy?" The MVP. He shouldn't have to tell her he'd won. She should have been there with him.

"I couldn't . . ." Her eyes were so weary. "I couldn't help but think it's all going to fall apart. News of Clayton's involvement in FITNatural, and the bet . . ."

"There is a rumor of his leaving the partnership. But that's all." He knelt beside the tub. "I've been keeping a close eye on the whole FITNatural story. It's starting to leak out. Just the part about some of their supplements being less than natural, and yeah, there's speculation of banned substances."

She tensed. She had a hell of a lot more to lose than that bastard Barry.

"Hey, but don't worry. I haven't seen anything tied to your *former* partner." He reached for her hand, brought it to his lips and placed a reassuring kiss on her palm. "I don't think anything is going to come of it until after the series. I don't think the league wants to do any-thing to hurt the ratings. Once the offseason starts, I expect the story to blow wide open."

"That's what I'm afraid of."

"Look you have nothing to worry about. You didn't invest in the company. He did. And except for Nathan Cooper, no one else from the Goliaths is involved. And Coop's not even with the team any-more. You got rid of him as soon as you could."

"What if he cracks? What if Clayton tells about the bet we made?"

"Did you actually exchange money or shares?" When she shook her head, he continued. "If you ask me, it was just a friendly wager, a way of energizing the team. Like when we go on the road. Baxter and I have a standing bet that whoever hits fewer RBIs buys dinner."

"I called off the bet, after I won." She gave him a slight smile. "But what if someone thinks I coerced him into selling his share?"

"For the good of the team, not because of any bet." He sat on the edge of the tub, still dressed in his champagne soaked T-shirt. "You haven't done anything wrong. You have nothing to worry about. Hell, you don't even need to worry about me, because I only look illegal."

"You know, there should be a law against you looking so good." Hunter cracked. She couldn't resist his charm, even when she was about ready to go out of her mind with worry. "Especially when you smell so bad."

She yanked him into the tub and he splashed down on top of her, but as always, he was careful not to hurt her. He removed the sweat and champagne soaked T-shirt and yanked off the athletic shorts he'd slipped on before coming over.

Marco was magnificent. Hard muscle and smooth skin. And those electric blue eyes. She was captivated from the moment they met. But like all good things in baseball and in life, this was only temporary. The season would end. And so would their relationship.

"Promise me you'll be there for the next celebration." It took a great deal of athleticism for Marco to fit himself into the enormous tub. He was a big man. A strong man. And an agile man. He maneu-vered so that he sat behind her, pulling her onto his lap. "Winning the pennant just wasn't the same without you. You should've been there.

For me. And for the team. You're as much a part of our success as anyone."

Hunter leaned against him, relaxing a little. She could feel his erection against her back.

"Let me think. How can I possibly make it up to you?" She tried to position herself over him.

"Maybe I should punish you." He grabbed her around the waist, holding her in place. So close to what she craved, yet just out of reach.

"Marco, please." Those words hadn't failed her yet.

He loosened his grip and moved his hand down to her hip.

"You think you can just wiggle your bottom and ask me nicely and I'll give you what you want?" His words were teasing, but his tone was almost bitter.

She whimpered as he slid his hand down ever so slightly.

"You think I'm that easy?" His erection throbbed against her backside. She wasn't the only one who wanted it. "That because I'm a man, I can't resist?"

"Marco. Please." Her voice shook with urgency. She wanted—no, needed him to touch her.

His hands were so large, his fingers were so close to her sweet spot. She squirmed, aching for him.

He moved his hand up, placing it over her rapidly beating heart.

"Promise me you'll come back to the clubhouse." He spoke softly in her ear. "Before every game, you'll be there for me. And the rest of the team. Please, Hunter."

She turned over to look him in the eye. His desire shone in the brilliant blue depths. But it wasn't just for sex. He wanted something more.

"Promise me, or I'll leave. Right now." He shifted as if to get out of the tub.

Hunter pressed her lips against him, desperate to keep him from leaving.

"I promise." She kissed him hungrily, sloshing water all over the bathroom floor.

He kissed her back, slowing the tempo. Grabbing her hips, he steadied her above him. Easing inside her, he moved with slow, deliberate thrusts. So different than in the beginning, when they were two bodies colliding in uncontrolled lust.

Now it was something more, and Hunter felt like she was drowning. She couldn't breathe. Couldn't swim away from the overwhelming feelings surrounding her. She knew she had four more games. At the most, seven. Then she would have to let Marco go. Let the Goliaths go. She would savor the memories as long as she could.

Marco was lacing up his cleats when the clubhouse door opened. Hunter stepped inside, looking almost like she wasn't sure she belonged there. She flashed a tentative smile at a few of the players. Johnny Scottsdale stood, and offered his hand. She gave him a firm shake and that was all it took for her confidence to return.

She shook hands, high fived, and congratulated the rest of the team. Slowly, she made her way toward Marco's locker. He was glad she made an appearance but he didn't like the uncomfortable position of not knowing how to act around her. He didn't want to hide his feelings, but he understood how their relationship could complicate things for everyone.

Especially when they were about to take the field for game one of the World Series.

So when she approached him, Marco ached with the need to touch her.

"I'm glad you came." He stood stiffly. "It means a lot to the team."

"Thank you for reminding me that we got here together." She fiddled with the long braid she'd wound her hair into. It wasn't as uptight as the buns she wore when he first met her, but it showed him that her confidence had wavered. She pulled her hair back as a way of restraining her ambition. He couldn't have that.

Marco reached for the elastic band that held her hair in place. He slipped it off and wove his fingers through the braid, undoing her attempt at holding herself back.

"Marco, please!" Just two words, and damn if his dick didn't grow rock hard even though she said it in protest instead of encouragement. "People are watching."

"Yes, Hunter. People will be watching. It's the World Series." He arranged her hair in soft waves around her face, letting it fall over her shoulders and down her back. "I think the world should see you as I see you. A strong, beautiful woman who can take on anything the league throws at her. You brought this team together. Each and every one of us is here today because you believed in us. Believe in yourself."

"Marco." She smiled, tears shining in her eyes. "Thank you."

"No. Thank you." God, he wanted to kiss her right now. But he didn't think he'd be able to stop. He had to look away, and it was a good thing he did, because Rachel Parker, the Goliaths' in-game reporter, had just stepped into the clubhouse.

Marco started to move toward her. Head her off before she could zero in on the tender moment, but Bryce beat him to her. He whispered something in her ear and Rachel smiled, shaking her head. She watched Bryce out of the corner of her eye, but she was intent on doing her job first, flirting with the shortstop would have to wait.

"Miss Collins." Rachel waved to Hunter with a reporter's smile. "Can I get a quick word with you before the game?"

"You'll be fine," Marco whispered, giving her an encouraging shove in the reporter's direction. And he'd be close by in case the questioning got too personal.

"Sure." Hunter smoothed the front of her jacket, squared her shoulders, and stood ready to face the camera.

"First of all, I want to congratulate you on bringing this team all the way to the World Series." Rachel smiled as if she meant it.

"Thank you, but getting here is only the beginning." Hunter looked around the crowded clubhouse. All the players were suited up, ready to take the field. "We're planning on winning it all."

"That would be something. The Goliaths have not won a World Series since coming to San Francisco. They've been close, with the heartbreaking loss in '98 and again in 2007."

"I remember it all too well." She closed her eyes briefly, before turning back to the camera. "But we've been working toward redeeming that loss ever since."

"You see the game differently than the fans. It is a business for you." Rachel tossed her hair and gripped her microphone more firmly. "But this year, it's also personal."

Marco stiffened. He needed to keep his focus on the game, but he was not about to allow this reporter, or anyone, to attack Hunter or make their relationship into something sleazy.

"It's always been personal for me." Hunter tucked a strand of hair behind her ear. "This team has always been like family for me. I grew up here. In this very clubhouse. And before that, at the old stadium. Instead of brothers and sisters and cousins, I had the Goliaths."

"But this year is different," Rachel's voice softened and Marco had to just stand there and watch. "Your father passed away at the beginning of the season. And I'm sure it must be difficult to have this level of success and not be able to share it with him."

"Yes. It is difficult." Hunter's smile wavered. "But it would have been a lot harder if I'd let the team down. I could have given up. Let things slide. But like I said, this team means a lot to me. It's not everything . . ."

She glanced over at Marco, and for a brief moment, he saw her love for him flash in her eyes.

"It's not everything, but it is important to me that the team has success. And continues to have success. We've built something here that, hopefully, will continue long after this series. Long after this season." She glanced around the clubhouse, a serene look on her face. "Yes, I want to win today. And tomorrow. And two more games after that. But more than that, I want to leave behind the same kind of legacy my father left. A team that we can all be proud of. Win or lose, I want people to feel good about coming out to the ballpark. I want parents to share memories with their children. To bring them to a game and tell stories about when they saw Johnny Scottsdale pitch a two-hit shutout. Or Bryce Baxter's monster home run. Or that incredible catch by Marco Santiago to save the game."

"And be able to say they were there when the Goliaths won their first World Series since coming to the West Coast." Rachel Parker seemed to get caught up in Hunter's excitement.

"Unless we win while we're in Texas." Hunter smiled, and then nodded to the cameraman, signaling her pregame interview was over. She walked out of the clubhouse, her head held high, a look of determination in her stride.

They were going to win it all. Marco just knew it.

Chapter 20

Hunter returned to her seat behind home plate after her interview with Rachel Parker. At first she worried the reporter would focus on her relationship with Marco, but she didn't even bat an eye when Hunter mentioned his name.

Instead, the conversation had been about what the team meant to Hunter, especially given her father's passing.

This team meant the world to her. And it wasn't fair she'd have to choose between what was best for the team and what was best for her heart. She'd choose the team every time.

She'd signed the contract releasing her share of the Goliaths to Dempsey. With Clayton Barry selling his share that would leave Dempsey as the sole owner.

He would have five days after the final game of the World Series to make good on his promise of signing Marco for five years. If Marco and his agent refused or he signed with another team, the sale between her and Dempsey would become null and void. Her forty percent would revert back to her and she would continue on as an owner.

Dempsey would still have controlling ownership, so he would have the final say on whether or not she came back as managing partner. They'd discussed her thoughts on the priority of re-signing other players, as well as which free agents she would have pursued if she were to stay on board. But she had a pretty good feeling about Marco signing the deal.

He would remain a Goliath. And she would be happy for him. Even if she couldn't be happy with him.

He would settle in San Francisco. The fans adored him. And he was the perfect fit for the spacious and challenging left field of their ballpark. He would end his career in the city where, hopefully, he'd win his first championship. Then when he was ready to walk off the field as a player, he would fit in with the organization's coaching staff.

Somewhere along the way, he would meet someone who was free to love him. Someone who didn't have to worry about conflict of interest or creating controversy simply by being with him.

Someone who didn't feel the pressure of the entire team on her shoulders. Someone who wouldn't worry about his teammates turning their back on him when they went through a rough stretch next June. She didn't want him to have to look over his shoulder, working twice as hard as he needed to just to prove he wasn't there only because he'd slept with the boss.

Hunter opened her scorebook and tried to focus on the game. She watched as the man she loved stood for the "Star Spangled Banner." He glanced over at her before taking his place in the outfield. He smiled, but things were different between them. Maybe they both knew their time together was coming to an end.

The first two batters were easily retired with a strikeout and a ground out to short. The third place hitter, a man known for his power to left field stepped up to the plate. He was ahead in the count when he hit a fastball to deep left field. Only one man believed it would stay in the park. Marco never took his eyes off the ball and tracked it down right at the wall. The ballpark shuddered in relief.

Hunter dropped her pencil and watched Marco return to the dugout, his teammates patting him on the back and joking with him as they prepared for the bottom half of the inning. A leadoff single, stolen base and walk set the table for Baxter's double and just like that, the Goliaths were up by two runs.

Marco took his spot in the batter's box. On the first pitch, he stroked a double down the right field line, easily scoring Baxter from second and providing what turned out to be more than they needed to win the first game of the series.

After the game, Marco gave his interviews with a smile but he didn't approach Hunter. Instead he sent her a text, telling her he was going out with the guys and then he was going to call it a night.

She shouldn't be surprised that he was ready to move on. She'd been pulling back from him for weeks now, ever since their relationship became public. Every time they'd made love, it felt like it could be their last. Looked like last night, it finally was.

She got into her car and drove to the house she'd grown up in. It felt different now, Marco had made his mark. Left his scent. And somehow convinced her to move from her childhood bedroom to take over the master suite. Except, she couldn't sleep there tonight. Not alone.

But she couldn't return to the room where she'd once left her baby teeth under her pillow either. She wasn't that little girl anymore. She'd finally been able to mourn her father, but she didn't know how she was going to get over Marco.

She hoped she could be like the players who took challenges in stride. The catcher who ended up having a darn good career playing first base. Or the pitchers who were able to make the transition from being a starter to working in the bullpen as relievers.

But she had a feeling she would never be the same. Like the Cy Young Award winners who struggled when switching to a new league. Or worse, the Gold Glove winners who ended their careers by serving as designated hitters.

Caught between the past and a future that looked lonely, Hunter settled on the sofa, expecting a sleepless night. One of many more to come.

Marco went out with several of his teammates. The married ones went home early but he stayed out with the single players. There weren't all that many. Just Baxter and Garcia and a couple of other guys.

He didn't want to be here. Witnessing the whole single life of a professional athlete was a sharp reminder of what he didn't want the next few years of his life to look like. But he feared it might be over with Hunter.

He couldn't let her risk the most important thing in her life. Her team. And this was her team. It needed to remain her team. With Barry out of the picture, and Dempsey in his seventies, Hunter would eventually have the team solely in her control.

Bryce went to grab another round, but he came back with two young women instead. A blonde and a brunette. One for each arm. He played the part of the rowdy playboy, but there was something in his eyes that told Marco he wasn't enjoying it as much as he wanted people to think.

"So what do you ladies think?" Bryce nodded in Marco's direction. "Will my good friend Marco be the hero of the World Series, or is he going to give a guy like me a shot at the glory?"

"You're Marco Santiago." The blonde eyed him like he was an ice cream cone and she wanted to take a nice long lick. "Is it true you're sleeping with the team's owner?"

Bryce dropped his arm from around her waist and gave him a look of apology.

"Not anymore." Marco nodded at his teammate and made his way for the door.

"Shit." He heard Bryce mutter behind him and he felt Bryce's hand on his shoulder as he pushed his way through the crowd.

"Hey man, I'm sorry about that." Bryce had shaken off the two women and followed Marco outside. "I was just trying to lighten things up. Keep things loose."

"You do that. Go back to the party."

"No, man. I don't know what I was thinking." Bryce tucked his hands in his pockets as Marco waved for a cab. "I don't even want that in there."

Marco just shrugged, feeling a chill in the night air.

"I want what you have with Hunter. I see the way she looks at you. The way you look at her. Like nothing or no one can ever get in your way."

"Except reporters. Fans who think our private life is something to talk about like our batting average or fielding percentage." Marco shook his head at the absurdity of it all. If either one of them had a different job, things would be simpler. "Would people give a shit if she was my landlord or if I was her gardener?"

"No. Probably not." Baxter kicked at some litter on the sidewalk.

"The fact that she's in baseball and you're in baseball . . . Man, it's gotta be harder on her. The fact that there are still guys who don't think a woman should be anywhere in this game other than back there."

He jerked his head in the direction of the bar, where the two women Bryce had picked up could very well have moved on to one of the other players by now.

"It's gotta be tough to be a woman in this business. You know there are guys who still think they can get away with harassing the female reporters. Sticking their junk in her face or making sexist comments, just to see if she'll crack under pressure." Bryce balled his fists and made a noise like he really wanted to hit someone. "I imagine it's gotta be even harder on a woman in the front office. I can just picture the guys who'll ask her if she chooses players based on their looks instead of their numbers. Hell, I was asked that just the other day. I ignored the dickwad and answered a real question about how you and I seem to play off each other, a little friendly competition about which one of us is going to hit more home runs in the series."

"Yeah, it's tough on her. And it's killing *us*." Admitting it out loud seemed to mark the final inning of their relationship. But like the loyal fan who stayed for the last pitch even with a ten run deficit, he wasn't willing to walk away until it was officially over.

A cab pulled up and Marco got in. He gave the driver Hunter's address out of habit, but then corrected his mistake. He went home to the apartment he'd spent some of the best nights of his life in. But he wouldn't renew the lease. He'd stay in San Francisco, but he'd look for a new place. Too many memories here.

He wondered if he'd have to hang it up after this series. He couldn't see how he could keep playing a game that would eventually come between him and the woman he loved.

He knew she couldn't sign him as a free agent. Even if it wasn't against the rules, it was a major conflict of interest. He got that now. He hadn't wanted to see it, but Hunter had known all along. Being with him could ruin her livelihood.

And his too. Even if he won it all, he'd still lose. They both would.

Hunter entered the clubhouse as Marco was packing up his locker. If they took two of the next three games, then this would be his last game in this ballpark. Out of the corner of his eye, he watched her congratulate his teammates before making her way over to his side of the room.

He knew he was being irrational, but every handshake, every smile, every pat on the back just further convinced Marco that she cared more about the team than she cared about him. And given the fact that he hadn't done much to contribute to tonight's win, his battered ego couldn't shake it off.

He tried to shove his MVP trophy into his bag before she could see it, but she caught him.

"What is that?" She approached him with a curious smile. She wore some soft, silky blouse cut low enough to engage his imagination but not so low as to provide a glimpse of anything he didn't want any of his teammates to see.

His heart sputtered as he tried to shove the damn thing deeper into his bag. "It's nothing."

"Is that . . ." She reached into his bag and pulled the trophy out of its hiding spot. "It's the MVP trophy. Why didn't you tell me?"

"You should have been here." Marco couldn't believe how much it hurt that she hadn't been there. "But you weren't."

He grabbed it out of her hands.

"Marco, I'm sorry."

At least she didn't say please.

"It doesn't matter." He was frustrated. Hurt. And tired. He was tired of having to pretend he could slip in and out of his feelings like he changed in and out of his uniform.

"I knew I was right about you." She took the trophy from him and turned it over in her hands. She smiled as she read the inscription.

"Nah, they could have given it to any one of us." The way her face lit up as she examined the trophy had him even more convinced that their connection was more about them winning than anything else.

"No. You've got something special. If we'd had you all year, I think you'd be in the running for league MVP."

"Doubtful." Marco took the trophy back. He didn't want it. He wanted Hunter, but . . . well, this wouldn't be the first time he didn't get what he wanted.

"That's one of the reasons the fans love you. You're a great ballplayer with just enough humility to keep it real. And next year . . ."

"Next year? There is no next year." He tossed the trophy several feet toward the nearest trash can. It hit the wall before dropping into the barrel.

Marco stormed out of the clubhouse and into the cool night air. He wanted to go home, but there were still a lot of fans milling around the ballpark. He normally enjoyed interacting with the fans: smiling, taking pictures, making their day.

But tonight, he didn't want to talk about baseball. Didn't want to discuss the game that had brought him and Hunter together and was now tearing them apart.

Hunter retrieved Marco's MVP trophy from the trash and was dismayed to find it was broken.

"You can fix it." Sully nearly made her jump out of her skin.

"No. I don't think so." The trophy was broken in two. Her heart, on the other hand, was shattered in a million pieces. "I think it's beyond repair."

She fought to keep the tears from rushing forward. She straightened and tried to keep from falling apart. Everyone else in the clubhouse was celebrating. Enjoying the high of being two wins away from the ultimate prize. Or what she'd always thought was the ultimate prize.

The ultimate prize had walked out of her clubhouse. And maybe even out of her life.

"I'll see what I can do." Sully took the smashed up trophy and placed a reassuring hand on her shoulder. "I bet it will be good as new by the time our flight leaves tomorrow."

"I won't be on the plane with the team."

"Why the hell not?" She'd never heard Sully raise his voice, at least not to her. Sure he'd chewed out his crew on occasion for not taking care of the equipment or the clubhouse to his very particular standards. But he was of the school that required a gentleman to watch his language around a lady. "This is just as much your team as anyone's. You worked just as hard to get us here."

"Yeah? Well, I forgot the most important thing."

"What's that?"

"It's just a game."

Chapter 21

"Welcome to Whittaker Field. I'm Denton Charles Whittaker the Third, but my friends call me Denny." The tall Texan sat down next to Hunter shortly before batting practice. After playing the first two games in San Francisco, the World Series had moved to their opponent's home field. "I hope you'll find our ballpark to your liking."

"It's the second best in the league." There was something about this man that was familiar. His eyes were a startling blue and his smile made her wonder if they'd met somewhere before. She must have seen pictures of him. He was the heir to Whittaker Electronics and Technology Corporation, who had made their fortune in pocket calculators before moving into computer components. They owned half of Texas, including the ballpark.

"Don't ever tell a Texan he's second best." He leaned over and flashed a set of dimples that probably charmed more than his fair share of ladies.

"Sorry, but San Franciscans prefer to tell it like it is." She wouldn't be one of them.

"I spent three years in Berkeley. Graduated from Cal." He must have thought that would impress her.

"I'm so sorry to hear that." Hunter turned her attention toward the visitors' dugout, hoping the team would take the field soon. She was already bored with this conversation. The man was obviously used to having women fall at his feet. He was handsome, fit, in his late forties, maybe early fifties. But he was no Marco Santiago. "I'm a Stanford girl."

"Ouch." Whittaker leaned back in his seat and she almost expected him to offer the whole ballpark to her. She planned on taking it, thank you very much, with a little help from her team.

"That's what you'll say when we take this series." She smiled and held out her hand for a formal introduction. "Hunter Collins, President and Managing Partner of the San Francisco Goliaths."

That was a lie. She was no longer president or partner. The contract had been received by the commissioner's office. She expected final approval within the next twenty-four hours.

"You're that confident?" He gave her a firm handshake and a friendly, if somewhat competitive, smile.

"Yes. I've put together a fine team." She leaned forward, as Marco stepped out on the field. Her heart beat a little faster as he strode toward her. "I'm proud of my guys."

"Marco Santiago seems to have come through for you." There was something in his voice that prickled the back of her neck.

"You had your chance with him. You let him go." She had every intention of hanging on to him. Well, the Goliaths would keep him.

"My company funded the ballpark. I have no say in who plays here." He sounded somewhat disappointed about that fact. "I would have never let him get away if I had any choice in the matter."

"That's too bad. I take full responsibility for every man in a Goliaths' uniform." And pride in each of her players.

Marco dropped his glove a few feet in front of her seat and approached with pure fury in his eyes. Wow. Was he jealous? An interesting twist on things. Maybe now he'd understand how she'd felt when women went all fangirl crazy on him.

"Leave Hunter alone." Marco glared at the man, his fists balled at his sides, the muscles in his forearms flexed. "Just stay the hell away from her."

"Look, son . . ." Whittaker leaned forward, a pained expression on his face.

"You gave up the right to call me that a long time ago." Marco gripped the railing separating the field from the seats. "When you abandoned us."

"Marco, I'm sorry. You have no idea how sorry I am." His voice was strained with emotion.

"Too late."

"You're his father?" Hunter looked at both men, and yes, the resemblance was striking. Marco had inherited his father's height and build. He'd most certainly inherited his blue eyes. "Wow."

"I am. But he wants nothing to do with me." Whittaker stood. He kept his eyes on Marco as he answered Hunter. "I guess I don't blame him. I just wish he'd give me the chance to make amends."

"You waited too long." Marco gripped the railing even tighter. Doing his best to keep from losing his temper. "You had eighteen years to make it up to me. To make it up to her."

"I tried. Believe me, I tried. But . . . You'll never forgive me, will you?" Whittaker shook his head and then headed up the aisle.

"Marco." Hunter's heart broke for him. "I had no idea."

"Yeah? Neither did I. Until he showed up the day I made my big league debut. Thought he could walk in here, in this very ballpark, and just start being a dad." Marco took a ragged breath. "He took advantage of her and then left her with nothing. He had everything and left her with nothing."

Marco took his bitterness back on the field. He would wait his turn for batting practice. Hunter was glad he had a way of working through his emotions. Because she had no way of helping him work out, at least not until after the game. If he'd still want her. She wasn't sure of anything anymore. He'd been so angry about her not being there when he'd been awarded the MVP. Yet, here he was, in a fury over her talking with another man. His father.

She couldn't walk away from him just yet. Not when he obviously had some unresolved issues with his father. He needed her. She'd go to him, one more time. No matter how much it would hurt when she'd eventually have to walk away.

As he waited his turn for batting practice, Marco couldn't help but overhear a reporter interviewing his manager. He usually ignored what everyone else had to say, but when the reporter mentioned "FITNatural," Marco turned his attention to what was said.

"Did you know of Nathan Cooper's involvement with FITNatural from the beginning?" The reporter had that tone they all got, like they thought they were performing a public service by exposing the dark side of sports. But maybe it was just payback for all the girls who'd overlooked them in high school to go out with the jocks.

"I'd never even heard of the company until the last couple of days." Javier was usually an easygoing guy, but Marco could hear the irritation in his voice. "I didn't worry about whether or not Cooper was one of the players involved because he's not a member of this team. Hasn't been with us at all this year."

"Did the organization know about his involvement?" The reporter asked. "How much did they know and when did they know?"

"I found out about the suspension a few hours before it went public. Fortunately we had enough depth in our farm system I was able to replace him in the bullpen." Javier sighed, which meant he was really pissed now. The man never had to raise his voice. Just arched a brow, crossed his arms, or shook his head in disappointment. His actions spoke volumes more than any loud-mouthed coach ever could. "As far as the organization, I think their feelings on the matter were made clear when they released him."

"He was designated for assignment." The reporter made sure everyone knew he'd done his homework. "Then he was part of the trade for Marco Santiago."

"Yes. He was one of the minor league players we sent away in exchange for Santiago. And I'm damn glad we got him. Between Santiago and Bryce Baxter, our offense has been prolific enough that we're two games up in the Series. I'd like to get back to work so we can try to make it three."

"What about the Goliaths' ownership group? Do you know of any connection between them and FITNatural?"

"Nope." Javier adjusted his cap. "I'm afraid I don't have any inside information. I'm just here to manage this team."

The reporter noticed Marco watching the interaction, and grinned.

"Marco Santiago." He turned toward him and the camera followed. "Do you have any inside information?"

"Nope." He repeated his manager's quote.

"You have a personal relationship with Hunter Collins."

Marco stood still, holding his favorite bat in his hands. Doing his damnedest to keep from taking a swing at this asshole. But that would only hurt the team. It would only hurt Hunter.

"You also had a relationship with Annabelle Jones, who is married to Clayton Barry."

"I knew Mrs. Barry. A long time ago." Could this day get any worse? "We were friends. Went out a couple of times, but like I said, it was a long time ago."

"Rumor has it that Clayton Barry is selling his share of the team."

"I suppose he has that right."

"And Mrs. Barry has filed for divorce."

"So what does that have to do with me? I'm a little busy here, I've got a game to prepare for." Marco gripped the bat tighter. "It's kind of an important game."

"With all these distractions going on, how do you stay focused?"

Marco glanced over to where Hunter was sitting. Alone, now. His father had abandoned his effort at hitting on her or trying to soften her up. Marco wasn't sure which. It didn't matter. Hunter mattered. She mattered a lot.

"I have my routines." Marco smiled, thinking of making love to Hunter. He decided he wasn't going to give her up. "Ways of staying loose. I've got my teammates behind me. And one goal in front of me."

Marco nodded at the camera, and turned toward the batting cage. Baxter was just finishing up, and when he stepped aside, Marco was ready for the first pitch.

He launched it deep into the center field bleachers. He hit several more, drawing cheers from the crowd. He hit and hit and hit the ball. Exactly what he needed to get his mind focused, to stop thinking about his father, the FITNatural scandal that was starting to heat up, and the fact that he only had two more wins before his tenure as a Goliath would come to an end.

Hunter watched a tight, tense game. Marco hit a sacrifice fly in the third, scoring the Goliaths only run in regulation play. Texas tied it up in the eighth and it wasn't until the eleventh inning that the powerful swing Marco displayed in batting practice finally found its way fair.

The Goliaths had won another close one and they were now only one game away from winning the championship. One game away from the end of the season. The end of Hunter's reign as president and managing partner.

She made her way into the clubhouse, searching for Marco. This could be their last night together, and she wanted to make sure she made the most of it.

Marco was finishing up an interview. His hair was still wet from his shower and he looked as sexy as ever. But there was a weariness in his eyes. It had been a rough day. His confrontation with the man who'd abandoned him had taken its toll. While he'd been able to take his frustration out by crushing the ball during batting practice, the pitching was too good for him to carry it over into the game. Until the last inning, when, finally, he was able to send them all home.

"Marco." She smiled at him, waiting for his interview to wrap up. His eyes lit up and she didn't care if everyone knew they were going to end up in bed together tonight. She walked over and kissed him the second the camera stopped rolling. She put her arms around his shoulders and was surprised at how tense he was. Almost as tense as their first night together.

"Let's go back to your room," she whispered in his ear. "I think you could use a rubdown."

"I can't." He tensed even more. "I promised my mother I'd meet her for dinner."

"Oh." Hunter couldn't hide her disappointment as she stepped back. "I guess I'll catch up with you later."

"No. Wait." He reached for her hand. "Join us. I'd like you to meet her."

"Sure." She would have liked a little more time to prepare, but she'd already met his father today, so she figured this would be much easier.

"Great." He ran his hand through his damp hair. "I'm sorry for how I reacted earlier. I should have given you a heads up. I just didn't expect him to use you to get to me."

"Why do you think that?" Hunter knew she'd have to tread carefully. "He was just making sure I was well taken care of. As a representative of the ballpark."

"Right." Marco clenched his jaw. "He knew exactly who you are and what you mean to me. He was trying to get on your good side. Trying to charm you into . . . something."

"If I didn't know better, I'd think you were worried. You thought he was flirting with me." She squeezed his hand to let him know she was joking.

"He was flirting with you?" Marco dropped her hand and glared at her. All the fury he'd had before the game returned.

"No. I don't think so. But now you know how I feel when I see women of all ages falling at your feet."

He was not amused.

"Marco, please . . ." She put her arms around his neck and pulled him down for a kiss. "Are you sure you don't want to meet your mother for breakfast?"

"Damn woman, you are very tempting." Marco untangled her arms from around his shoulders. "If we hadn't gone extra innings, maybe . . ."

"I guess we'll just have to eat quickly." She ran her hands across his chest. Damn, he was one sexy man. She was going to miss him.

They took a car to the restaurant and did a little making out in the back of the limo. Hunter was disappointed when the car pulled to a stop. Now she'd have to meet Marco's mother with the flush of arousal on her face. Nice.

Marco checked in with the hostess and found out his mother was already seated. They were led to a table near the back, out of the way, and Marco stopped short.

"Son of a bitch." He dropped Hunter's hand and glared at the man she'd met earlier nuzzling the neck of a beautiful dark-haired woman who blushed and giggled like a teenager.

"Marco. There you are." She smiled and Hunter could see some of her features in Marco. He was a perfect blend of the two of them. His father's blue eyes and his mother's dark hair. His mother's flawless skin and his father's strong jaw. "And this must be your special lady."

She stood and offered her hand.

"Isadora Santiago, but my friends . . ." She blushed and smiled at Marco's father. "My friends call me Izzy."

"Nice to meet you, I'm Hunter Collins." She shook hands with the woman who'd raised Marco all on her own.

"What is he doing here?" Marco just glared at the man, rage radiating off him in waves.

"Marco. Please. Calm down." Izzy put her arms around her son, but he stood stiff. "I thought it would be good if we all had a nice talk."

"No. I won't sit at the same table with him."

"Marco. Sit down." Her voice was soft, yet commanding. The kind of voice no son would dare disobey.

He held a chair for Hunter before taking the seat next to her. He never took his eyes off the man across from him. His father.

"I'm sorry, where are my manners." Izzy smiled at Hunter. "Have you met Denny? Marco's father?"

"We met earlier tonight. At the ballpark." She gave Whittaker a polite nod.

"I hope you enjoyed the game." He smiled, and it almost reached his blue eyes.

"Yes. I did. I enjoyed all eleven innings. Especially the last one." She placed a hand on Marco's thigh. His muscles were tight, tense with agitation.

"Yes. We watched the game together." Izzy smiled at Marco's father. "Denny invited me to his luxury box, and we had a chance to catch up."

Marco grunted. His displeasure with their way of catching up was more than obvious.

"I've been trying to win her back for thirty years." Whittaker ran his hand up her arm and draped his arm around her shoulder.

"We've been corresponding for a couple of years now." Marco's mother spoke directly to Hunter. "Well, he's been corresponding for a couple of years. E-mails, telephone calls, that kind of thing. But I kept putting him off. I was too afraid I'd be unable to resist his charm."

She leaned her head against his shoulder.

"I was right. I couldn't." Izzy smiled at Hunter, like they were two old friends, talking about boys. "Marco is just like his father that way."

"I'm nothing like him." Marco set his fists on the table. "I would never abandon a woman and her child. Ever."

"I didn't want to abandon you." Whittaker leaned forward, with enough regret in his voice that Hunter felt sorry for the man. "I wanted to marry her. Wanted to spend the rest of my life with her. But we weren't given the chance."

He reached out and took Izzy's hand.

"When my parents found out we were seeing each other, they sent me away. To California."

"I didn't know I was pregnant at the time." Izzy added, as if it made a difference.

"If I had known, I would have done anything." Whittaker sounded truly sorry, but the damage had been done. "Anything."

"When I found out I was going to have a baby I went to his mother, hoping she would send him a letter, letting him know. But she never sent it." Izzy wiped tears from her eyes. "She offered me ten thousand dollars to make my problem go away."

"But you never took the money." Whittaker reached for her hand.

"No. I didn't take the money. I couldn't. Even if I hadn't been raised with strict religious convictions, there was no way I could..." She placed her hand over her abdomen, protective of the baby who had grown there. "But then she told me if I tried to contact you, she would send me and my entire family back to Mexico."

"She was here legally." Marco stared the other man down. "There was no reason for them to send her back."

"Yes, I was here legally." She gave Marco a sad little smile. "But my brothers, my cousins...I couldn't risk my family. I figured they'd take care of me. Take care of us."

"But they didn't, did they?" Marco was so angry. So bitter. "We took care of ourselves."

"Yes, you did. Despite the way my family, *my mother*, continued to meddle in your lives." Marco's father pulled Izzy closer. He spoke directly to her now. "Every time you started to get settled somewhere, they worried I'd find you. So she'd get you fired. And then my father would make sure you heard of a job somewhere else. Somewhere just out of my reach."

"You had money. You could have kept looking." Marco wasn't buying it. Hunter wasn't sure if she was either.

"You don't know what my mother was like. She had plans for me. Big plans. She wanted a Whittaker in the Governor's mansion, maybe even the White House. She sent me to California. Even picked out a wife for me." He bowed his head in shame. "It didn't last a year. I couldn't forget about Izzy. I couldn't ever love anyone like I loved her. Still love her."

"Nice story. Too bad it's all lies." Marco pushed back from the table and spoke to his mother, looking at her as if he was seeing her for the first time. His eyes glistened, the tears turning them an even more startling blue. "I thought you were smarter than that. I thought you were stronger than that."

He shook his head and walked out of the restaurant.

"Please, excuse us." Hunter rose and followed him out.

"Hunter, wait." Marco's mother stopped her before she could leave. "I'm so sorry. For everything. If I'd known he was bringing you here tonight . . . He's never introduced me to a woman he was dating. You must be very special."

Hunter didn't know what to say. The whole situation was beyond her experience.

"I shouldn't have tried to force this on Marco. He's always been such a sensitive boy." Izzy shook her head. "But a good boy, just the same. He's worked so hard, his whole life, trying to take care of me. You have no idea how hard it was to convince him to go to college instead of signing with the first team who drafted him. He wanted to take care of me. To make sure I didn't have to work so hard."

Pride shone in the woman's eyes.

"He went to college, though. And he graduated. That's something I'm so proud of."

"I can see why you would be proud of him." Hunter wished she could embrace this woman. Be the daughter she'd never been able to be. "He's a good man. And a hell of a ballplayer."

"He is good." Izzy beamed with admiration for her son. "Very good. But I'm afraid he doesn't know the first thing about love. About the kind of love between a man and a woman. I am sorry for that."

He wasn't completely ignorant, but Hunter wasn't going to discuss their tenuous relationship. Not when she was still trying to figure it out for herself.

"I know Marco thinks I'm foolish." Izzy sighed. "But I've only been foolish once in my life. It brought me the greatest heartache I've ever known. And the greatest joy."

Hunter was still at a loss for words. So she nodded and smiled, encouraging the other woman to go on.

"Try to talk to him. Get him to listen. I've been given another chance at love. And I'm going to take it."

"Good for you."

"If Marco can't accept us together . . ." Izzy's voice cracked. But then she took a deep breath and looked Hunter square in the eye. "I'll be heartbroken. But I'm not going to let anyone come between us. Not even my son."

Marco made it almost to the curb before he was approached by a couple of fans. He signed autographs and did his best to pretend he wanted nothing more than to take a picture with his biggest fans from Yreka, California.

He sent them off with a souvenir and a smile. They laughed and commented on what a nice young man he was before disappearing into the restaurant. Guilt slammed into him as the doors closed. He'd left Hunter back there to deal with his parents. Both of them. Together. What the hell was up with that?

He leaned against the wall just outside the door. The thought of that man putting his hands on his mother made him sick. But then again, he wouldn't be here if they hadn't gotten together in the first place.

Still, he could never, ever, forgive the man for abandoning them. When he finally found out who his father was, and the kind of money he'd come from, Marco had been even more furious than when his father was just a nameless, faceless, *gutless* sperm donor.

There were so many things he wanted to say to the man, but none he could say in the presence of a lady. So he walked away.

"Marco." Hunter caught up with him just as the car pulled up to the curb. "Wait. Please."

One little word and he'd do anything for her. Except apologize to the man who'd made his childhood one struggle after another. One move after another. And while his baseball career had hardly been a struggle, he had moved around far more than he'd liked.

He wanted stability. Roots. A family.

"Hunter. I'm sorry. I couldn't spend one more minute with that man." Not when he reminded him of everything he'd never had.

"You didn't even give him a chance to explain."

"What's to explain? He abandoned us. Went on with his life."

"She loves him."

"It's not enough."

"No. I guess it isn't." Hunter stepped back as the driver opened the door, waiting for them to get in.

"We've got a game tomorrow." Marco motioned for her to get in the limo. He hoped with all his heart she'd come back to the hotel with him. "Could be our last one."

"Yeah. It could be." Hunter got in, making room for him next to her. What she didn't say was that this could also be their last night together.

Chapter 22

The next morning, Hunter dressed slowly and carefully. She didn't want to wake Marco, but she also took her time because she knew this would be the last morning she'd wake up in his bed.

She should have let him leave the restaurant last night. Not followed him out and come back to the hotel with him. But she'd thought she could change his mind. Make him see that his forgiveness meant a lot to his mother. And his father.

But he wouldn't talk about it. His childhood hurt and resentment had too big of a hold on him. And if he wouldn't talk to her, she had no reason to stay.

"Hunter, wait." Marco stirred. He rolled over and with painful understanding in his eyes, he sighed. "You're leaving."

"Yeah. Big game tonight." She tried to focus on that. This could be her last game as part of the Goliaths' family.

"You're still mad at me about dinner last night." He sat up, raking his hands through his sleep-ruffled hair.

"Yeah. I am." She might as well get it all out while she could. "Do you have any idea what I would give to have just one more meal with my father?"

"Oh, Hunter." He moved toward her, putting his arms around her and holding her. Holding on for dear life. "I'm so sorry about your father. I know you miss him. I know it must be hard on you right now without him."

"He left me, you know." She let herself fall into Marco's embrace, resting her head against his strong chest.

"He didn't do it by choice." He stroked her hair, saying all the things that should have been comforting. "He'd be here right now if he could."

"No. I mean, he left me when I was a baby."

"I'm sorry."

"He divorced my mom and left me with her. He thought I'd be better off with my mother."

"I didn't know."

"Well, I wasn't. She never forgave him." Hunter turned around. Facing him so she could look into his eyes. Make him see this was important. "She never forgave him and it killed her."

"Hunter, I . . . I'm so sorry." He pulled her close to comfort her, but she didn't want comforting right now.

"She was always taking pills, I assume they were antidepressants, I don't know. One day she took too many." When he tried to reach for her again, she stood up. She walked over to the window. "So I was sent to live with my father. A man I didn't remember, but had only heard of as being this horrible person. Every bad word I'd ever known was associated with my father."

"But you two ended up being so close." She could hear him shift on the bed, as if he was leaning toward her.

"It wasn't always that way. I hated him at first. Because of what he'd done. I didn't care what his reasons were, I only knew he was the reason my mother cried all the time and would take pills so she could sleep and one day she took all of them so she wouldn't have to cry anymore."

"Hunter." He was behind her, his arms around her again. She let him. She leaned into him, absorbing his strength.

"The first few months were horrible. I cried myself to sleep, and I think he worried it was hereditary. Her depression." She closed her eyes, remembering all of it. Those first few nights in the strange house. The way she'd wake up in the middle of the night and find him sleeping in a chair at the foot of her bed. And she'd watch him, fascinated, just waiting for him to turn into the horrible monster her mother had described. "He took me with him everywhere. To his office. Meetings with clients. He didn't trust me with a babysitter."

She let Marco hold her. Let him love her one last time.

"One day he took me to a baseball game." She turned around and offered him a smile.

"And it made you happy." Marco held her close. "Sully told me the story. About how you found baseball and you loved it so much, your father bought the team for you."

"It was much more complicated than that." Yet, it was also that simple.

"You love the game. Love the team. It's so much more than a business for you."

"It's everything. The Goliaths are my family. My identity." Hunter moved out of his embrace. She needed to distance herself. From him. From the team.

"So tonight's game is pretty important to you."

"Yeah." Even though it was no longer her team. She'd checked her phone earlier. Sure enough, there was the e-mail from the commissioner's office. She had a feeling he'd hold off making an announcement until the games ended. Commissioner Wagner did everything he could to keep the focus on the field as long as there were games in progress. But once the offseason hit, he'd make sure to keep interest in the game. He liked to spread announcements around, so that there wasn't a week that went by without some baseball news.

He'd taken office vowing to clean the game up once and for all, but with the amount of money at stake there would always be some willing to risk it. Even with the expanded testing and stiffer penalties for repeat offenses, there were still players trying to cheat the system. Not to mention their fans, their teammates, and anyone close to them.

Still, she knew Wagner wouldn't want anything to taint the final games of the World Series. So if he knew of the connection between Clayton Barry and FITNatural, it wouldn't come out until after the offseason began. She hoped he'd approve both Barry's and her sale of ownership long before any ties between the *former* Goliaths' ownership was linked in any way with the scandal.

Hopefully, by the time the team reported to spring training the following February, people would have also forgotten about the affair between the former managing partner and star outfielder Marco Santiago.

"So will I see you after the game?" Marco asked. He seemed to sense her pulling away.

"Maybe you should spend some time with your mother. She came all this way." Although she had no idea how far she'd traveled. For all she knew, Marco's mother lived just down the street.

"I think she has other plans."

"She'd rather spend time with her only son."

"She'd rather be with him." The venom in his voice told her he wasn't about to forgive his father any time soon. "I don't want anything to do with him."

"That's too bad. She loves him."

"What do you know about how she feels?" Marco's anger returned. "You don't know her. You don't know anything about her."

"You've known her all your life, yet you won't even give her a chance to explain." Hunter was saddened by his stubbornness. "What if there were circumstances they couldn't control? Factors that made it impossible for them to be together?"

"Doesn't matter. They should have found a way to be together."

"They have. Now."

"It's too late." Marco's refusal to forgive broke her heart.

"That's too bad. Because you're the one who's going to lose the most." Hunter shouldered her purse and walked out.

What should have been the best day of Marco's life was starting out to be one of the worst. Hunter was right. He was going to be the big loser here. But it's not like he could take thirty years of disappointment and just forget about it. Forget about their struggles. Forget about all the moving around. About all the nights he'd heard his mother cry herself to sleep.

He wasn't by far the first kid to grow up without a father present. But that didn't make his life any easier.

As he looked around the luxury hotel room, he realized his life was a lot easier than most. Baseball had given him a damn fine way to make a living. And his mother had been the one to sign him up for baseball. She'd been the one to take off work to get him to practice. To work overtime to buy him a new glove.

He always thought buying her a nice house and sending her money whether she asked for it or not was a good enough way to pay her back.

But maybe he should at least give her a chance to tell her side of the story. It didn't mean he was going to embrace the man who'd abandoned them thirty years ago. Nor did he like the idea of the man embracing his mother.

He sucked it up, and gave her a call to invite her to lunch. Just the two of them.

"Did you ever get any dinner last night?" His mother asked as she kissed his cheek.

"Yes." He held a chair for her and waited for her to sit before taking the seat opposite her.

"And what about your lady friend?"

"I took care of her." He wasn't sure if she was fishing for details on his love life or making sure he'd been a gentleman after he left. He certainly didn't want to talk about her love life.

"Still such an angry young man." Mom shook her head and tsked under her breath. "At least you still have baseball to keep you out of too much trouble. I was always thankful for that."

"I'm not angry." What the hell? "I've never been angry. It's just unfair that you had no one to help you raise me. Especially when he had so much."

The waitress arrived to take their order. His mother smiled and laughed with the woman, acting as if they had been friends forever. She'd always had a way with people. Drawing them in. Making them feel like the most important person in the room. He supposed he'd inherited some of her charm. But he always got the feeling that his fame was a big part of the attraction.

"You don't know how lucky—"

"Yes, I do." He cut her off. "I do know how many of our friends and neighbors had it worse. How many guys like me ended up in a gang instead of on a team."

"Oh, Marco." Her voice held a soft, almost achy tone. "Yes. We were lucky that way. You were always a good boy. A little rambunctious at times, but good boy."

"You were a good mom." Now his voice sounded a little achy. "A real good mom. I just wish . . . I wish it was easier for you. It should have been easier on you."

"You think if we lived in the Whittaker mansion our lives would have been easy?" She laughed, like she had when he was a kid and suggested she marry slugger Juan Gonzalez. "No. I think in a lot of ways we had it easier."

"Not possible."

"I'm glad you never knew your grandmother. Edith Whittaker was an unhappy woman." He'd never seen his mother speak ill of another. Ever. "She had ambitions. Ideals she felt everyone around her should live up to. Heaven forbid a person in her employment make a mistake. Silver showing a speck of tarnish. Linens not perfectly starched. A window with a single streak was cause for dismissal."

Marco couldn't picture his mother committing any such crimes. She'd always been an immaculate housekeeper. Even if the house they were living in was hardly more than a shack, she'd kept it spic and span.

"But when she couldn't find anything wrong with my work, she watched me even closer." She spoke of the woman with the kind of disdain Marco felt for his father. "I got the feeling she thought I was going to entice her husband."

She stabbed her salad with a shudder.

"Imagine her horror at finding out I'd seduced her son, instead." She smiled, a secretive, somewhat risqué smile. "Oh, she had such high hopes for her baby boy."

"He took advantage of you." Marco couldn't picture his mother as anything other than an innocent victim.

"We took advantage of each other." She blushed, taking a sip of her iced tea. "It was love at first sight. Really. I was putting fresh sheets on his bed, not expecting him to come home from college until after my shift had ended. He showed up unexpectedly. Took one look at me and we just knew."

Marco would have thought she was completely crazy, except . . . He recalled his first meeting with Hunter. The powerful connection that he couldn't shake even after he found out who she was.

"She sent him away. Before we had a chance to make plans. Before I knew I was pregnant with you. He never knew about you."

Marco wanted to believe her, but he'd constructed the story in his head so long ago. He wasn't quite ready to let go of the way he'd imagined the truth.

"He tried to find me. But every time he got close, I'd lose my job. Edith had something to do with that on more than one occasion."

"You're kidding." It seemed too convenient to blame it all on one person. A woman who was so heartless she'd put a young mother and child on the streets.

"No. I wish I was. But fortunately, D.C., your grandfather, knew what she was up to." She pressed her napkin to her lips. "He made sure there was always another job. Usually with housing somewhere. He was the one who paid my hospital bill when you were born."

"Why didn't he tell his son?"

"I think he thought he was doing enough." She continued to eat her lunch. "He wasn't thrilled with the idea his perfect son had a child outside of marriage. He, too, hoped Denny would have a career in politics. I don't know. The two of them are still working things out."

"So he went his whole life not knowing about me?"

"He found us once. But your uncle Manny was visiting. He was teaching you how to ride a bike. Denny thought we were a family, so he left without . . ." His mother reached for her water glass. "He didn't want to get in our way. He thought we were happy. And, you know what? That day we were."

"Why are you telling me all this? It doesn't change the past. It doesn't make up for all the times we had to move. All the times we had to start over with nothing but the clothes on our backs and two suitcases apiece." By the time he'd started high school he'd vowed if he ever met the man responsible for their nomad lifestyle he'd beat the tar out of him. Fortunately, he'd matured enough to control his temper.

"I love you, Marco. With all my heart. But . . ." She reached across the table and patted his hand. "I hope you can accept my relationship with the man I love. With your father. I know you felt his absence in your life. But you managed you grow into a fine man. A mother couldn't ask for a better son."

"But you're asking me to just accept him in your life?" He wanted to be as forgiving, as loving as she was.

"I'm asking you to try." She gave his hand a squeeze.

"I'll try. For you." He squeezed back. "But if he hurts you again . . ."

Marco dropped her hand. The ass kicking would be much harder to resist.

"Thank you." She smiled, looking more beautiful than ever. "So, tell me about your lady friend. How did you meet?"

"She picked me up." At his mother's look of surprise, he chuckled. "Literally. She's the one who traded for me. She's the managing partner of the Goliaths."

"That must be an interesting job." His mother's interest was genuine. But she would have said the same if he'd told her she was a teacher or doctor or a maid.

"Yes. She's good at it, too. But . . ." His stomach churned at the thought that he'd made her job so much harder. "I don't see how she can re-sign me. Not with our personal relationship. I may be playing in my last game tonight."

"Oh, Marco. I hate to think of you going to another team. You seem so happy in San Francisco."

"I am happy. But I can't stay." His gut tightened even more. "I can't go anywhere else, either. So I guess I'll be retiring soon."

"Don't be ridiculous." She laughed. She didn't believe him. "What does your agent say about this idea?"

"He's not my agent." Marco was in uncharted territory. He'd never been without his agent since shortly after he was drafted. He'd never been without a contract. The thought of not playing baseball was almost inconceivable. "He refused to negotiate with the Goliaths. And I won't play for anyone else."

"You're quitting? Baseball?"

"Yes. I can't play for Hunter. Not without people giving her a hard time. She's already being harassed by some people. Making jokes about the size of my bat. Asking her how long it took me to get to third base. Bullshit like that."

"Do you honestly think you can protect her by quitting?"

"What else can I do?"

"That's something you're going to have to figure out for yourself." She smiled like she always did when she wanted him to learn an important lesson. Some of those lessons had hurt like hell, but he'd managed to learn them all the same. He just hoped he could figure out a way to keep Hunter from losing her team because of him.

Chapter 23

Hunter watched as the Goliaths dominated the next night, easily taking the series in a four game sweep. She stuck around long enough to accept the World Series trophy and to congratulate Bryce Baxter on being named most valuable player. He'd played well, hitting six home runs, three doubles, and a total of eleven RBIs. She'd suggested that Marvin Dempsey extend his contract, but it was totally up to him.

She knew he'd re-sign Marco, though. It was part of their agreement. And even though he'd leveled off a bit in these last four games, she knew he'd come out of it next season. He was just hitting his prime and as long as he stayed healthy, he would give the club at least five more good years.

Her work here was done. She gave a brief interview, and then slipped away quietly.

Her life's work had ended in triumph, yet she felt completely empty. She'd won the World Series, yet lost so much more.

The only consolation was in knowing that Marco would be taken care of. He'd be able to end his career in a city that loved him. They'd embraced him from the moment he stepped foot in the ballpark. And he'd repaid them by bringing home a championship.

She wished them a long and happy future together.

Now she needed to embark on her own future. A future without baseball. A future without Marco.

The limo took her back to the hotel. She packed her things and checked out, heading down the stairwell to avoid running into any of the players on their way back to the hotel. No such luck. She came across Bryce Baxter making out with a woman who looked an awful lot like Rachel Parker. But neither one of them looked interested in where she was going or why she was sneaking out the back way.

Her flight to Paris didn't leave until eight the next morning, but she wanted to make sure she got there in plenty of time, so she switched to a hotel closer to the airport. Yeah, that was why. It had nothing to do with not wanting to run into Marco before she fled the country. He was right. Love wasn't enough.

Marco half-heartedly joined in the locker room celebration. He spent most of the time trying to avoid getting too much champagne in his eyes so he could search for Hunter. He'd lost sight of her shortly after the on-field ceremonies awarding the team trophy. Even though he hadn't had the best series, going three for eleven with runners in scoring position, his defense was solid and he was still sought out for interviews.

By the time the reporters had cleared out, he realized so had Hunter. He showered and changed into dry clothes and headed back to the hotel. He didn't even know what room she was in, she'd stayed with him the last two nights, so he headed straight for the front desk.

He approached a female desk clerk. She was older than him, by maybe five or ten years, but she looked friendly enough. "I need to know what room Hunter Collins is in."

"I'm sorry sir, I can't do that."

"Please?" He smiled, turning on the charm he used to wield as skillfully as his bat. "It's important I talk to her, tonight."

She looked at his big blue eyes, his dimpled smile, and sighed. She bent over her computer workstation, clicking away.

"I'm sorry sir, there's no Hunter Collins registered at this hotel." She offered an apologetic smile.

"Look, I know you're just doing your job. And most of the time we appreciate it." He leaned forward, hoping she'd see that this was a matter of great importance. "I'm with the team. I need to speak to her right away."

He reached for his wallet, hoping he could get her cooperation after he flashed his ID.

"I know who you are, Marco Santiago." She said his name with a little sigh, making it sound like "San-ti-*aaah*-go." "I remember when you were drafted in the second round. It was a sad day for the state of Texas when they traded you."

"Thank you. So can you give me the room number now?"

"I'm sorry, but Ms. Collins is not staying at this hotel. She checked out about an hour ago."

"Shit." Marco rubbed his hands over his face. "Sorry. I was hoping to catch her tonight."

"Is there anything else I can do for you?"

"No." He hung his head in defeat. "Not unless you happen to know where she went. No. I know where she went. She went back to San Francisco."

"I suppose she's got a lot of work to do. Planning the victory parade, designing your World Series rings." She smiled, thinking he'd give a damn about those things. All he cared about right now was finding Hunter. Convincing her that love was enough.

"Thanks. Look, if she calls . . ." Wishful thinking. "If she calls for me, put her through. I don't care what time it is."

"I'll do that, Mr. Santiago."

He went straight to his room. Straight to bed, even though he had no illusions of getting much sleep. But he was exhausted. His body knew better than to waste any energy tossing and turning. Tomorrow he'd face the biggest challenge of his life. A challenge he must win.

The phone jolted Marco out of a deep, yet unsatisfying sleep.

"Hunter." He sat up, a little disoriented. "What time is it?"

"It's seven thirty in the morning," a male voice told him. "And this is Marvin Dempsey. I need your agent to give me a call directly. As soon as possible."

"I don't have an agent." Marco rolled his neck from side to side. Man, he was stiff.

"In that case, meet me downstairs. The main restaurant. In a half an hour."

"I'll be there in twenty minutes." Marco hung up the phone. He'd only met the man a couple of times, but Hunter had known him her whole life.

Marco made it to the hostess station in fifteen minutes. He'd showered, dressed and took the stairs two at a time. He hoped Dempsey would have some insights on how he could get Hunter to talk to him.

Hunter's partner arrived only a few minutes after Marco. The waitress hadn't even returned with the coffee yet.

"Glad you could meet with me." Dempsey extended his hand. Marco stood and shook.

"Have a seat." Marco slid back into the booth and waited for the other man to get comfortable.

"So what happened with your agent?" Dempsey asked after the waitress left with their orders.

"We had a difference of opinion. Besides, I know what I want."

"Good. Then let's get down to business." The other man took a leather portfolio out of his briefcase and opened it up. "I'm prepared to make you a qualifying offer. The Goliaths want to keep you in left field for quite some time."

"Where's Hunter?" There was a time when Marco would have been itching to know what kind of offer was on the table. "I need to talk to her."

"I'm afraid you'll have to negotiate with me, and me alone."

"I see. She's hiding out so we can make a deal." Marco relaxed a little. She was trying to protect him. And her team. "She doesn't want to be directly involved in contract negotiations so no one can claim that the Goliaths made any promises outside the lines."

"Hunter Collins is no longer affiliated with the Goliaths organization." Dempsey spoke loud enough for the waitress and anyone sitting nearby to overhear.

"What are you talking about?" Marco leaned forward, keeping his own voice low.

"She sold her share of the team to me."

"No. She wouldn't." Marco wondered if the man was getting senile. He was in his seventies, he looked healthy, but . . .

"Yes. She did." He looked Marco right in the eye. There was no confusion, no sign of disorientation.

"I don't understand."

"Oh, but you will." He leaned forward. "See, our Hunter is a crafty one. I've known her since she was in pigtails. And let me tell you, she's one of the most intelligent, hardest working people I know. She's also the most loyal. How many young women would go straight from college graduation to caring for an ailing parent? She should have been off having fun, seeing the world. Instead, she came home and made Henry's last years . . ."

Dempsey took a drink of his coffee, but not before Marco noticed a shine in his eyes.

"Henry was one of my oldest and dearest friends. He loved two things more than anything in this world. This team. And his daughter."

"So how can you call yourself his friend and take this team away from his daughter?"

Dempsey sat back in the booth and laughed loudly enough that the nearby patrons looked their way.

"She made me." He chuckled, softly this time. "She forced me to buy her out. But she had a condition. The sale is only valid if I sign you to a minimum five-year deal."

"You're kidding." Maybe Marco had been too hasty in dismissing his agent. Surely he'd know if such a condition was even legal.

"Nope. If I fail to sign you, the sale is null and void." Dempsey seemed a little too pleased with the idea.

"So I won't sign. End of story. She gets her team back and everybody wins." Marco sat back, folding his arms over his chest. No way was he going to let Hunter give up her team.

"No. No one wins if you do that."

Marco gave him a puzzled look.

"She wants this." Dempsey leaned forward. "Believe me when I say she thought long and hard before making this deal."

"But she loves this team." This made no sense. She loved the Goliaths, yet she was willing to let them go. Did she love him, too? Even though she walked away?

"Yes. And she knows that having you in left field for the next five years or more is the best thing for everyone."

"Not for her." Marco uncrossed his arms. Rested his hands on his thighs. "I can't do it. I can't take away everything she's worked for."

"But it's what she wants." Dempsey sounded so calm. Like he made negotiations like this every day. "She made that very clear."

"She may think it's what she wants, but come spring training, she'll be sorry. She'll miss it too much." Marco couldn't do that to her.

"You care about her?"

"I can't let her give this up for me." Marco raked his hands through his hair. "I love her."

"Son, you're going to cost me a lot of money." The other man shook his head. "Whatever your next contract is, I'll owe her."

"I won't sign another contract." Marco placed his hands flat on the table. "I can't play anywhere else."

"Yet you're refusing to play here."

The waitress arrived with their breakfast, giving Marco a chance to douse his eggs in hot sauce. He took a few bites, trying to think. Was he really ready to give up on baseball? The game he'd played since he was six?

"What if I take a lesser deal?" Maybe there was a win-win for all of them. "Say three or four years. That way, she doesn't lose her team, you don't lose your money and . . . and I can keep playing."

"So you do want to play ball. Good. That's good." He cocked a bushy white eyebrow. "But what about when your contract is up? She'll have to go through this agony all over again. Questions about your relationship will resurface. Not to mention the other players that come along. People will wonder if she's choosing players based on their talent, or something else. You don't want to put her through that do you?"

"No." Marco hated the pain he'd caused her, simply by loving her. "But if she's my wife, no one would dare say anything."

"Your wife?"

"Yes. I don't know why we're sitting here debating over a four or five year deal, when what I really want is a lifetime." There. He'd thought about it. Come to a conclusion. And now all he had to do was figure out how to make it happen.

"You really love her?" Dempsey held his poker face.

"Yes. Now tell me how I can convince her that I can't live without her."

"Sign the contract. Five years. Or more." He cracked a smile. "She was thinking you're good for another seven, but she wanted to give you some negotiating room."

"Five years should do it. Let's see the contract."

Fifteen minutes later, the deal was done. Marco Santiago would finish his playing career in San Francisco. He hoped he'd done the right thing.

"One more thing." Marvin Dempsey folded the contract up after the hotel's on-site notary service had made it official, and placed it in his briefcase. "I'm getting older. Thinking about retiring someday. But my kids don't love baseball. They like the game, don't get me wrong, but they don't love it."

"I suppose some people don't." Marco wasn't sure why he was getting a lesson on family preferences.

"Well, I wouldn't feel right about giving Hunter's team to someone who wouldn't take care of it." Dempsey nodded. "So I was thinking of gifting back her share, say ten percent for every wedding anniversary."

"That's very generous of you, but I'm planning on sticking around long term. You'll end up with nothing in about ten years."

"Exactly." He leaned forward, a twinkle in the old man's eye. "I drew up the contract so that she'd get everything she deserves. You. The team. She'll be a minority owner as long as you're playing, so all that political stuff won't be an issue. Then when you retire, you'll help her run the team. Think you can do that?"

"Yes, sir. Just one problem."

"What's that?"

"I don't know where she is," Marco admitted. "If I'm going to marry the woman, I need to find her first."

"Ahh, yes. I must be getting old. Minor details starting to slip."

"So?" He needed to see her. To hear it from her that she wanted this.

"Try Paris."

"Paris, Texas?" He'd lived there for a time as a kid. Fourth grade, or maybe it was fifth.

"No. Paris, France. She mentioned something about wanting to look at art." Dempsey shrugged. "Don't ask me why."

"I've got to get to the airport." Marco stood and started for the exit. He took a deep breath and turned around, extending a hand toward his future wife's former partner. "Thank you. For everything."

"Good luck, son. But I don't think you'll need it." Dempsey sent him off with a wink and a smile.

* * *

Hunter's flight was delayed. Just what she needed, more time to sit in the airport thinking about how she was making a huge mistake running away from Marco. She'd already had more coffee than she could stomach, but it was a little early for a drink.

She walked over to the bar, if only to kill some time. Maybe she could talk herself into a mimosa. How was she going to fill her days, if she was already having trouble with an extra hour?

She glanced up at the TV over the bar. They were showing highlights of last night's game. Bryce Baxter's home run, Johnny Scottsdale's eleven strikeouts, and Marco Santiago's spectacular catch in left field that killed the only rally Texas had all night.

Did she really think that running off to another country was going to do her or Marco any good? She wanted to give him the space to take care of his contract business, and then what? If she'd been smart she would have left a ticket to Paris for Marco so he could join her. Now that she wasn't president of the San Francisco Goliaths, she had nothing better to do. Did she really want to walk around Paris looking at art?

She'd rather be anywhere with Marco.

If he'd still have her.

She approached the counter at the gate.

"Excuse me," Hunter made a decision. "I'd like to cancel my ticket for this flight."

"I'm sorry for the continued delay." The clerk tried to remain polite, but she'd been dealing with disgruntled passengers for the last forty-five minutes. "If you'll just be patient with us for little bit longer, we'll be boarding shortly."

"It's not that." Hunter gave the poor woman a sympathetic smile. "I've decided not to go to Paris, for personal reasons."

The clerk reluctantly took Hunter's boarding pass, her shoulders slumping when she saw it was a first class ticket.

"I know it's extra work for you, and I apologize for that." Hunter didn't want special treatment, she just wanted to get out of there. "But I can't get on this flight. I can't leave . . . I can't leave him."

The clerk sighed. "It will take me a few minutes to process your request. In the meantime, you are welcome to make yourself comfortable in the lounge."

"Sure. I'll be right over there." Hunter made her way over to the bar. The TV was still tuned to ESPN, but instead of highlights of last night's game, they showed a teaser shot of none other than Clayton Barry before cutting to a commercial.

She ordered a drink and sat down, wondering what bad news awaited her next.

"Could you turn that up?" She offered a generous tip along with her request.

The bartender pocketed the cash and turned up the volume.

Hunter took a sip of her tequila sunrise. A mimosa wasn't going to cut it.

The studio reporter gave a quick overview of the FITNatural scandal before cutting to a live feed from the commissioner's office. Clayton Barry stood in front of the building, a briefcase in his hand, and a weary expression on his face.

"Mr. Barry, can you tell me if your involvement with FITNatural will cast a shadow over the San Francisco Goliaths' recent World Series victory?" The reporter shoved a microphone in his face.

"The Goliaths earned their victory." Barry stood tall, almost defiant. "They have every reason to be proud of all they've accomplished."

"Surely the involvement of an owner in the biggest PED scandal can only cast doubt over the four game sweep."

"First of all, my investment in what I believed to be a legitimate nutrition and fitness company was one hundred percent personal." Barry straightened his tie. "I made the mistake of not fully investigating the nature of the business. I was led to believe the company was legitimate, and because of school ties and a misguided sense of loyalty, I provided capital with hope of return on my investment."

"So you're saying you didn't know you were providing steroids to the very players you held the contracts on?"

"I was a minority investor in the Goliaths' baseball team. I was mostly a silent partner, meaning my involvement was purely financial. I have since sold my share to long-standing partner Marvin Dempsey."

"So you dumped your share of the team in the wake of this scandal?"

Hunter took a long drink, maybe she should get on the plane to Paris after all. That way she wouldn't feel like she'd let her father down. And her team. And the entire city of San Francisco.

"No. I sold my share for personal reasons." He ran his hand through what was left of his hair. "My wife has filed for divorce. Rather than drag the team and the fans through our personal problems, I wanted to do the right thing. I sold my share because cash is so much easier to divvy up."

"So your partners aren't involved in FITNatural?"

"No. They are not." Clayton looked directly into the camera. Almost as if he was looking right at Hunter. "I made a mistake, and I truly regret that my association has cast a shadow on the team. I felt honored to work with Henry Collins, Marvin Dempsey and most recently, Hunter Collins. If I was half the man she is . . . Well, I wouldn't be here today, giving my testimony to the commissioner's office in hopes of cleaning up the game."

He nodded toward the camera, and then turned to head inside.

Hunter finished her drink, almost feeling sorry for Clayton Barry. But right now he was the least of her worries. She needed to get to Marco. To let him know that sometimes love was enough.

Thirty minutes later, she stood on the curb, looking for the car she'd ordered to take her back to the hotel. And hopefully back to Marco.

A sleek black limo pulled to a stop in front of her. The driver jumped out and took her suitcase. He opened the passenger door and Hunter got in.

"Oh, Marco, you scared me!"

"You scared me, too." Marco's heart beat rapidly. "I was afraid I'd lost you."

"You found me." God, she was beautiful. Her hair was messy, like she'd been tossing and turning all night. She'd tried to contain it in a loose ponytail, but several strands had escaped, framing her face like a halo. "How did you find me?"

"Marvin Dempsey." Marco wanted to reach for her. To pull her onto his lap. Like he'd wanted to do the very first time he'd met her. "We met this morning."

"Good. I'm glad." She gazed down at the floor. "So, how was your meeting?"

"I accepted the offer. But Hunter . . ." He reached for her hand. "I can't believe you gave up your team. For me."

"Don't be silly. I did it for the team." She looked up at him, and he could see how much it cost her to give it up. "They need you."

"Do you need me?" He held her hand to his lips, but hesitated. "Do you love me?"

"Yes." She closed her eyes when he brushed the back of her hand with a kiss. "And yes. I love you."

"Then why were you leaving? Why Paris?"

"I convinced myself that it would be easier on you if I wasn't around." She opened her eyes and smiled. "That you could take care of business and not have to worry about the league or the union or any of that."

"I'm not worried about any of that." He placed a finger under her chin and tilted her head up so he could look directly into her eyes. "I'm sure my baseball contract will hold up under scrutiny. But there is a matter of negotiations that fall far outside the structure of organized baseball."

"I'm no longer affiliated with the club." It killed him to see her act as a martyr. "You'll have to negotiate with Dempsey."

"I don't want to marry Marvin Dempsey." Marco took both her hands in his. Her hands were steady, his were shaking. His heart pounded in his chest. "I promised you a ring, darling. One with a ridiculous amount of diamonds. What do you say I give you two? One for the World Series, and one because you mean the world to me."

Marco slid off the seat, and knelt before her. He was about to negotiate the most important contract in his life. One that was more valuable than any other.

"Hunter Collins, will you do me the honor of becoming my wife?"

"Yes. Oh, Marco . . ." She threw her arms around him and he buried his head in her sweetness. She wore a suit, like the first time they'd met. Only this one was softer, more feminine. The jacket was cut to emphasize, rather than hide, her curves. Her deep rose blouse dipped low enough to entice without giving up all her secrets.

"I'll make it worth your while. You'll see." Marco kissed her. Victory had never been sweeter. He was the luckiest man in the world.

"I'm counting on it." Joyful tears glistened in her eyes.

"Don't worry; your team is in good hands."

"I know. I picked these hands myself." Hunter brought his hands to her mouth, kissing his palms, making him want her more than ever. "So far, I've not been disappointed."

"I wasn't talking about me." Marco groaned. He'd checked out of his hotel room, thinking he was on his way to Paris. He'd need to get another room. Fortunately, the hotel should have plenty of openings, since the team would head back to San Francisco this afternoon. "I meant Dempsey. He's a tough old bird."

"Yes. Yes, he is." She smiled, seemingly at peace with her decision to let the team go.

"He wouldn't take no for an answer."

"Why would he have to?"

"I wasn't going to sign." Marco turned to face her. He had to let her know he was willing to sacrifice for her. "He told me about your deal. About the contingency. I tried to quit. I still can. I'll walk away right now. It's not official until the league approves it. I'll call Dempsey right now. You can have your team back, and I'll be your house boy." Marco reached for his phone.

Hunter grabbed it from him, tossing it on the seat next to her.

"I need you on the field. You can still be my house boy after the game." She ran her hand along his thigh. Oh yeah, he'd gotten a good deal. He'd end his career in San Francisco. He'd spend the rest of his life with Hunter.

"I won't let you down," he promised.

"I know." She climbed on his lap, kissing him. Loving him. Believing in him.

Epilogue

The Goliaths' victory parade marched down Market Street, ending up at city hall. Hunter stepped to the podium.

"Thank you, San Francisco!" She had to practically shout into the microphone, the crowd was so loud. "This has been quite a season. For the team. For the city. For me, personally."

The crowd hushed.

"As many of you know, my father, Henry Collins, passed away this past April. The beginning of a new season was marred by the loss of someone very dear to me and many in the Goliaths' organization."

She squared her shoulders, strengthened by the knowledge that she had made her father proud. She could walk away on top. She glanced over at Marco, sitting in the front row of players. He nodded, giving her a slight smile of encouragement.

"But this team kept going. They kept me going. Together we only got stronger. We did it. Together." She hesitated, taking a deep breath. "But it's time for me to step aside. I sold my share of the team, and I'll no longer serve as president. But don't worry. You're in good hands. Marvin Dempsey has been a mentor and a good friend, and he'll take care of this team. This World Series Championship team."

After what seemed like minutes of stunned silence, the crowd cheered.

"Now, I'd like to introduce your team, starting with manager, Juan Javier."

Javier gave a brief speech, before Hunter introduced the rest of the coaching staff. She introduced the pitchers next, and several of them spoke to the crowds. She stepped back up to the microphone.

"Your left fielder, Marco Santiago." The crowd erupted into cheers as Marco strode to the podium, but instead of grabbing the microphone, he grabbed Hunter. Swept her into his arms and kissed her before the million or so fans in attendance. The fans went nuts, applauding, whistling, and shouting, "Get a room!"

"Thank you." Marco flashed his most charming grin to the crowd before turning his full attention to Hunter. "Thank you, Hunter. You've made all my dreams come true. Any kid who's ever picked up a baseball has dreamed of playing in and winning the World Series. You brought me here. You believed in me. As a ballplayer. As a man. And since you've agreed to marry me, I take it you'll believe in me as a husband."

The cheers grew even louder.

"I love you, Hunter Collins." He kissed her again for all the world to see.

Bryce Baxter approached the podium.

"It's going to be hard to follow that." Laughter broke out amongst the spectators. "Bet you didn't know you were invited to the world's largest engagement party."

He waited for the crowd to settle.

"But that's the way it is. Love comes out of left field and if you're lucky, like these two, if you're lucky, you can make the catch."

Turn the page for a special excerpt of Kristina Mathews's

Better Than Perfect

Life Beyond the Game . . .

Johnny "The Monk" Scottsdale has won it all on the baseball diamond. He's even pitched a perfect game. Known for his legendary control both on and off the field, his pristine public image makes him the ideal person to work with young players in a preseason minicamp. Except the camp is run by the one woman he can't forget . . . the woman who made him a "monk."

Alice Harrison once traded her dreams so that Johnny Scottsdale could make it to the Majors—and then her dreams fell apart. Now here comes Johnny back into her life, just when she's ready to finally go after her dreams. This time she's not letting up. Even if she has to reveal what she's kept secret for too long from her son and Johnny. She's can't be sure how things will turn out, but she's not leaving until she swings for the fences. . . .

On sale now!

Chapter 1

"Pitchers and catchers report to spring training in thirteen days, twenty-one hours and seventeen minutes," Hall of Fame broadcaster Kip Michaels announced, and the crowd went wild. "Kicking off today's Fan Fest, I'd like to introduce one of our newest players. Two-time Cy Young Award winner, perennial All-Star, and the last man to pitch a perfect game. Give a warm San Francisco welcome to Johnny 'The Monk' Scottsdale."

Thirty thousand people were expected at the ballpark today. A great crowd—for a baseball game. But instead of working the count, Johnny would be working the crowd. Answering questions. Signing autographs. Putting himself out there in a way he wasn't entirely comfortable with. He was as nervous as the day he'd made his professional debut fourteen years ago. Butterflies? Try every seagull on the West Coast taking roost in his stomach.

Focus. Breathe. Let it go.

"Thank you. I'm thrilled to be here." He'd much rather face the 1927 Yankees than sit in front of a camera and a microphone talking about his game instead of playing it. "I hope I can help the team bring home a World Series Championship."

He tried to relax his shoulders. Tried to hide his nerves. The Goliaths could be his last team. His last shot at a ring. His final chance to prove himself and leave a legacy that went beyond the diamond.

After fielding a few questions about what he could bring to the team, and deflecting some praise about his success so far, Johnny was released to another part of the park to sign autographs. Little Leaguers approached with wide eyes and big league dreams. Tiny tots with painted faces squirmed with excitement about getting cotton candy while their parents shoved them forward to collect an autograph. A shy boy with a broken arm asked him to sign his cast. The look on his face was more than worth the discomfort of being in the spotlight for something other than his on-field performance.

Johnny had signed the big contract. The team paid him a lot of money to pitch every five games. They also paid him to interact with the fans, to be an ambassador for the game he'd loved for so long. The game that had saved him from a completely different kind of life.

He shared a table with another new player, shortstop Bryce Baxter. They were set up near the home bullpen along the third base line. Several other stations were set up around the park, giving fans a chance to get up close and personal with the players. Some tried to get a little too personal.

"So you're the hot new pitcher." A busty brunette leaned over the autograph table, wearing what appeared to be a toddler-sized tank top. The team logo sparkled in rhinestones and she was obviously well aware of the attention she drew. "I'd be more than happy to show you around."

"No thanks. I'm pretty familiar with the city." He held his pen ready, although she didn't seem to have anything to autograph. Nothing he was willing to sign, anyway.

"I could take you places you've never been." She leaned over even more.

Johnny kept his head down, trying to avoid gazing at what she had to offer. He reached for a stock photo, scrawled his signature across the bottom, and slid the picture forward, hoping she'd take the hint and leave.

"You forgot your number." She pouted.

"Sorry. I don't give that out." Johnny wished he could retreat to the locker room. Get away from her and the crowd that seemed to be growing. He never understood why people would wait in line to make small talk and take his picture. He gripped the black marker, needing something to do with his hands. If he only had a baseball, he could roll it around in his palm. Feel the smoothness of the leather, the rough contrast of the raised stitches. Find comfort in the weight and the symmetry of the one thing he could always control.

His teammate inserted himself into the conversation. "Do you know who this is? The one and only Johnny 'The Monk' Scottsdale."

"The Monk?" She drew her gaze over Bryce, then glanced at Johnny before settling on Bryce once more.

"He's a god." He flashed a grin indicating he was more than willing to play her game. "Me? I'm a mere mortal." Bryce leaned toward her, clearly enjoying the interaction.

"You're new, too." She scooted over to his side of the table, dismissing Johnny's rejection as strike one. She must think she had a better chance of scoring with Bryce.

"I am. I think I left my heart somewhere in the city. Could you help me find it?" He slid one of his photos across the table to her.

"I can help you find whatever you're looking for." She took the pen from him and wrote something on the inside of his forearm. Her number, most likely.

Bryce grinned as if he enjoyed having a stranger tattoo him with a permanent marker.

"Bring your friend, too. If he's up for a challenge."

"I'll see what I can do, sweetheart." Bryce tipped his cap and winked at the woman.

Johnny exhaled, realizing he'd been holding his breath during the entire conversation.

"Thanks man, I owe you one." Johnny shook his head, as relieved as if Bryce had just snagged a line drive with two outs and the bases loaded.

"So it really isn't an act." Baxter eyed him carefully. "You really do walk the walk."

"What walk?"

"The celibacy thing. It's for real." A lot of guys thought he was full of it. That it was just for show. A way to get attention, and women. But once they realized he was genuine, most of the other players accepted him. Some even respected him. "You really don't mess around."

"No. I don't. I'm not perfect, but I try to stay out of trouble." Johnny removed his cap and ran his fingers through his hair. Since they were both new to the team, their booth wasn't as crowded as some of the others. They had a chance to catch their breath. He was able to finally sit back and enjoy the perfect weather. It was one of those glorious Northern California days when the sun came out to tease, dropping hints of spring and the fever that came with it.

"You looked like you were a little uncomfortable there." Bryce, on the other hand, seemed to relish the attention.

"I know it's part of the job, but it's not the part I'm good at."

"You let your game speak for itself. That's cool." Bryce reclined in his chair, looking as relaxed as if he was sitting in his own back yard. "Some of us have to use our charm to make up for lack of talent."

Johnny laughed. Baxter had plenty of talent. And more than enough charm to go around.

"She was pretty fine, though." Bryce continued to check her out as she walked away, collecting ballplayer's numbers like kids collected baseball cards. "Exactly what I need to get me in shape for spring training."

"Is that so?" Johnny managed to avoid the whole groupie scene. His entire career had been about control, both on and off the field. The Monk kept his cool. The Monk never got rattled. And The Monk maintained a spotless reputation. He had to, considering where he'd come from.

"There he is. Come on, Mom." A kid, about twelve or thirteen, rushed up to the booth, practically dragging his mother by the arm.

Johnny slipped on his best fan-friendly smile.

"We're, like, your number one fans." The boy was practically bursting at the seams. "Right, Mom?"

The boy's mother stepped forward, taking Johnny's breath away.

He'd had several reasons to come to San Francisco. Eleven million obvious ones, and several others that he'd done his best to articulate to the fans. There was only one reason he should have stayed away.

"Alice." Just saying her name sent a line drive straight to his heart. Even fourteen years later.

"Congratulations on your new contract. I know you're going to have a great year." She sounded like any other fan, wishing him well.

She just marched right up to his table to ask for an autograph. A freaking autograph? Like he meant nothing to her.

A slight breeze blew her hair around her face. She tried to smile as she tucked a loose strand behind her ear. Blond, straight, silky—and if he remembered correctly—oh-so-soft. She wore modestly cut jeans and a soft blue sweater that on anyone else would have looked plain and proper. He didn't need to glance at her left hand to know she was off limits. Yet, she still moved him like no other woman ever could. Made him long for what he'd had. What he'd lost. What he'd tried for years to forget.

"Wait." The boy gaped at her. "You guys know each other? For real?"

"Yes. Johnny was . . ." She held Johnny's gaze just long enough for him to catch a flicker of regret. She turned to her son, who was about an inch or two taller than her. "He was your dad's college roommate."

"You knew my dad?" The boy seemed more impressed by that than the fact that people waited in line for his autograph.

"Yes. I knew him." Johnny swallowed the lump in his throat. "Before he married your mom."

"Cool." The kid smiled and nodded his head, like it was no big deal. "I mean, I know you played for the Wolf Pack when they went to Nevada, but I had no idea you guys were, like, friends."

Sure. Friends.

"Zach." She placed her hand on his shoulder, ready to steer him away. "I'm sure Mr. Scottsdale is a busy man. Let's leave him alone."

They'd once been as close as two people could be. But now he was Mr. Scottsdale.

The boy shrugged, dismissing her and looking up to Johnny with admiration. "It's totally awesome to meet you."

Johnny nodded, giving his most sincere smile, even though seeing Alice, and her kid, hit him like a 97-mile-an-hour fastball.

They started to walk away.

"Give my best to Mel." As if he hadn't already done that.

Alice turned around.

"Mel died. Eight years ago." A pained expression flashed across her face.

"I'm sorry. For your loss." Johnny said the words. He wanted more than anything to mean them, but he'd carried that resentment around for so long, it had become as much a part of him as his right arm.

"Thank you." Alice gave him a sad little smile. It was forced. Polite. The kind of smile she'd give a stranger. "It was good seeing you. Really good."

"Yeah. Sure." He could say the same, but he'd be lying. Seeing her again only reminded him of everything he'd sacrificed.

The minute she'd seen Johnny on the stage, Alice's heart had swelled big enough to fill the stadium. There he'd been, larger than life. Damn. The man looked good. Better than on TV. Better than she remembered. He'd gained some muscle. A lot of muscle. Even without the jersey, there'd be no doubt he was an athlete. He moved with the kind of confidence and grace that came with being totally in tune with his body. Like he'd once been totally in tune with hers. She ached at the memory, but shook it off, uncomfortable having such thoughts with her son sitting next to her. Like Johnny had clearly been uncomfortable onstage, addressing the media and the crowds. He never did like to talk about his game. He'd simply let his talent speak for itself.

Just as she'd predicted, women lined up at his booth. They all wanted his autograph. Some of them wanted a little more. She hadn't been able to handle it back then. And now? What he did was his business. Especially since she'd been the one to walk out on him.

"Mom. Are you okay?" Zach was protective of her. And a little too observant.

"I'm fine, Zach." She shook her head to clear the fog of memories that rolled over her. With only the briefest look into his eyes, she couldn't forget the three years they'd spent together, nearly inseparable. Studying. Hanging out. Making love. "I'm surprised to see him, that's all."

"But you knew he'd be here." Zach had that tone, the unspoken *duh*. They'd been coming to Fan Fest every year since Mel's death. She'd known Johnny would be here. She just wasn't prepared for the impact of seeing him again. She'd thought she'd put those feelings behind her. Packed them away with her college sweatshirts and student ID card. "You were so excited when you heard it on the radio.

Your favorite player finally becoming a Goliath. Why didn't you tell me you guys were, like, friends?"

"I didn't want you to think it's a big deal." She tried to place her hand on his shoulder, but he squirmed to avoid the contact. That was new. Not unexpected, given his age, but she missed her little boy. The first time they'd come to Fan Fest, he'd held her hand. Until they'd gotten to the miniature version of the ballpark. He'd joined the t-ball game like he was born to play.

"It is a big deal." Zach looked at her like she was hopelessly out of touch. Something he did a lot these days. "Mom, you actually know Johnny Scottsdale."

There it was. The star-struck admiration bordering on worship.

"I *knew* him, Zach." Alice tried to keep her tone neutral. She couldn't betray her emotions. A wave of regret washed over her. The question of what might have been. "But that was a long time ago."

"Wouldn't it be cool if he came to the foundation's minicamp?" Zach couldn't know why it would be such a bad idea.

She'd hoped to avoid him. Avoid digging up the past. And the question that had plagued her more and more as Zach grew. "I already have a pitcher lined up. Nathan Cooper. He's done it for years."

Alice had worked for the Mel Harrison Jr. Foundation since its inception, a little more than a year after her husband's death. The initial donations were privately funded, set up to provide grants to community schools and youth organizations. As the foundation had grown, they were able to provide services for greater numbers of children, but the more successful they'd become, the less contact she had with the kids.

Until a few years ago, when the team had approached her about setting up a minicamp for youth players. It evolved from a Saturday demonstration and meet-and-greet to a weeklong afterschool program where the ballplayers worked directly with the kids, helping them learn fundamentals of the game while boosting their confidence with the attention and mentorship of the pro athletes.

"Cooper's alright." Zach sounded disappointed, bordering on whiny. "But he's not Johnny Scottsdale."

"Zach, we made a commitment to Nathan Cooper."

"And Harrisons always keep their commitments." Zach parroted the family motto. She could tell by the tone of his voice he had to restrain himself from rolling his eyes.

"Yes, Zach, Harrisons keep their commitments." No matter what. She'd made a commitment to Mel, to the Harrison family. She'd hoped her feelings for Johnny would eventually fade. She'd made her choice. A desperate one at the time, but once she'd committed to Mel, she wouldn't look back. She still couldn't. "Cooper's a good player. A good guy. We can't just tell him we don't want him anymore."

"Well, maybe they could both do the pitching clinic," Zach suggested. "Since Cooper's a lefty, maybe it would be better to have a right-handed pitcher too."

"Johnny's a busy man. He doesn't need us bugging him." And she didn't need to be reminded of what she'd given up.

"Yeah, but he probably doesn't know very many people here yet." Zach sounded hopeful. Like they'd be doing Johnny a favor. "It would be good for him to get involved in the community."

"Zach. He doesn't need us." She'd made sure of it.

"But . . ." Zach couldn't let it go.

"I think it's time for some lunch." Lately, food seemed to be the best distraction.

"I could eat." Zach shrugged. "You want to split some garlic fries?"

"You know I do." The ballpark's signature fries had become a tradition. But if she ate a full order herself, she'd be sorry later.

"Can I get two hot dogs, then? Or maybe some nachos?"

"You're that hungry?" Wasn't it only yesterday that she begged him to eat? Playing airplane with the spoon or bribing him with a toy to take three more bites.

"Yeah. I guess meeting Johnny Scottsdale increased my appetite." He grinned at her. For a second there, he reminded her of someone she used to know.

"Oh, Zach . . ." She sighed, her emotions getting the better of her. Seeing Johnny for even a few minutes had her all mixed up.

It had been easier when Johnny was on the other side of the country. When he'd been nothing more than a box score. An image on TV. She'd followed his entire career. From his earliest days in the minor leagues, to his first start in Kansas City, to when he was traded to

Tampa Bay. She'd watched him. Cheered for him. Wished him nothing but success.

"Oh please, Mom. Don't go there." She was embarrassing him. As she often did whenever she talked about how quickly he was growing up. Becoming a man. Neither of them was quite ready for it, but that didn't matter.

She put her arm around him but felt him struggling with the idea of pulling away. Reluctantly, she let him go, knowing it was only a matter of time before he wouldn't need her at all.

"Order whatever you want. Just don't complain about a stomach ache later."

"I won't." He ordered a hot dog, nachos and a root beer.

She stepped up behind him and ordered her hot dog, the garlic fries and a Diet Coke. She struck up a conversation with the lady behind the counter while they waited for their order.

"Geez, Mom. Why do you have to talk so much?" He'd waited until they were at the condiment station before complaining.

"I was only being friendly. There's nothing wrong with that." She unwrapped her hot dog and placed it under the mustard spout.

"Yeah, then why weren't you very friendly with Johnny Scottsdale?" He kept his head down, concentrating on his food. She'd learned to pay attention more when he seemed least interested in making conversation. "You actually knew him in college and you barely said a word to him."

She hit the pump on the mustard a little too hard and it splattered all over her sweater. She quickly grabbed a napkin to wipe up the stain.

"Is it . . . Is it because he reminds you of Dad? Does seeing him make you sad?"

"Oh, honey." She put her arm around him, pressing him against her. How could she possibly explain why seeing Johnny again was so painful?

"It seems kind of weird that they didn't keep in touch after college." Zach had no idea how weird it would have been if they had. The three of them had been the best of friends. How many times had they let Mel tag along on their dates? Or how many times had she made herself at home at their place? But Johnny had been at the heart of their little group. And when he'd moved on, she and Mel turned to each other.

"Johnny was trying to make it to the big leagues." She used the same story she'd told herself over the years. "He had to work very hard to get to where he is today. Mel had a job here in the city, and I was busy raising you. We just drifted apart, that's all."

"But, maybe you and Johnny can be friends again." He had a tiny hesitation in his voice. Telling her there was more to the story than he was willing to share.

She waited. Pushing him would never get him to open up.

"Maybe . . ." Zach took a long slurp of his soda. "Maybe he could tell me more about my dad."

Well, that was a mistake. By bringing up his dad, he'd upset his mom. Zach could tell because she got really quiet. They sat in the stands to eat their lunch and watch the next round of interviews. She nibbled on her hot dog and absently picked at the garlic fries. He ended up eating most of them, which was fine. He loved garlic fries. But it was weird with her not talking. Normally she would chatter on and on about the upcoming season and especially all the new players. He'd expected her to be really excited about Johnny Scottsdale. She was probably an even bigger fan than he was.

She'd actually cried when he pitched his perfect game. Cried and hugged Zach like they'd been there. But she barely said a word to him when they met today. And they didn't even get an autograph.

Now, she was all quiet, and he wouldn't be surprised if she said she wanted to leave soon. He'd seen what he wanted to see. Johnny Scottsdale's first interview as one of the Goliaths, and then he'd gotten to meet him. Sort of.

Kip Michaels stepped onstage to introduce the next set of players. He was one of the best. He never had anything bad to say about an opponent, but he was a Goliath to the core. He also managed to throw out a few tips for young players during every game. He'd point out simple things, like keeping balanced in the batter's box or following through on a pitch. Plus, he'd been there. Way before Zach's time, but he'd pitched in the majors for ten years. So he knew what he was talking about.

"Thank you, San Francisco!" Nathan Cooper stepped up to the mic for his turn in the spotlight. "It's going to be a great season. I guarantee it."

Yeah, he was alright. Kind of a showoff, though. Like it was more about him than the team. Cooper played to the crowd, making them laugh and cheer and get pumped up for the season. Even if he was kind of obnoxious, he was a pretty good pitcher. Most of the time.

Zach glanced over at his mother. She was trying to rub the mustard stain out of her sweater. He wondered if that would be her excuse for leaving early. He wouldn't mind. Not really. He just wished he could have talked to Johnny Scottsdale more. He had a lot of questions. Mostly about baseball. Like what it was like to pitch a perfect game.

He had questions about his dad.

He barely even remembered him. Only a few fuzzy memories—mostly good—of a guy in a suit taking off his tie and getting down on the floor to play with the Thomas the Train set. He remembered watching movies and going to the park, but he didn't think he'd ever played catch with his dad.

He'd played catch with a few different major leaguers. As part of the minicamp. He never really felt like he was part of the program though. It was more like he tagged along, just because he could. Because his mom ran the show and his grandparents had started the whole charity thing after his dad died.

Some of the other kids had it real tough, though. Single parents who worked two jobs just to pay their rent. So they didn't have time to play catch with their kids. There were foster kids who never lived in one place long enough to be part of a team. Some of the kids had dads in the military, serving overseas in Afghanistan or places like that.

Zach felt kind of bad, taking up a spot for a kid who needed it more. At least he didn't have to worry about money. Or his mom didn't have to worry, anyways.

"Hey Mom?" He had an idea.

"Don't tell me you're still hungry." She smiled at him, but she was kind of distracted.

"No." Not really. But he would be after dinner. They'd probably have a big salad or vegetable stir-fry—something healthy to make up for all the junk food. "I was just thinking. Maybe I'm getting too old to be in the minicamp."

"You're not too old." She folded up her napkin and wrapped up the last of her unfinished hot dog. "There will be plenty of other kids your age."

"I guess." He wasn't as excited about it as he'd been the last few years.

"You don't have to do the minicamp." She tried to sound like it didn't matter to her, but he knew she'd be disappointed if he wasn't there. "I hope you're not quitting because I haven't asked Johnny Scottsdale to join us."

"That's not it." He grabbed the last garlic fry. Except maybe that was part of it. "I just don't know how much more I can learn from the same guys."

That kind of made him sound like a jerk. Like he thought he was some great baseball player already. That's not what he meant. He just didn't know how to say it without sounding like he was spoiled or something. How many kids got to work with real Major League baseball players every year? Not many. For most of them it was a once-in-a-lifetime kind of thing.

"If you don't want to come, that's okay. You won't hurt my feelings." She said that, but she didn't like when he didn't want to do stuff with her. It was hard for him to tell her he'd rather be with his friends. She always worked so hard at finding fun things to do together. Maybe it was because he didn't have his dad around anymore and she felt like she had to make it up to him. Or maybe it was because she didn't have his dad around and she was lonely.

"I'll come," Zach said. But he didn't really want to.

Johnny plopped down in front of his locker to change out of his jersey and into his street clothes. He was wiped out, but not in a good way like after a game. His muscles were sore from tension, not exertion. He was still reeling after his encounter with Alice. For years he'd pretended they were both dead to him. Come to find out, Mel had died. And even though they hadn't spoken in years, it still came as a big blow. The man had once been Johnny's best friend. Almost a brother. And now he was gone. Was it an accident? A long and painful battle with disease? Whatever the cause, Alice was left to raise their son alone.

Alice was a mother. Not a big surprise. She'd always loved kids. She was going to be a teacher. Until she'd married Mel and didn't have to work. Mel was rich. Came from money and probably couldn't help but make even more money once he graduated and went to work for his father, helping make other rich people richer.

It bothered him more than he wanted to admit. Her having a kid. Not that Johnny had ever really wanted to be a father. But maybe a part of him would have wanted to be the one to give her that gift.

He was wrestling with that thought when his manager, Juan Javier, approached him.

"Just the man I need to see." Javier had been a catcher during his playing days. A pretty good one too, until his knees gave out. But he was still in good shape. Still had a commanding presence.

"Sure, what do you need?" Johnny didn't know the man well enough to determine whether he should address him by his first name, last name or just call him "Skip." His reputation around the league was that of a player's manager. Well respected and well liked, with a thorough knowledge of the game and an uncanny ability to get the most out of his players. Johnny looked forward to working with him.

"I need a hero." Javier parked himself next to Johnny. "Got word this morning that Nathan Cooper didn't pass a drug test. He's out fifty games, unless he appeals."

Did that mean Johnny would be moved to the bullpen? Cooper was a relief pitcher, a left-handed specialist. Johnny was a right-handed starter. At least he had been his entire career.

"Don't worry, you're still a starter." Javier clapped him on the back. "This is a PR nightmare. At least it didn't leak out this morning. That would have put a dark cloud on the Fan Fest."

"So what can I do?"

"Your reputation is spotless. It's one of the reasons the team was so interested in signing you." They didn't call him The Monk for nothing. His composure on the mound was only part of the story. "We had a few years where . . . well, you catch the news. The fans are sick of this stuff. Sick of the cheaters. We need someone like you. Someone the kids can look up to."

"I try to be one of the good guys." Johnny shrugged. It's all he'd ever wanted to be. He wanted his name to be associated with honor, integrity and respect.

"Russ Crawford, from the front office, had Cooper lined up for this charity event." His manager placed a sturdy hand on Johnny's shoulder. "We don't want a guy suspended for drugs representing us to the community."

"No. We don't." Johnny never understood what would drive a guy to take such a risk. Or why there were still guys who felt they could get away with it. He balled his fists, thinking about how much harder the rest of them had to work at proving they were clean.

"We need someone to take his place. I thought you'd be perfect." He gave Johnny a friendly pat on the back.

"I was perfect once in my life." Twenty-seven batters had faced him. Every one of them had walked back to the dugout shaking their heads. None of them had reached first base. No hits, no walks, no errors.

"You and only about twenty-three other guys." Javier gave him a smile of admiration. Of respect. Not only for Johnny, but for all the players who'd come before him. "But you're not just perfect on the field."

That was his reputation. No wild parties, drugs or women. When he went out with his teammates, he stuck with one beer. Just to be one of the guys. Then he would return quietly to his room. Alone. He politely refused advances and room keys from his female fans.

"What kind of charity thing are we looking at?" *Let's get to the point.* What really mattered. As long as it wasn't a speaking engagement. He could pitch in front of a sold-out stadium. Or an empty one where the few fans in attendance tried to make up for the lack of numbers with an abundance of noise. But talking to a room full of people? No thanks. He'd much rather run the bleachers, drag the field, or even cut the grass by hand, one blade at a time.

"It's a minicamp for youth players," Javier explained. "They come to the ballpark after school and we take them through a few drills, demo mechanics and basically share your knowledge of the game."

"That sounds like something I could do." Johnny was just beginning to think about what he might do after his career was over. Coaching was something to consider; it would keep him in the game. But he wasn't sure if he'd be any good at it. He didn't know if he could explain things in a way others would understand. He could show them, though. He could demonstrate what worked for him.

"So you'll do the pitching clinic." It wasn't a question. The new guy on the team had to prove himself, no matter his reputation, and picking up a teammate was a good way to do just that.

Johnny nodded. Why not? Anything to keep his mind off Alice and Mel. And their kid.

"Tell me about the kids." Johnny didn't have a lot of experience with kids. Like, none. Even when he'd been a kid, he didn't really know how to relate to them. He was the quiet boy in school and in the dugout. "How old are they?"

"I think anywhere from about nine to twelve or thirteen."

"Old enough to tie their own shoes, then." In other words, about Zach's age.

"Yet still young enough that they don't think they know everything," Javier added with a slight smile. "About baseball, at least."

"So these kids should be coachable." When he'd been that age, he'd soaked up every tip and tidbit of information about the game. He'd been eager to learn and apply the knowledge to his rapidly growing skills.

Could he be the kind of mentor he'd had back then? Could he pass down his knowledge of the game to the next generation? He hoped so.

"They're good kids. Some of them may have caught a bad break. Single parent homes, families fallen on hard times. Some of these boys might be homeless or in foster care." Javier was starting to make Johnny a little nervous. He'd been one of those kids. He'd known hard times. Lived with a single mother who'd worked too much. Without a father or a man to look up to.

Until his coach had stepped up.

"I guess you've got your man." Johnny hoped he could be the kind of man these kids needed. "Just give me the time and place."

"I knew I could count on you. The camp starts Monday. Here's your contact at the Harrison Foundation." The manager handed him a slick business card. Johnny's heart seized as he read the name.

ALICE HARRISON, DIRECTOR

"She's a great gal. Professional. Knowledgeable." Javier seemed not to notice all the air had been sucked out of the room. "You'll love her."

Oh yeah. Johnny had loved her. He'd once loved her even more than he loved the game.